TROUBLETWISTERS

— BOOK TWO —

THE MONSTER

TROUBLETWISTERS

— BOOK TWO —

THE MONSTER

GARTH NIX
— AND —
SEAN WILLIAMS

SCHOLASTIC PRESS · NEW YORK

Library of Congress Cataloging-in-Publication Data available

ISBN 978-0-545-25898-2

10 9 8 7 6 5 4 3 2 1   12 13 14 15 16

Printed in the U.S.A.   23
First edition, June 2012

The text was set in Sabon.
Book design by Christopher Stengel

To Anna, Thomas, and Edward,
and to all my family and
friends — Garth

For the boys — Finn, Ryan, Seb,
and Xander. And for Nick, who I
hope will never grow up. — Sean

TABLE OF CONTENTS

TROUBLETWISTERS

BOOK TWO

THE MONSTER

STRANGENESS IN THE NIGHT

It was quiet in Portland, the calm, still quiet of a small town at two o'clock on a rainy Monday morning. The streets were empty, there was no traffic, and the only sound was the soft tap dance of the rain and the slow background beat of the surf rolling in on Mermaid Point.

Through the predawn silence, something moved in the middle of River Road — something huge and dark and struggling. The length of a bus, but not as high, it propelled itself, awkwardly and with great effort, sideways up the slight slope toward Main Street.

As it drew near the next streetlight, it raised one strange, dark eye — and the light went out. The thing opened its great maw to let out a soft, almost yawning hiss of satisfaction, then dragged itself on, leaving a trail of slime and a line of fizzled-out streetlights behind it.

Soon, its destination became clear. It was heading toward a big, old house on the slope below the Rock — a house with a widow's walk around a high-pitched roof, topped with an eccentric weather vane shaped like a crescent moon with several attendant stars.

Right now, even though there was no breeze, the weather vane was wavering between southwest and north-west — pointing in the rough general direction of the thing squelching ever closer to the house.

The creature paused at the intersection of Parkhill Street and Watchward Lane, and its huge, wide mouth opened again. But this time its whole body convulsed, ripples moving through its form like shaken jelly.

A moment later, with one final, particularly violent spasm, it vomited up half a dozen partially digested rats. The thing sniffed at them warily, then continued on its way, crushing its rejected dinner as it slid up the lane.

It moved faster as it neared its goal, helped by another shower of rain that made the cobbled lane wet and eased the monster's strange progress. Bright arc lights suddenly flickered on down at the marina and the fish market, urging the creature to greater speed. The night was ending, the boats were coming in, and soon there would be people about.

The monster needed to hide. Fortunately, it knew exactly where to go.

CHAPTER ONE

THE MONSTER OF PORTLAND

It's kind of hairy like a gorilla," said one of the boys, whose name Jack Shield hadn't quite managed to remember yet, even after a week of being in the same classroom.

"No, it isn't," scoffed Miralda. She was the mayor's daughter and the self-proclaimed expert on everything to do with the town. "Everyone knows it's as big as an elephant and has a shell like a giant insect. And it has a really wide mouth and teeth like a shark."

"What does?" asked Jaide Shield, who'd gone to get a drink of water the moment Mr. Carver had let the class out for lunch, and had missed the beginning of the conversation.

"The Monster of Portland," said Kyle. He'd been unfriendly from the first moment the twins had started at the school, so it was no surprise when he added, "Nothing you'd know about."

"True," said Jaide, as if she didn't care. "I don't believe in monsters anyway."

"Yeah," added Jack. "I guess *we're* too old for that stuff . . . Kyle."

"You wouldn't say that if you'd seen it," insisted Miralda. "The Monster of Portland is real."

"Who *has* seen it, then?" asked Jaide.

"My brother," said Kyle.

"My aunt," said Miralda. Several other children gathered together in the playground to chime in that various relatives or friends had seen the monster, but no one claimed to have seen it themselves.

Jack and Jaide shared a quick, secret glance. When the twins said they didn't believe in monsters, neither was telling the entire truth. They knew that such things were very possible. In the previous week they had battled hordes of insects and rats, and creatures made up of many different living things, including a vast squid monster and a woman who had living rat heads coming out of her shoulders — all the work of an enemy so terrible it was known only as The Evil.

The twins' father's mother, whom they called Grandma X, was the local leader of a secret international order called the Wardens that had dedicated itself to fighting The Evil. But that wasn't all Jack and Jaide had discovered since moving to Portland. Just as The Evil had mysterious and terrifying powers, so, too, did the Wardens, powers they called Gifts. Most amazing of all, Jack and Jaide were developing Gifts of their own — magical powers they couldn't entirely control.

"How come everyone's talking about this monster thing today?" asked Jack, as casually as he could. Inside, he was both excited and a little bit frightened. If there was a monster about, surely this meant that The Evil was back, despite Grandma X's assurances that they had beaten it last time.

"The new girl saw it last night," said Miralda.

"What?" said Jaide. "I didn't see —"

"Not you," said Miralda impatiently. "The *new* new girl, the one who started today. Tara. You know."

Jack and Jaide turned out of the huddle to look at a girl who was coming out of the school. Mr. Carver had introduced her that morning, but they hadn't had much of a chance to look closely at her. She was tall, and had glossy black hair cut in a very fashionable style, as well as expensive-looking clothes. Unlike Jack and Jaide's old school, the Stormhaven Innovative School of Portland did not have uniforms, but even so, about two-thirds of the other students seemed to have an unspoken agreement to wear particular kinds of clothes.

"Hi," said the new girl as she approached the huddle, which, taking the lead from Miralda, immediately broke apart, leaving just Jack and Jaide behind.

"Hi, I'm Jaide. This is Jack."

Jaide didn't need to explain that they were brother and sister. Though they were not identical — Jack had the darker complexion and hair of their father while Jaide took after their mother, who was a fair-skinned redhead — they did look very much alike.

Jack held up a hand in greeting and raised the corner of his mouth in a fractional smile.

"I'm Tara," said the girl. "Tell me — is Mr. Carver always that weird? The tin whistle and the 'Happy Song of Beginning' . . . I mean, come on."

Catching herself, she added, "Uh, sorry if he's, like, your favorite teacher or something."

"Not likely," said Jaide. No matter how often he insisted, they would never call Mr. Carver by his first name, Heath. "We're new as well. We only started a week ago."

"Oh, thank goodness I'm not the only one," said Tara. "I have to start at a new school almost every year, so I've had lots of practice. But never at one this small."

"Why do you have to move schools so often?" asked Jack. Tara didn't look like a troublemaker, but then it could be hard to tell. One of the most innocent-looking kids at his last school had been expelled for taking the principal's car for a joyride.

"My dad is a property developer," Tara explained. "He's always finding some great new opportunity, so we have to move while he gets it built. Then he sells whatever it is and off we go again."

"Our mom's a paramedic on a rescue helicopter," said Jaide, feeling a little twinge of competitiveness. "And Dad is an antiques expert."

"Well, he's come to the right place. This whole town is an antique."

"He's not here at the moment," said Jaide, falling into their cover story. "He's away overseas, looking for some lost masterpiece, and we've come to stay with our grand-mother for a while."

"Where does she live?" asked Tara.

"You can see it from over there."

Jaide led the way to the corner of the playground and pointed east. Though the most obvious landmark was the huge hill of stone that thrust up out of the headland, which was appropriately called the Rock, to the north of this they could also see the top of Grandma X's house, from the roof with its weather vane down to the widow's walk. There was also a huge Douglas fir behind the house, which, weirdly, wasn't always visible, though today Jaide could see it clearly.

"No way," said Tara, suddenly clutching Jaide's shoulder with a deadly grip. "Not the big, old house on Watchward Lane?"

"Yes," said Jack, feeling slightly left out of the girls' instant bonding. "What do you know about it?"

"Only that my dad's bought the wrecked-up place next door. He's going to rebuild it himself while his next big development is on hold. Hey, you must be the kids whose old house exploded! You're famous!"

Inside, Jack groaned. He'd made a mistake on his first day of school, when Miralda had grilled him about his and Jaide's origins. Everyone had seemed perfectly sympathetic as he had recounted the story of the destruction of his family home in a gas explosion and their sudden flight to Portland. He had left out all the real facts, of course, like the intrusion of The Evil, and the twins' instinctively using their Gifts, which had gotten out of control and contributed to the disaster.

Gifts getting out of control was pretty typical for young Wardens and the reason they were called troubletwisters. That was why they had come to Portland. The accidental awakening of their Gifts in the city had drawn The Evil to them, and they would remain vulnerable until their Gifts settled down and they learned to use them properly, under the instruction of Grandma X.

Jack was soon glad that he *had* left all that out, because Miralda had decided that even the basic cover story was a source of enormous amusement, which she had immediately shared with all the other kids. Jokes about gas and unintended explosions had haunted him and his sister ever since. It had taken days for Jaide to forgive him.

"We'd rather not talk about it," his sister said now, shooting Jack a withering look.

"It is true, though, isn't it?" Tara said, studying both of them in turn. "I mean, how awful! It's lucky you weren't killed."

Or worse, thought Jaide. Their house blowing up had been just the beginning of their struggle with The Evil. If it could take one of them over, The Evil would get to use the troubletwisters' Gifts for its own purposes, absorbing them in the process.

"I'm not sure *lucky* is the right word," Jack said, looking down at the ground. He was thinking about his father, who had saved them that first time. Hector Shield was a Warden like Grandma X. But Wardens could have children only with non-Wardens, and their mother, Susan, hadn't known about Hector's powers or responsibilities until they were married. She had tried to keep the truth from the twins until it was clear that their Gifts were going to come regardless of what they were told. Now Grandma X was teaching them, and Hector wasn't allowed anywhere near, in case his Gifts unbalanced theirs and caused a disaster.

"What big development is your father working on, Tara?" asked Jaide, to change the subject.

"Oh, the old building near the railway station," she said. "It was a sawmill once, then it sat empty for years and almost fell down. Dad bought it and he's going to turn it into apartments, once the town council stops arguing about it. It's going to be called Riverview House."

"More like swamp view," said Jack. "Or rock view, since Little Rock will be right across from them."

Little Rock was a hill of rough stone, a smaller version of the Rock, since it was only about a hundred and twenty feet high. It had a railway tunnel through the middle of it. Though the regular trains had stopped long ago, there was a tourist steam train that ran once a day each weekday, and twice daily on weekends.

"Riverview sounds better," said Tara. A slight frown passed across her face. "I hope it does, anyway. Dad's last development didn't work out very well."

"Where was that?" asked Jaide.

"Over in Scarborough," said Tara. "You know the shopping mall? Dad and some partners built it, but there was a problem and he's not part of it anymore. I think he lost a lot of money. We still live in Scarborough, though."

"What?" asked Jack. "That's at least a forty-minute drive away. Why come to school here? It's not that great a place."

"Because Dad has to be here all day, from the early morning," said Tara. "And my mom has to stay behind, because she's got a new shop that's open really long hours."

"Our mom is away for three days at a time," said Jaide.

"Sometimes I *wish* my mom would go away that long," Tara said with a dramatic roll of her eyes. "Do you miss your mom when she's gone?"

"Yes," Jaide admitted, even though the truth wasn't as simple as that. When their mom was away, the twins could continue the exploration and use of their Gifts without interruption. The less their mother knew about their secret new life, the better. "When she's away, it's just Jack and me . . . and Grandma."

"Well, I guess that sucks."

Jack cleared his throat. The girls were bonding again and he could feel himself being squeezed out of the conversation.

"Hey," he said, remembering how they'd ended up talking to Tara in the first place, "Miralda said you saw this 'Monster of Portland' thing last night. Did you really?"

"I'm not sure," said Tara. "I just asked her if there was a circus in town, because when I was waiting in the car for my dad last night, I saw something really big near the railway station. But the streetlights were out, so I couldn't see it clearly, and then when I got out to have a better look, it had gone."

"Was it really as big as an elephant?" asked Jaide, recalling Miralda's description. "With insect skin and shark teeth?"

"I don't know about all that stuff," said Tara, looking doubtful. "But it *was* big. I was sleeping in the backseat and at first I thought I dreamt it, but when I brought it up this morning, everyone started talking about this monster of theirs. . . ."

"You don't really believe all that, do you?" asked Jaide with sunny skepticism. "It's just a story."

"Something the locals tell to give each other a scare," added Jack.

"I guess so," said Tara, relaxing again. "I mean, it has to be, right? Monsters aren't real."

"Of course not," said Jaide, even though she knew the exact opposite was true. "Oh, listen — there's the music for the end of lunch."

"What *is* that?" asked Tara. The song being played over the school loudspeakers sounded like wind wailing through the cracks in an old door.

"That thing Mr. Carver plays — it's not a tin whistle," said Jack. "It's a nose pipe. This is one of his songs, called 'Back to Learning.'"

Tara laughed. "No way!"

"Really," said Jaide. "You wait. There's different songs for recess and lunch and home time. Sometimes he walks around us as we work, playing for inspiration. I think he's the only one who ends up feeling inspired."

"Dad is not going to believe this," said Tara.

The three of them started to walk back to class. Behind Tara's back, Jaide mouthed several words to Jack. She almost didn't need to, because he already knew what she was thinking.

We have to talk to Grandma X about this monster!

CHAPTER TWO
HAZARDOUS
HOMEWORK

When the end of school came, Jaide and Jack were the first out the door, scooping up their bags and hurrying on up the path. Tara called "Bye!" after them, and Jaide waved as they fled. Jack was too busy watching the trees across the road as he always did, looking for any sign of The Evil. That was where it had first attacked them, dragging him into the sewers underground on a tide of ants and rats. Just thinking about it still made him feel nervous and unsettled.

They raced each other to Parkhill Street, where they turned right. Watchward Lane lay between a hardware store and a secondhand bookshop called the Book Herd, which had a front window full of adventure novels from the 1950s and incomplete encyclopedias from some time before that. The twins kept an eye out for Kleo the cat, who at least notionally lived there, but she wasn't visible. The only living creature around was Rodeo Dave, the bookshop's mustachioed owner, who waved from the open doorway as they ran by.

Up the cobbled lane they went, under a whitewashed arch topped with weatherworn gargoyles, then along a curving gravel drive. Their grandmother's house appeared from behind a long line of poplars that cast creepy shadows across a scraggly lawn. The faded bricks and shingled roof that had once seemed strange and threatening to them were now a welcome sight. The house provided a secure base of operations for their grandmother's secret work in Portland. From the widow's walk, they could see across most of the small town, and the weather vane next to it had proven a handy indicator of The Evil's presence on more than one occasion.

Jack reached the front door first, as he always did in the race home from school, unless Jaide tripped him along the way. The door was unlocked. They burst inside with a loud clatter of shoes on polished floorboards, threw their bags into the den, and hurried down the hallway.

"Grandma! Grandma!" they both called out.

"She's not here" came the voice of their mother from the kitchen.

Immediately, the twins knew that they had to contain their excitement. If their mother noticed, there would be too many questions that they couldn't answer, with consequent difficulties. Grandma X had "helped" Susan forget the worst parts of the twins' recent adventures, and they didn't want to do anything that might make those memories return.

"Do you know where she went?" Jaide carefully ventured.

"She didn't say." Susan Shield emerged wiping floury hands on an apron. "How was your day?"

Both twins skidded to a halt in the middle of the hallway, staring at her as though they had seen a ghost.

Jaide said, "Mom, what are you doing?"

"Cooking, of course."

"But," said Jack, "you never cook."

"That's not true. I do occasionally."

She turned and went back into the kitchen, with the twins cautiously following, as if something horrible might be lying in wait. "With my shifts giving me four days off in a row, I have to find something to do with my spare time. I thought you'd be excited."

"That depends," said Jaide. "What are you trying — I mean, what are you making?"

When Hector Shield was home, Susan wasn't allowed anywhere near the stove. Her disasters were legendary, including scones that could be used as paperweights years later, steak as tough as plastic, and baked potatoes on which she'd sprinkled sugar instead of salt (Jack had quite liked those).

"I'm making a cobbler," she said proudly. "I found it in one of your grandmother's recipe books. Mamma Jane used to make it for me when I was a kid. You'll love it."

"I thought a cobbler made shoes," said Jaide, thinking about things Susan had made in the past that tasted like old shoes.

"It's also an old word for a kind of pie," replied Susan.

Jack looked around the kitchen and tried to be enthusiastic. The room was a mess. Every cupboard was open, and every drawer, too. A giant pot sat on the stovetop, splattered with dark green gloop. The table was covered in dishes and exotic instruments designed to beat, whip, and blend even the most reluctant ingredients into line. Jack didn't recognize any of them, and he hugged his arms close to his chest to ensure none of the mess got on them.

Some of Susan's cheer faded. "Unfortunately, your grandmother doesn't have any modern appliances — nothing that works on electricity, anyway — so I've been using trial and error. I *think* I've got it worked out now . . . and the oven appears to be behaving itself at last. . . ."

Jaide peeked over the lip of a baking dish broad and deep enough to wash a dog in and saw a glutinous mass that she thought might — or might not — be a cobbler-in-waiting.

"Do we have to eat it?" she asked.

"Don't be like that," said Susan, her face falling even farther. "I'm making it for you as a treat."

"But we didn't ask you to."

"I know you didn't, but that doesn't mean you won't like it." Susan put her hands on her hips. "I mean, I know we're here for a reason, and your grandmother is a very good cook, and you need her to . . ."

Her voice faltered, and her eyes lost focus for a second, as though she had momentarily captured a memory, only to lose it again.

"That is . . . I mean, I ought to be able to look after you, too . . . shouldn't I?"

"Yes, Mom," said Jack, braving the mess to give her a hug. It had been little more than a week since their old home exploded, but already it felt as though they were living separate lives. Every aspect of their troubletwister training, from their Gifts to the house's special properties, had to be kept hidden from their mother. It was a kindness, really, since she couldn't cope with the truth.

Jaide joined him, letting her mother squeeze her around the shoulder. "Can we go play now?"

"No, I want you to do your homework."

"But we don't have any homework to do," said Jack triumphantly.

"I know Mr. Carver never assigns any," said Susan, "but that doesn't mean you can't do some anyway. Look in your room. I've downloaded and printed out some math problems. Do them now and there'll be cobbler when you've finished."

"But, Mom —"

"No buts, Jaide. It's either that or help me clean up in here. Not that this was all my mess. The kitchen was in a terrible state before I even started. Your grandmother has been steaming up some rather odd greens in that big pot. Now, I've finished with the mixing bowl, so you can wash that up, for starters —"

"Homework's fine, Mom!" chorused the twins, as they beat a hasty retreat.

On their beds were two pages each of closely spaced exercises. Jaide barely glanced at them. She threw herself onto her bed. If there was one thing she hated more than her mother's so-called cooking, it was math.

"This isn't *fair*," she said.

"It's not so bad," said Jack. He was good with numbers, and had already completed the first three problems in his head, just by reading through the questions. "The sooner we start, the sooner it'll be finished."

That was one of their father's pet sayings. Jaide didn't appear to be listening.

"I mean, there are so many better things we could be doing," she muttered, kicking one sneakered foot against a pole of her four-poster bed, making the knob on top rattle in a very satisfactory way. "If Grandma was here, I bet we wouldn't have to do this."

"She'd only make us work on the *Compendium*," said Jack. The *Compendium* was the repository of knowledge every Warden needed to possess to help them fight The Evil. Over the past week, Jack and Jaide had spent hours writing up their own experiences for the benefit of others and reading about previous encounters until their eyes crossed with exhaustion.

"Yes, but at least that's *interesting*. That's what we're here for, isn't it? Not to do adding and subtracting. We won't need any of this stuff when we're Wardens."

Jack put his pencil down and thought about that.

"We might, you know," he said. "I mean, being a Warden is a secret job, so we'll have to have ordinary jobs as well. Dad has his antique-finding business. I know it ties in with being a Warden, but he must need it for money, and to look normal, I guess."

"Normal?" Jaide scoffed. "Since when does Dad look normal?"

"Okay," Jack replied, picking up his pencil again. "I'm just saying that even when we're Wardens we'll still need ordinary jobs and everything."

"Maybe," Jaide agreed, grudgingly. She thought about being a Warden, and wondered what her cover identity might be. "It depends where we have to go to fight The Evil. If we get to go somewhere interesting, like Africa, I could be an archaeologist. Or if it's to a tropical island, I could be a marine biologist."

There were a number of special places all around the world, like Portland, where The Evil found it easier to get through and take over living things. The Wardens blocked these entry points by establishing magical wards. But the twins didn't know where these places were. They didn't even know where three of the four wards were in Portland, or what they were.

The only thing Grandma X had told them about the wards so far was a simple rhyme:

SOMETHING GROWING
SOMETHING READ
SOMETHING LIVING
SOMEONE DEAD

There was a ward for each of the four points of the compass, but the twins only knew about Portland's East Ward, because they'd had to fix it. Formerly a charm magicked into a bronze plate in the lighthouse, the "something read" ward was now a piece of romantic graffiti written by their parents before getting married, invested with magical powers from the twins' Gifts.

The twins had tried to work out what the other wards might be, but Grandma X wouldn't tell them, and discouraged them from guessing. She just said, "You know your Gifts can disturb the wards, my dear troubletwisters. So until you have control of those Gifts, it is best that you do not involve yourselves with them. There is a time for everything, you know, and now is not that time."

After the restoration of the East Ward, The Evil could no longer come through from its own dimension or world or wherever it properly belonged, and everything had gone back to normal.

Or so Grandma X told them. But if there really was a monster in Portland, it must have come from *somewhere*.

"Never mind The Evil," muttered Jaide, finally reaching for the pages to start her homework. "We need protection from our own mother. . . ."

They worked in silence until the last math problem was completed and checked. Jack finished first, but he didn't go on about it to Jaide. She was already cross. When they were done, they put the completed pages on their mother's bed, then paused for a moment at the top of the stairs, taking stock.

From below came a faint burning smell, the sound of clattering dishes, and the occasional, puzzled exclamation.

"She sounds busy," whispered Jaide. "Let's not disturb her."

Jack didn't argue. Together they tiptoed down the stairs and out the front door, then circled around the north side of the house, well out of sight of the kitchen window, until they reached the backyard. The rain of the previous night had cleared, leaving the ground only slightly damp. They climbed the tangled roots of the Douglas fir and debated what was to be done about their missing grandmother. They had been home from school for a full hour and still she hadn't appeared.

"Her car's gone," noted Jack, peering into the shady corner of the yard where the yellow Hillman Minx usually sat.

"And so are the cats," said Jaide. She stood on her tiptoes to peer over the fence bordering the yard, in case the cats were hunting next door. Aristotle and Kleopatra were their grandmother's Warden Companions, and they were often prowling about. "Kleo's always here to keep an eye on us when Grandma's out, like she doesn't trust us. . . ."

Over the south fence they could see the old, fire-blackened house that had been empty since before the twins had arrived in Portland. This was the house Tara's father planned to develop. It was a twin to Grandma X's ancient home, but built on a much narrower block, which made it seem smaller, somehow, crowded in on all sides. They had been warned to stay well away from it because it wasn't safe.

"Kleo?" called Jack, just in case the cats were close but out of sight. "Ari?"

There were no answering meows, just the soft sighing of wind through pine needles.

"Now what?" asked Jaide, slumping down onto a particularly large root. "Should we go looking for the monster ourselves?"

"We don't even know if there really is a monster," replied Jack. "Besides, we have to stay here to suffer from Mom's pie."

"We could look it up in the *Compendium* —" Jaide started to say, before Jack interrupted her.

"No, we can't," said Jack. "Grandma told us not to go into the blue room when she's not around. We'll just have to wait."

The blue room was the house's hidden lower level, entered by a second front door only Wardens and trouble-twisters could see, or via a magical corridor that led from the second floor to the basement in a single step.

"But there's nothing to *do*," Jaide complained. "I wish we still had our trampoline."

Their trampoline had been blown up along with their old house and all their other toys, and it was one thing Jaide particularly missed. She liked nothing better than being airborne.

"Yeah, well, if you hadn't kicked the soccer ball into the tree yesterday —"

"It wasn't my fault the branch got in the way!"

"But if you hadn't been cheating, it would never have gone that high in the first place."

"Cheating how?"

"By using your Gift."

"I would never do that." Jaide jumped to her feet, inspired rather than offended by the accusation. "But that's how we'll get it down again. Come on!"

CHAPTER THREE
A NOSY NEIGHBOR

Jaide dragged her brother out of the shadow of the tree and shaded her eyes to peer into the upper branches. They had found the soccer ball in a closet the previous day. It was old and slightly flat, but they had pumped it up with a bicycle pump discovered on a previous expedition, and had kicked the ball around for an hour before it went up into the tree. Now it seemed impossibly high, a tiny black-and-white speck caught firmly in the crook of two branches.

She really hadn't been using her Gift to give the ball even the slightest extra boost. It had just seemed to shoot off her sneaker like a rocket. Perhaps she had hidden soccer talents, too, she thought.

"Are you sure we should do this?" asked Jack. "Grandma —"

"Grandma keeps telling us we'll never get our Gifts under control unless we practice them."

"Yeah, but inside, where no one can see."

"We're pretty well hidden here," Jaide pointed out.

"I suppose —"

"Good!" exclaimed Jaide, without waiting to see what Jack was actually going to say. He sighed, shrugged his shoulders, and gestured for his sister to do whatever it was she wanted to do.

Jaide took a deep breath and lifted her hands up, palms out to face the ball. The sun, one source of power for her particular Gift, shone brightly upon her, making her feel warm and full of energy. A faint breeze — which also reinforced her Gift — tickled her arms and face and set her red hair dancing. This was the fun part — starting, feeling the Gift stirring in her, slowly letting it build up before she unleashed it, hopefully under control.

In front of her, a miniature whirlwind spun up out of thin air, hurtling around and around like an elongated top.

"Go on," she told it. "Get the ball, and *don't* do anything else."

The tiny twister stretched upward and then, moving erratically at first but then more steadily, began to ascend toward the tree's upper branches.

Jack watched her from the edge of the tree's shade, feeling slightly envious. Jaide could *do* things with her Gift, practical things that had an immediate effect on the world. All he could manage when the sun was up was skulking about in shadows. His Gift was fed by darkness and the deeps of the earth.

Feeling left out, he stepped back into the shade of the tree and concentrated on being invisible. The afternoon sun was still bright, and the dense foliage above him cast a thick net of shadows. Diving into them was like pulling a veil down over the world, because when he became one with the darkness, ordinary light seemed to slip over him, too, like water off a duck's back. Daytime became dull and thin, and the night as deep as a magical well.

The shadows gathered where the branches of the tree met the trunk. He reached into them, slipping from point to point with the ease of breath. He was a Shadow Walker, someone who could go wherever shadows led, popping in and out of existence — and in this case, that could be right up into the top of a tree.

It suddenly occurred to Jack that he could race Jaide to the ball and, if he was careful, bring it down himself.

Shadow-Jack darted silently up the trunk like a dark, human-shaped lizard, grinning at the thought of how he would surprise his sister.

Meanwhile, the tiny twister danced higher, twitching and tying itself in knots. Jaide kept her eyes carefully on it, and used her upraised hands to bat it in the right direction as if she were wielding a motion-guided remote control. Grandma X once had her nudge individual dust motes back and forth in shafts of golden sunlight, but this was much more fun — and considerably more challenging. She could feel her Gift uncoiling in her like a tiger roused from sleep, and she whispered calming thoughts to it.

"Easy, easy . . . not too fast . . . that's it . . . no, gently — gently . . ."

The tiny twister came level with the ball, and trembled there for an instant, as though deciding whether to collapse or go sweeping off into the sky. Jaide gritted her teeth, *willing* it to behave. All it had to do was nudge the ball firmly enough to knock it out of its perch. She could do it with the tip of a finger. Why should using her Gift be different?

By then, Shadow-Jack was two-thirds up the tree. He saw the twister waving an arm's length from the ball and put on a renewed burst of speed. It was getting harder the higher he went, as the branches became thinner, letting in more light. He felt simultaneously stretched and squeezed as he jumped from perch to perch. *Just another jump*, he told himself. Just one more, and the ball would be in reach.

Jaide was concentrating too closely to see her brother.

"Nearly there, nearly there . . . that's it . . . Yes!"

The twister reached out with one tendril of air to touch the trapped soccer ball. The ball shivered in its perch, and the branch shivered with it, sending sharp swords of sunlight into Shadow-Jack, ripping him apart.

"Jaide, be careful!" he cried out.

"Don't worry," she said, thinking he was still on the ground behind her. "I've nearly got it. One more push —"

The twister came closer to the ball, shredding needles as it went, letting in even more sun.

"Jaide!" shouted Jack. He felt sick, and strange, neither in his physical body back next to Jaide, nor in his shadow-form, but somewhere horrible in between.

An electric blue nimbus sprang into life around the soccer ball. With a roaring noise like a jet taking off, the twister exploded into a full-strength whirlwind as big as the tree, blowing off most of its needles.

Jaide was thrown back, even as she shouted at the twister.

"Stop! Listen to me! Why won't you do what I tell you to?"

The wind roared and the tree groaned, roots knotting and clenching in the soil at its base. The Evil's bulldozer attack the previous week had weakened it. Jaide could see roots lifting out of the ground. It looked like at any moment the tornado might lift the entire tree away.

"Stop!" screamed Jaide. "STOP!"

The twister didn't obey. It got worse. The tree groaned like a wounded animal, the wind shrieked, and somewhere deep inside both noises Jaide heard Jack shouting, too.

Only then did she wonder where he was. He had been standing right next to her, but now . . .

Jaide looked around wildly, no longer concentrating on the twister. There was a kind of dim, shadowy version of Jack near her, but that was all. It was as if most of him had disappeared, leaving only an outline.

Then she saw him up the tree, *inside* the whirlwind. Or rather, she saw his shadow-form.

"Jack!" she shouted. "Get back in your body!"

There was no answer. The whirlwind was too noisy for Jack to hear her, and any second now it looked like the tree would topple over, taking Jack with it.

Jaide shut her eyes and concentrated, willing the whirlwind to stop with every particle of power she possessed.

Jack was attempting to get control of his Gift as well. He tried to get back into his normal body, but there was too much sunshine. Every time he got into a little patch of shadow, the tree would twist and move and the sun would break across, hurting him.

I have to make shadow, Jack thought desperately. *I need to create a shadow to block the sun long enough for me to get back to my body.*

He didn't know if he could make a shadow. Closing his eyes, he reached for his Gift and tried anyway.

The soccer ball sent out a bolt of lightning that went straight up into the sky, and the sharp, acrid smell of ozone spread through the air.

Above Jack's shadow-self, a cloud of darkness began to form. It spread sideways and ballooned around him, taking in the tree, the twister, the yard. Then, without any conscious direction from him, it suddenly enveloped the entire town.

The twister fell silent. The air stopped moving. The great Douglas fir uttered a last, plaintive growl as it settled back in place.

The soccer ball fell out of the branches and rolled across the ground toward Jack and Jaide.

It was suddenly cold. Jaide opened her eyes and blinked in the sudden darkness. What had happened?

"Jack? Jack . . ." she whispered in the silence. The darkness had to be his doing. But she felt a sudden, terrible fear that perhaps they'd done something awful. Maybe they'd let The Evil in.

Jack felt himself snap back into his body. He opened his eyes and looked up at the tree. Despite the darkness, he could see, after a fashion. It was rather like looking at a fuzzy black-and-white negative image, all white outlines and no detail.

He realized immediately that this was much more than just their Gifts going out of control. There was something not right about the soccer ball. He could see it now, sending out fizzing sparks. Was it a trap?

"Jack? Bring back the sun."

Jack looked across. Jaide was kneeling down, clutching her legs, making herself as small as possible. Only then did it occur to him that he'd made more shadow than he'd intended.

"Uh-oh," he whispered. He bent his head and concentrated, feeling the shadow. It was almost as if it was part of him, some extension of himself.

"*Come back*," he whispered, reaching out with his hands to pull the darkness back toward him, like drawing up a blanket on a cold night. The shadow responded, returning to its maker.

Jaide stood up as the dark sky peeled back to reveal the sun once more. She shivered and looked at Jack, who lowered his arms and met her gaze.

"I'm sorry," she said.

"It wasn't your fault. Do you think anyone noticed?"

"Noticed?" said a man's voice from the other side of the fence. "I reckon the whole town must have seen it!"

The twins spun around, guilt and fear making their hearts pound.

A middle-aged man with an expensive haircut was looking over the makeshift fence, stretching up to get a good look. He was wearing an old baseball cap with a three-M logo on his head, tipped back on his immaculate hair. The cap looked very out of place with his brilliantly white shirt, gold tie, and dark, pin-striped suit.

"Have you ever seen anything *like* that?" he said, turning his attention to the twins.

"It isn't what you think," said Jaide, torn between wishing Grandma X was there to offer the man a hot chocolate and make him forget about everything, and hoping Grandma X never ever found out about what they had done wrong.

"Not what I think? Nonsense! What else could it have been?"

"Uh, I don't know," said Jack, who didn't like the way the man was looking at him. He was studying them entirely too closely, and he hadn't blinked once.

"Well, then." The man abruptly changed the subject, gesturing toward Grandma X's home. "You live here, huh?"

"Yes," said Jaide, also beginning to feel defensive. That feeling grew only stronger as a barrage of questions followed.

"Do you go to school in Portland, too?"

"Yes, but what —"

"I'm new here. Perhaps you can help me."

"I don't know —"

"There's a woman — Renita Daniels. She was supposed to meet me here but she hasn't shown up. Have you seen her at all?"

The twins exchanged an anxious glance. They knew exactly who he was talking about. Rennie was the town handywoman who had been taken over by The Evil. The last time they'd seen her, she had rats growing out of her shoulders and had tried to kill them, before falling off the top of the lighthouse.

"We haven't seen her," said Jack.

"She disappeared," Jaide added.

"When?" the man asked them.

"In the storm."

"That big blow a week ago? I wondered why I hadn't heard from her. You see, she has something of mine, and I'd very much like to get it back."

CHAPTER FOUR

DEVELOPMENTS OF A DUBIOUS NATURE

That will be quite impossible," said a firm voice. "Rennie is missing. It is feared that she was swept out to sea in the storm, and is very likely to be dead."

Three pairs of eyes converged on the house's back entrance, where Grandma X stood with one hand on the door frame. She was a tall woman with thick silver hair, and was dressed in blue jeans, a white shirt, and cowboy boots. Next to those boots, one on each side, stood two cats, one gray and straight-tailed, the other a ginger tom whose head was held low to the ground, ready to pounce.

"And you are?" asked the man.

"The grandmother of these children."

"Ah!" The man straightened to his full height — which could have barely been five and a half feet, given the way he was clinging to the top of the fence. His smile was sudden and entirely too friendly, as though he had taken off a mask and replaced it with a new one. His teeth were far too white and regular to be natural. "The owner herself! My company has been trying to get in touch with you. My name is Martin M. McAndrew —"

"I know who you are."

"Well, let's get straight to it, then. I want your house."

Jaide stiffened and Jack felt a lump turn to ice in his stomach. Martin McAndrew's eyes weren't the ghastly pure white of The Evil, but after a statement like that, there was no way his intentions could possibly be good.

To the twins' surprise, Grandma X didn't explode, or turn him into a cockroach. She just smiled back. But if smiles could be warning shots, this would have whizzed over his left ear and taken his cap with it.

"Tell me, Mr. McAndrew, why were you asking the children about their school?"

"Because they might know my daughter, Tara. She just started."

"And what do you want with poor Rennie?"

"I hired her a fortnight ago to help with the renovations here." He waved at the empty, fire-blackened house behind him, his smile faltering for just a moment. "My company, MMM Holdings, still deeply regrets that terrible accident with the bulldozer, and we want you to know that our offer for your house still stands, Mrs. — uh —"

"Thank you. Lastly, what do you think you just saw in the sky?"

"Just then? It was an eclipse, of course."

"An eclipse?" echoed Jack in surprise.

Martin McAndrew turned his attention back to the twins. "What else could it have been? The sun going out like that, then coming back again. Remarkable!"

Jack hastily nodded. "Yes, it sure was."

"I'm surprised it wasn't on the news, but I've been very busy lately . . . distracted. I'm rebuilding this house here as a personal thing, just a sideline, but you might have heard of my latest big project — Riverview House. There are still some retirement units left, you know, and we'll be back at work on them very soon. Perhaps we could arrange some kind of swap. . . ?"

"I really don't think so," said Grandma X. "Jack, Jaide, come inside now. Your mother has made you a . . . treat."

The twins backed away toward the house, not quite ready to turn away from Martin M. McAndrew.

"Nice to meet you, kids," he said with a jokey salute. Once he dropped down behind the fence, the twins hurried inside, ushered into the laundry room by their grandmother while the cats ran after McAndrew, as though to see him off.

The twins conducted a hurried conversation entirely in whispers, so Susan wouldn't hear.

"That's Tara's dad?"

"He doesn't look a bit like her!"

"He's so creepy."

"And did you see the way he smiled at us?"

"I thought we were dead for sure!"

"Don't be ridiculous, Jackaran and Jaidith," said their grandmother, doing her best to interject herself into their excitable exchange. "He's just a property developer. An insidious and unlikable breed, but not actually dangerous."

"But it was his bulldozer that almost flattened us!"

"And he was looking for Rennie —"

"And he wants your house —"

"And he saw what happened when we —"

Jaide elbowed Jack firmly in the ribs, but it was too late.

"What did he see, troubletwisters?" asked Grandma X sternly.

Jack lowered his gaze and looked at the floor. Jaide met her grandmother's eye squarely and said, "We used our Gifts, and something went wrong. We don't know what. It was like something interfered with us."

"It was the ball," said Jack, raising his head. "Tara's dad did something to it — I'm sure of it. He rigged it so we would reveal ourselves, and he was right there to catch us when we did."

"That's an interesting theory," said Grandma X. "It's a shame the facts don't support it."

She raised her right hand, which held the deflated remains of the ball. Clearly written on the limp rubber were three letters written in a childish hand.

HJS. Their father's initials.

"I don't need to ask you where you found this," she said. "It's been moldering away in that box ever since your father was a teenager — but time doesn't change the fact that it was once owned by a Warden. A troubletwister then, of course, but his Gift is what matters. The ball has some of his power in it, and it reacted to you when you used your Gifts near it. You must be careful what you play with around here — just as you must be wary of strangers, but not to the point of imagining things that simply aren't there. A person of dubious morals and practices he may be, but Mr. McAndrew is not The Evil."

"You said that some people ally themselves with The Evil even though they're not taken over," said Jaide, not yet willing to let go of the theory. Martin McAndrew was definitely guilty of *something*.

"And he's working on a big development," said Jack. "What if he digs up one of the wards or . . . or pours concrete over one of them!"

"He won't, trust me. I have taken steps. And don't you worry about the wards. It's dangerous for you to go anywhere near them. And it's dangerous for them, too."

"How can we avoid them if we don't know what all of them are?"

"First of all, don't practice your Gifts unless you're under my supervision. Secondly, if you do find something strange happening, immediately back away and come home. Thirdly, don't even *think* about the wards. Do you understand?"

Both twins thought of the promise they had made their father — to do anything their grandmother asked them, no matter how strange or annoying.

"Yes, Grandma," Jaide said.

"Can you fix the ball?" asked Jack. "So we can play with it?"

"I think it would be best if I bought you a new one." Grandma X smiled.

"Thanks, Grandma!" said Jack. "You're the best."

Grandma X's smile widened. She tousled Jack's hair, then looked piercingly at Jaide.

"Is there something else I can do for you, Jaidith?"

"Uh, yes," said Jaide. "I . . . we . . . wanted to ask you about the Monster of Portland."

"Is it real?" Jack asked. "Is it some creature of The Evil?"

Grandma X's smile faded, though there was still a slight twinkle in her eyes. She knelt down and gathered both children into a quick hug.

"People in Portland have been talking about their monster since your grandfather was a boy. Probably longer. But none of them have ever seen such a thing. All I can say is that if there was a creature of The Evil stalking about the streets, I would certainly tell you about it. Now, come into the kitchen and see what your mother has made — and then I have something for you that I hope will help you burn off some of your restless energy, so it is not directed into your Gifts."

The twins obeyed, torn between their reluctance to eat their mother's cooking and the rewards that would follow.

Sure enough, when they entered the kitchen they found the air thick with smoke and their mother trying to put on a brave face.

"Here we are, kids," she said as she unveiled the charred lump sitting on a wire tray in the center of the table. "I was missing a couple of ingredients, and that oven still has a mind of its own, but I think this'll be delicious. Shall I cut you the corner piece, Jack? I know that's your favorite."

"Go out the window," yowled Ari from the sill, his tail lashing. "It's not too late."

"Don't listen to him," said Kleo, sitting prim and upright on the sideboard. "He just wants more for himself."

"Not me," Ari said, with a shiver that ran from nose to tail. "I'm off to find something more edible, like a three-days-dead mouse."

With that, he followed his own advice, leaping out the window and running off into the garden.

"He really does have the most abominable manners," sniffed Kleo.

"Listen to those cats meow," said Susan. "If only we could understand what they're saying."

"I expect they'd only talk about food," Grandma X said. "And perhaps the benefits of a good scratch under the collar."

She looked at each of the twins and winked. That was just one of many secrets they had to keep from their mother, along with the blue room, their Gifts, and everything to do with The Evil. Jack and Jaide really wanted to ask Kleo where the cats had gotten to that afternoon, but the twins had to pretend that they heard only mews and yowls.

Grandma X produced antique tea plates from a cupboard while Susan carved the cobbler into pieces, with some difficulty. Jack did indeed like the corner piece of fresh cakes, because they were the crunchiest bits, but he struggled to get his teeth through the burned crust that had formed over this one. Inside, he found lumps of fruit and nuts in a doughy paste that hadn't quite cooked through.

"Deliffoush," said Jaide through a mouthful that proved to be particularly difficult to swallow.

"Yes," said Grandma X. "Very good, dear. But don't eat it all, children. It will be dinnertime soon."

Jack gratefully put his slice back on the plate, only half eaten. Even Susan herself looked relieved as she did the same.

"I guess it's later than I thought," she said. "It's easy to

get distracted, cooking. Are we going to have those . . .
um . . . Chinese greens you've been steaming?"

"Greens?" said Grandma X with an eyebrow raised. "I
thought we'd just have fish and chips. I'm quite busy and,
well, I think you've done enough cooking for one day."

"But I thought . . ." Susan indicated the giant pot still
sitting on the stove.

"Oh, that's just where I dyed some old jeans."

"Bright green?"

"For community theater, dear. This year the Portland
Players are putting on *Peter Pan*. Perhaps we'll go see it
when it opens next month."

"Er, yes, perhaps." Susan got up to clear away the
plates. "Well, I'll just clean up here while you show the kids
what you got them today."

"If you like. Come on, Jackaran and Jaidith, and see
what's in the back of the car."

Revived by the reminder of their presents, the twins
thundered out of the kitchen and up the hall. Grandma X
and Kleo followed at a more sedate pace.

Outside, the twins fought over who would open the car
door. Jaide won, and she swept it open to reveal two metal
contraptions that were so entangled she didn't immediately recognize what they were: black wheels, worn leather
saddles, rubber squeeze-bulbs connected to long hornlike
devices, and wire shopping baskets fixed to two broad
handlebars.

"Bikes!" said Jack and Jaide at the same time.

"I picked them up this afternoon," said Grandma X as
they struggled to slide the tangled bicycles out of the car

without damaging anything. "Careful of your fingers. The green one is for Jackaran, the purple for Jaidith. I hope that's right. I thought they'd be good for getting to and from school."

With a metallic rattle, the bikes touched the ground and untangled into their new owners' arms. They were larger than they had looked in the car, and heavy, too, spotted here and there with bright red rust. Jack couldn't help but be disappointed by how old they were, although he shouldn't have expected anything else; everything Grandma X owned was an antique. Jaide was very pleased with her color, and the old-fashioned horn. Experimentally, she squeezed the rubber bulb, and jumped at the bright *hoh-onk* it emitted.

"Thank you, Grandma!" she said, hopping onto the seat. It was just the right height. "Can we go for a ride now?"

"Helmets," replied Grandma X, handing over two entirely new bicycle helmets, just out of their plastic wrap. "From your mother."

Jack and Jaide took the helmets, looked at them, swapped the ones they'd been given, and put them on.

"Can we go *now*?" repeated Jaide.

"I suppose so," Grandma X said with an amused smile. "Remember what I told you before, and make sure you're back before the sun goes down."

"Okay!" said Jaide, putting her weight on the pedals and taking the bike once around the car.

Jack followed more cautiously, half expecting the handlebars to drop off the moment he tried to steer. Fortunately they didn't, and in fact the bike rode smoothly under him, wheels crunching musically on the gravel.

"Don't go anywhere you shouldn't!" Grandma X called after them as they cycled down the driveway.

Kleo ran after them to the beginning of the lane. There she stopped and sat, tail twitching. The twins were already disappearing around the corner and onto Parkhill Street, barely wobbling on their new wheels and happily tooting their horns at each other.

"Do you think the bikes will keep them distracted for long enough?" asked Kleo as the Warden of Portland came up behind her.

"One can only hope," said Grandma X, already turning to go back into the blue room and the difficult task ahead of her. "Herding troubletwisters is a very uncertain craft. I must give them space to grow, and hope they do not break anything important. Least of all themselves."

CHAPTER FIVE

SECRET SECRETS

Jack and Jaide sped down Dock Road, past the fish market, and onto Main Street. Pedaling furiously, they swept over the iron bridge and took a right opposite Town Hall onto the track that led around the coast to Mermaid Point. Jaide's hair streamed out behind her, and Jack whooped every time he took a bump. They'd had bikes in the city, but there had been so few places they could ride this fast. There were always cars to worry about, and traffic lights, and it was easy to get lost if they went too far from home. Portland had none of those problems. For the first time, they learned that life in a small town could really suit them — even without the magical elements that Grandma X was so-slowly revealing to them.

At the turnoff for Mermaid Point, they braked to a crawl.

"Shall we take a look?" asked Jaide.

"At what?" Jack replied.

"The Point. Remember, it looks like a person? A woman, Grandma X said. Maybe it's one of the wards."

"We're supposed to stay away from them!"

"How can we if Grandma X won't tell us where or what they are?"

Jack thought about that.

"I guess she doesn't think we can get near them," he said. "Or else she's watching us and will step in if we get too close."

Both twins looked around. There were no people nearby, and no cats lurking about. But that didn't mean Grandma X wasn't watching by some magical means.

"Let's keep on riding," said Jack. Secretly he was a bit concerned that the rocky shape at the end of the point might really be one of the wards, and he didn't want to go near it just in case Grandma X *wasn't* keeping an eye on them.

"I suppose we did tell her we wouldn't go near anything that might be a ward," said Jaide.

"*You* did," said Jack with a grin, putting on a sudden burst of speed and shooting ahead.

They followed the track to the Wide Beach parking lot, where they turned left and headed inland. Here and there they saw evidence of the storms that had gripped the town a week ago, when Grandma X and The Evil had waged battle over the twins. Piles of branches awaited cleanup crews; odd little sand drifts reached long fingers over the path, where the ocean had spilled across the land.

The small hospital farther up looked busy, with lots of cars in the parking lot, and a steady stream of people going in and out. It had looked deserted when the twins had first arrived.

Behind the hospital was a retirement home and a pre-school, neither of which they had noticed before. A cheery old man with one arm and not a single hair on his head waved at them as they went by, and they honked their horns in response.

Instead of returning by Main Street, they crossed it and cycled through a series of streets named, they guessed, after long-dead dignitaries of the town. Some of the names they recognized from the cemetery, including Govey, Treddinick, Camfferman, and, lastly, Rourke. Rourke Road ran along an old estate and a swamp that also bore the same name.

"Whoever he was," Jack said, "he must have been important."

"Or she," said Jaide as they swept back to the iron bridge across the river.

At the intersection of Main and River, directly in front of the school, Jaide slammed on her brakes and skidded to a halt.

"What're you doing?" asked Jack, coming to an abrupt halt beside her.

She pointed up Main Street to the end of the block, where it turned left and became Dock Road.

"We *could* go home the way we came," she said, "or we could go this way."

This time she pointed up River Road, past the willows.

Jack suppressed his automatic shudder. "Why that way?"

"Do I need a reason?"

"No . . . wait . . . you want to go past the old sawmill!"

"Maybe." She smiled and spun her pedals with the foot that wasn't holding her bike upright.

Jack looked up at the horizon.

"It's almost sunset."

"Are you game?"

"Grandma said not to go anywhere we shouldn't."

"Yeah, but she didn't tell us anywhere in particular. Besides, if we're back before the sun really sets, she'll never know."

"All right, then." The shadows were lengthening fast, but Jack figured they had enough time for a quick ride-by. "Race you!"

They waited a moment for a delivery truck to pass them, then shot up River Road, working harder along a slight uphill gradient. Jack had already noted that Jaide was slightly better at riding than he was, so he put extra energy into distracting her, pointing out birds flying to their nests, odd domestic scenes glimpsed through un-curtained windows, even suggesting that she had a better bike because Grandma X liked her more. The distractions and bickering disadvantaged her just enough that they were neck and neck as they turned onto Station Street and saw the old sawmill ahead.

They slowed, taking stock of it from a prudent distance. It had once been an imposing structure — that was clear from the thick, exposed beams that showed how high its sloping roof had been and how wide and long it had stood. Now, much of its exterior planking had been removed and lay in rough piles dotted around the site. Yellow construction machines sat abandoned in an orderly row down one fence line, near a management hut that sat dark and unattended. There were no trees around the site, no vegetation at all beyond the odd blade of grass in the sandy, industrial soil, which had been perfectly leveled in preparation for the next stage of development.

Behind the site stood the dark peak of Little Rock, with the sun setting fast behind it.

Jack shivered without knowing why. Then he noticed the banner hung from a shiny new flagpole at the southeast corner of the block. The banner was facing the other way, but with the evening sun shining through it, the twins could easily make out what was on it. There Martin McAndrew's three-M logo was depicted as a line of peaked rooftops. Below that was the slogan, which was meant to say:

BUILDINGS TO LIVE IN.

But from the twins' perspective, seeing it reversed, it spelled out:

.NI EVIL OT SGNIDLIUB

The capital letters were highlighted in a bright green that made the word ***EVIL*** almost glow in the twilight.

"Grandma's wrong about that McAndrew guy," whispered Jaide. "She has to be."

Jack wasn't so sure. Jaide did have a tendency to leap into things, and surely, if McAndrew was an agent of The Evil, he wouldn't advertise it in this way.

"It could just be a coincidence, couldn't it? I mean, it's not really evidence."

"Let's find some evidence, then!"

Jaide leaped off her bike, letting it fall on the side of the road.

"Hey! Wait!" Jack called out. But she was already across the road and slipping through a narrow gap in the fence. Jack hurriedly propped his bike against a street sign and followed.

It was getting dark fast. Jaide opened her eyes as wide as she could in order to tiptoe safely around planks and trestles, over power cables and bags of nails. A dark rectangular stack of corrugated iron snagged her hoodie as she went by, making her heart leap into her throat. The site was quiet and apparently empty, but she couldn't be sure of anything where The Evil was concerned. With every moment, the dusk got deeper and deeper. . . .

To Jack, the light was perfectly sufficient. With the sun hidden, he felt at home and confident. He glided silently and swiftly to Jaide's side, and was gratified by her slight gasp of surprise.

"Don't *do* that," she hissed, gripping his arm tightly as he led her deeper into the site. "See anything suspicious?"

He shook his head. Together they went around one corner of the sawmill and followed its southern wall to the back of the block, where a cement mixer and a mound of heavy bags loomed out of the shadows. Several deep trenches had been dug behind the sawmill, possibly to extend its foundations and thereby allow it to be expanded. Jack warily skirted the nearest one. Even with his excellent night vision, he couldn't see its bottom. Anything could have been hiding there.

"What's that smell?" Jaide asked suddenly. "Crushed ants?"

Something squelched underfoot.

Jack looked down.

"Yeeuck!"

He jumped backward out of a puddle of brackish liquid, dragging Jaide with him. The puddle was several long steps across. Floating in the liquid like tiny, sad icebergs were a dozen half-dissolved rats.

"What is it?" asked Jaide, struggling to see anything on the ground through the thickening gloom.

"Uh . . . you don't want to know."

"I *do* want to know, Jack. That's why I asked."

He told her and she blanched.

"Oh, that's . . . gross."

Headlights washed over them, and they ducked behind a portable toilet. A car had pulled up outside the building site, and was sitting there with its engine rumbling.

"We should get out of here," said Jack, dazzled by the glare.

"But we can't go back that way." The gap they had squeezed through was close to the main gate, where the car was parked.

"There must be another way out." Jack peered about him. "There," he said, pointing at the fence line on the other side of the site. "I think I see something."

They scurried from shadow to shadow as they heard the sound of a car door opening and closing behind them. The padlock on the main gate rattled, and then the gate itself was opening, hinges squeaking faintly in the still evening air.

Jaide tripped over a sudden dip in the ground. "Ooof!"

"Shhhh!"

"Sorry."

"Wait — what is this?" Jack's keen night-sight had picked up something odd about the dip Jaide had stumbled over. It didn't look deliberately made. Everywhere else, the ground was perfectly flat, but here the ground was churned up as though by something heavy — something that had been dragged along, creating a trench with bunched-up earth on either side.

"Who cares?" whispered Jaide. "Keep moving!"

"No, wait!" He followed the trench backward, toward the fence. There were secondary marks on either side, like giant scratches.

Jack gasped when he saw the fence itself. A giant hole had been ripped through it.

"Jaide — look!"

Even in the twilight, Jaide could see the hole. "Great!" she said. "That's how we get out."

Dragging him after her, she ran through the rent in the fence and off the building site.

They had barely reached the road when they were caught in another set of headlights.

They froze like rabbits.

With a loud engine roar, the van behind the lights lunged toward them, wheels spinning. Jack and Jaide split up and went in opposite directions, sprawling desperately out of the way. The van went between them, and Jaide caught a brief glimpse of the logo painted on its side before it sped off down the road, turned right at the next intersection, and disappeared into the streets of Portland.

MMM. Buildings to LIVE in.

"It was him!" she gasped, ignoring the sting of her grazed hands and knees. "He tried to kill us!"

"Why would he do that?" asked Jack, scrambling painfully to his feet.

"Because he's part of The Evil, of course!"

Jack stared back at the giant hole in the fence. He didn't know what was going on, but he did know they would be in trouble when they got home. And the later they were, the bigger the trouble would be.

"We'd better get moving," he said.

Jaide groaned. "Our bikes — they're by the front gate."

"We'll have to go quietly, then."

Taking Jaide's hand, he led her along the fence line, to the corner bordering River Road. There were streetlights there, and they hurried through the pools of relatively bright light until they reached the intersection with Station Street. From there, they could see their bikes where they had left them. Across the road, parked by the site's main gates, was a car they both instantly recognized.

A yellow Hillman Minx.

"Uh-oh," breathed Jaide.

" 'Uh-oh' indeed," said Grandma X from behind them.

Jack's heart practically burst out of his chest, and Jaide jumped so hard her Gift kicked in and started to lift her into the sky, before Grandma X reached up and pulled her down by her ankle and set her firmly on the dirt.

"Grandma!" she said. "You frightened me!"

"Good. What are you doing here? You're supposed to be home by now."

"We . . . got lost," Jack said, improvising wildly. "Then I dropped something. We were looking for it back there, under the lights."

"I don't believe you. You came here to snoop on Mr. McAndrew, didn't you?"

"Yes!" said Jaide, made bolder by what she knew was the absolute truth. "He's evil for sure! Why won't you believe us?"

The sound of Grandma X's tapping foot was startlingly loud in the falling night. "I'll believe you when there's something sensible to believe. I'll tell you this one more time, and you must accept it. Mr. McAndrew is not under the influence of The Evil. You've seen his eyes; they're perfectly clear. Besides, all four wards are intact and working, so The Evil cannot get into Portland without my knowledge. Now, I may not agree with Mr. McAndrew's policies on renovations and redevelopments — in fact, I have argued against them many times at council meetings — but that does not make him an ally of The Evil. Just human. And that is forgivable, if not very likable at times."

Neither twin could meet her firm, reproving stare. They dropped their gaze, and only then did Jack notice the green-stained apron Grandma X was wearing, and Jaide the large, empty soup pot at her feet.

They glanced at each other, communicating clearly and without words: *What?*

"Uh, Grandma," said Jaide. "You've got a soup pot . . ."

Grandma X looked at the pot and picked it back up.

"I came in a hurry," she said. "Now get your bikes and head home before your mother begins to worry."

She ushered them back to their bikes, and then crossed to the parked car. Its engine was idling, the harsh electric glare of its headlights still spilling across the dead soil.

Grandma X opened the back door and tossed the pot onto the backseat.

"If you only came out here looking for us," said Jaide, unable to suppress her curiosity, "why did you go through the gate?"

"I didn't, dear."

"But we heard you."

"You didn't hear me," replied Grandma X firmly. She looked around carefully, and added, "It must have been someone else."

She climbed inside the car and firmly shut the door behind her.

"Straight home, both of you," she ordered through the open window. "I'll be right behind you all the way, so don't even think about taking any shortcuts."

With that, she reversed the Hillman back about twenty yards, its headlights fully illuminating the twins, as if she might confine them within the light.

Jaide ground her teeth together. Trying to get Grandma X to admit that she was wrong was like arguing with a brick wall. They'd definitely heard someone, and there was no one else around. It must have been Grandma X.

"Come on," Jack said quietly. "She's right about getting home. If Mom gets mad, she might take the bikes away. Or something even worse."

"All right." Jaide climbed on and kicked the pedals into motion. "But there's something going on here — I just know it."

"I know it, too. Did you see those tracks back there? They were huge!"

Jack was thinking of tracks he'd seen once on a beach while on vacation. His father had explained how when the moon was right, sea turtles dragged themselves out of the water to lay their eggs in the sand.

"I reckon the monster was right here, tonight."

Behind them, the Hillman Minx crept forward, like a sheepdog beginning to drive a flock. Jaide looked behind her, scowled, and then pushed off. As they rode away, she half turned to Jack and muttered, "She said the monster doesn't exist."

"No," replied Jack thoughtfully. "She didn't actually say it doesn't exist. She said something like she'd tell us if there was some kind of Evil monster creeping around."

Jaide wrinkled her nose.

"I wish she'd just give us a straight answer sometime. Does that mean there *is* a monster?"

"I don't know. But I guess Grandma doesn't want us to go looking for one, either way."

"Secrets!" spat Jaide. "There's just too many of them in this town."

They rode in silence for a moment, deep in thought.

"What if there are different kinds of secrets?" Jack said. "There are secrets like the wards, which we'll learn about one day and which we know we have to avoid right now. We don't know anything about them, really, but we know they exist."

"Like there being other Wardens," said Jaide. "Or that Dad is in Venice, only we don't know exactly what he's doing."

"Yeah. And then there are the other kind of secrets — secrets we're not allowed to even know exist. Because it'll be bad for us, or we might make things worse . . . or maybe just because Grandma doesn't trust us enough yet."

"*Secret* secrets?"

"Secret secrets," Jack confirmed.

"There might even be secret secret secrets," said Jaide. She tried to elbow Jack to emphasize the joke, and their bikes almost collided. A warning beep from the Hillman made them separate again and keep straight.

"Secret squared secrets," said Jack, as they turned right onto Main Street.

"Secrets to the power of secret," said Jaide, straight back.

"Secret times infinity," said Jack.

The sun was completely down now, and the night still and cool. Stars were beginning to come out between a light scattering of clouds.

"You know," said Jaide with new determination in her voice, "as well as not saying whether the monster exists or not, Grandma also never said we can't look for it."

"I guess not," replied Jack as they rode onto the drive

of the house and had to suddenly grip their handlebars more tightly and focus on riding through the loose gravel. "So what do we do?"

"If she won't tell us more about the monster, we'll just have to find someone who will."

CHAPTER SIX

DARK TIMES RECALLED

If Susan Shield detected any abnormal tension around the table that night, she said nothing about it. She had been out getting dinner when the twins had returned home on their bikes, and had therefore been none the wiser about their lateness. As they unwrapped the newspaper and divided up battered fillets and perfectly greasy chips, she asked them if they had enjoyed their bike ride, and they replied that they had.

"The one and only time I came here while your father and I were dating," she said as they ate, "we went on a long bike ride to Scarborough and back. It took hours."

"Why didn't you take the train?" asked Jack.

"I don't know. Time didn't seem to matter so much back then." Her eyes were focused on something far beyond the kitchen walls, and only with an effort did she force herself back to the real world. "There's plenty of cobbler left, when you've finished."

"Thanks, Mom," said Jaide.

"Yeah, awesome." Jack tried to smile, but he didn't need a mirror to know it came out all wrong.

"I suspect they're still full from the cobbler they had before," said Grandma X, patting Susan's hand.

"They can take a piece each to school tomorrow in their lunch boxes."

"Perhaps we could give some to Mr. Carver, too," suggested Jaide with an innocent expression.

"What a good idea." Grandma X smiled. "I'm sure he'd love that."

After dinner, it was Jack and Jaide's turn to do the dishes, but there was no sign of the mysterious soup pot and its thick, green stains, just ordinary plates, cups, and cutlery. Having done their homework and their chores, they would once have looked forward to watching some television, but Grandma X wouldn't allow one in the house. Susan was using her laptop, so the twins had two options: play a board game or read.

"Can we read the *Compendium*?" Jack asked Grandma X when Susan was distracted.

"Of course," replied Grandma X. "A very good idea. Your mother is going back to work tomorrow, and we have much to do while she is gone."

Grandma X ushered them up to their room, promising to return with the *Compendium* when she could.

"Do you think we'll find anything about the monster?" Jack asked as they took the first turn on the stairs. "The *Compendium* never really does what we tell it to."

That was one of the most annoying features of the Wardens' repository of knowledge regarding The Evil. The trick was to think of what you most wanted to know, then open to a random page. Supposedly, the *Compendium* would lead you straight to the information you needed. More often than not, though, the twins found themselves staring at recipes for exotic teas or methods of translating ancient entries into a language they could understand.

The only really useful thing they'd found was a way to quickly heal Jaide's injured finger — which had been savaged by the Oracular Crocodile — but it still tingled at unexpected times. Her fingernail had also turned slightly silver, as if she'd painted it, and the color could not be removed.

"Well, maybe we've just been asking the wrong way," she said. "Or we haven't needed to learn something badly enough."

"How do you think it tells the difference?"

"I don't know. We just have to concentrate harder, I think."

They read ordinary books until Grandma X came in with the *Compendium* several minutes later.

"Your mother will be up in an hour to turn off your lights," she said, putting it on the rug directly between them. "Make sure it's out of sight by then, won't you?"

They promised they would. Jack brought his quilt over to sit with Jaide in front of the *Compendium*. As always, he felt a tingle of anticipation before opening the enormous blue folder. Within lay all the secrets of the Wardens and their long fight against The Evil. Who knew what it would reveal to them this time?

"Think of the monster," Jaide told him, remembering how Grandma X had helped her find Jack when he was lost in the sewers, by holding a clear picture of him in her mind. The trouble was, they didn't have a terribly clear picture of the monster to go on. "What do we know about it?"

"It's big," Jack said. "And it drags itself along."

"It might have shark's teeth and an ant shell."

"And it might be hairy like a gorilla."

"It can't be all those things at once," Jaide said. "Can it?"

"Maybe that's why they call it a monster."

"But there's a word for that particular kind of monster, I think." She sighed. "Let's just open it."

They took one corner each to reveal what lay within the *Compendium*. There, on the page facing them, was the word *chimera* and a drawing of a creature with two heads, one that of a lion, the other a goat, and a snake-head for a tail.

"Oh, yeah," said Jaide. "That's the word I was looking for. *Chimera*."

Jack turned the page. There was a drawing of another chimerical beast, this time part eagle, part lizard. "Do you think these are real?"

"I don't know. We're not looking at photos, after all. Someone could have just made these up for fun."

"We're looking for real monsters," Jack told the *Compendium*. "Don't show us anything that doesn't exist."

The next few pages contained images of mushroom clouds and dictators.

"Ha-ha," said Jaide, turning the pages faster. "Very funny. You know what we mean."

"Wait," said Jack, sticking his finger onto a photo before it could whizz by. "That looks like the Rock."

"What? Where?"

The page was a rather gory one about whalers — men in sailing ships who had slaughtered whales by the thousands in generations past. Dead center on the page was a faded black-and-white photo of a tiny coastal town, featuring two ships moored at the mouth of a narrow harbor, with a huge whale carcass being winched up a kind of broad boat ramp, and a crowd of people standing around in awkward poses.

"There, see?" said Jaide, pointing to the very right-hand edge of the photo. "That's Mermaid Point."

Jack squinted. "It is! But there's no lighthouse or iron bridge. This must have been taken years ago!"

"And there's a clock tower, look. Isn't that where Main Street runs now?

"I think you're right." Jack peered even closer to the photo, straining to make out details from the ancient grays. "But how did they take this? I mean, it's like an aerial photograph, but way before there were planes. . . ."

He looked at Jaide. The same thought occurred to both of them.

"A Warden took it," they said together. "A flying Warden!"

"Must have been a better flier than me," added Jaide with a sigh.

Jack didn't answer for a moment. He tapped a barely legible line of writing at the bottom right of the photograph.

"Or not one at all. It says here, 'The town from above. Third balloon ascent, 1872.'"

"Oh," said Jaide. As so many times before, there was

an ordinary explanation. Perhaps this meant that there was one for Martin McAndrew's *EVIL* sign, too. "Why's it in the *Compendium*, then?"

"Look at the guys around the whale. Check out their eyes."

The figures around the whale were tiny, the photograph having been taken from at least a few hundred yards away from them, and perhaps fifty yards up. But when she looked as close as she could without them turning into tiny, blurred splotches, she saw that every single one had strangely large eyes.

Eyes that were entirely white, without pupil or iris.

"Their eyes are white," she said. "They must have worked for The Evil."

"No, they *were* The Evil. There's no working for The Evil when it's taken you over. You're just part of it. Forever."

Jack's voice was hard and flat, and it was Jaide's turn to shiver. All of a sudden he felt like a stranger to her, a distant, grown-up Jack very different from the four-minutes-younger brother she knew better than anyone. He often went like this when reminded of the times he had come face-to-face with The Evil in the stormwater drains below the town, particularly those times when she hadn't been there to help him. She knew there were details he hadn't told her. A large part of her never wanted to know what they were.

Jack, for his part, was remembering a cold voice echoing through dank tunnels: *Come to us, Jackaran Kresimir Shield. Be with us. Be one of us. . . .*

"Do you think there were any Wardens back then?" Jaide asked.

"Of course, or none of us would be alive today. Besides, it must have been a Warden who took this photograph. Even from a balloon."

The *Compendium* suddenly shivered, then slammed shut. Before the twins could react, it slid across the floor and under Jaide's bed, like an insect that had suddenly been exposed to the light.

Their bedroom door opened. Both twins were gaping at the empty floor, but their heads whipped around as their mother entered the room.

"What are you two up to?" asked Susan with a smile.

"Uh, yoga," said Jaide quickly. "We learned it at school. Mr. Carver is very keen on yoga."

"I used to do yoga with your dad," said Susan. "We went to a class every Tuesday night for quite a few years. Hey, we can do some together —"

"Oh, I'm pretty tired," said Jaide hurriedly. Inwardly, she was cursing herself. Mr. Carver was indeed very keen on yoga, and led a class at lunchtimes for students and staff. Now she'd have to go to one to learn a few moves.

"I'm tired, too," said Jack, feigning a yawn.

"All right. Another day, then." Susan patted them each on the head and said, " 'Jamas and teeth."

"What about dessert?" asked Jack hopefully as Jaide hurried off to the bathroom. Dinner already seemed like hours ago, and his stomach was feeling hollow.

"Well, there's that cobbler. You can have a bit before you go to bed, if you like."

"Oh, no, thanks, Mom," he said.

She tilted her head to one side and smiled at him. "It's okay if you don't like it. You don't, do you?"

"Um, no. Not really. Sorry."

"That's okay, Jack. I'm not offended." She gathered him into a tight hug. "If your father were here, he'd make the best cake in the world, and then he'd say 'tamas and jeeth,' which he still thinks is hilarious, and then he'd chase you up and down the stairs until you were too excited to sleep for a week. . . . Despite all that, I miss him, and I know you miss him, too. Am I right?"

Jack nodded.

She let him go, but only so she could hold him at arm's length and try to meet his eyes.

"You've been very quiet since we moved here. Even quieter than usual. Don't be afraid to talk about stuff," she said. "You can tell me anything, you know."

Jack nodded again, knowing full well that if he told his mother even a small fraction of what he had learned, her mind would probably explode.

"Okay. Thanks, Mom."

That seemed to satisfy her. She ushered him to the door.

"When I come back from work," she called after him, "we'll do something special."

"You'll buy us a cell phone each?" asked Jaide, coming back up the hallway.

"You know the answer to that. Not yet — and besides, they don't work in this old house."

"But everyone else in our school has one. Even Miralda King!"

"Well, you're not Miralda King. You're Jaide Shield and you're just going to have to wait until you're a little bit older before having something like that. There's no way we could afford the bill you two would rack up, texting each other."

Jaide jumped into bed, making the heavy frame rattle. "We could text Dad."

"If he ever remembered to switch his phone on . . . which he doesn't."

Susan kissed Jaide on the forehead and turned off the main light. "You can read for a while, if you want. I'll send your grandmother up to say good night."

Grandma X poked her head in just as Jack was pulling the covers up to his neck. She was wearing her dirty apron again, only this time it had orange-yellow stains on it as well, the same color as curry powder.

"Good night, troubletwisters," she said. Bewilderingly, she had the *Compendium* under her arm. Jaide bent down and looked under her bed, but there was nothing there. "Sleep well, and dream sensible dreams."

"Grandma," said Jaide before she could leave, "did the whalers bring The Evil to Portland, or was it here all along?"

Grandma X stopped in the doorway. "What makes you ask that?"

"We saw an old photo in the *Compendium*."

She nodded, but her face was shadowed so they couldn't see her expression. "Well, you know that Portland is one of those places where the boundary between our world and The Evil's is particularly thin, so —"

"Yes, but was it humans who made it thin, or was it always like that?"

"That is a very good question, Jaide. One we will discuss at length when the time is right."

Then she was gone, boots tramping smartly up the stairs and through the doorway that led to the blue room, where the *Compendium* was stored for safekeeping.

"She *always* says that," muttered Jaide. "It's not very helpful."

"Neither was the *Compendium*."

"It's just a book. She's a person, and she's supposed to be teaching us."

"She *is* teaching us," said Jack, reasonably. "Only not always what we want to learn."

Jaide grunted and rolled over onto her side, clearly not wanting to talk about it anymore. In moments, she was breathing slowly and evenly.

Jack wasn't feeling anywhere close to sleepy. His mind was snagged on the day he had first learned to shadow-walk, when The Evil had almost caught him.

Your inner nature wishes to join us, it had said, *and if you do, you will become something far more powerful than any mere Warden. . . .*

Picking up the dusty old book from his bedside table — *Jeopardy at Jute Junction*, which had his father's name written on the inside sleeve — he opened it and read perfectly well despite the near absence of light.

The book was exciting and drew him in. Almost enough to drive the memories of that horrible whispering voice from his mind.

Almost, but not quite.

CHAPTER SEVEN

THE PRIDE OF CATS AND HUMANS

Jaide was woken two hours later by the most awful noise she had ever heard.

It sounded like a choir of ghouls wailing right outside her bedroom window, holding long, wavering notes in tortured harmonies, then sliding up and down the scales in something like unison. It was chilling and horrible and utterly alien. She didn't know what was making such a sound, but she knew it couldn't possibly be coming from a human throat.

"Jack!"

The moon was up, and she could just make him out, unconscious with a book lying limp over his face.

"Jack, wake up!"

He snorted and jerked upright. The book fell to the floor with a thud.

"Where? Who?"

"Shhhh!"

"Yow. Are you making that terrible noise?"

"Of course not. But I'm glad you can hear it, too. I thought I was dreaming!"

"I wish you were. What on earth is making it?"

"What do you think? It must be the monster!"

A stab of ice went through Jack's stomach. It was one thing to speculate about a hideous figure from Portland's folklore, quite another to have it rampaging about the house.

"It can't get in, right?"

"Of course not," she said. But Jack knew the look on her face really meant *I hope not.*

"But we can't just sit here," Jaide continued. "This might be our one and only chance to find out what it is — and when we know *that*, hopefully we can convince Grandma to do something about it."

That was true. Nerving himself to see something horrible beyond belief, Jack knelt on his bed and peered out the window.

The front garden was empty.

"See anything?" Jaide asked.

"No. We'll have to go up on the widow's walk."

"All right."

The hideous wailing got even louder and more penetrating. Jaide wanted nothing more than to dive under the rug and cover her ears, but instead she forced herself to swing her legs out of bed and hunt across the shadowy floor for her father's old dressing gown. She tied it firmly around her waist and slipped on a pair of woolly slippers. When she was ready, Jack was waiting for her by the door with sneakers on and a windbreaker pulled untidily over his head.

The door opened without a sound, and they slipped out into the hallway. Tiptoeing across the creaky floor, they crossed the stairwell, but before they could begin to ascend, Jack tapped Jaide's shoulder and whispered, "Wait a sec."

Jaide heard him move off but couldn't see him. At night, he was almost invisible to her more ordinary eyes. Something squeaked to her left, and she saw their mother's door inch open for a second, then click closed again.

A second later, Jack whispered, "Mom's asleep," into her ear, and Jaide stifled a soft scream. "How is that even possible?" he asked.

"I don't know," she said, barely hearing the words over the hammering of her heart. "But let's go before she does wake up."

They hurried up the stairs as quickly as they dared. The empty eye sockets of the masks on the next floor watched them blankly as they reached that level. For the first time, Jaide wondered why anyone would make masks of normal human beings, instead of owls or devils or the like. Perhaps, she thought, they were based on real people. That would explain why none was exactly the same. . . .

"Grandma's not here," Jack said, "and she's not in the blue room."

Again, Jaide started with fright. She hadn't even noticed him leave to check out the blue room, or come back. "Where could she be?"

"I don't know. Up on the roof already, perhaps?"

Jack took the lead, guiding Jaide along the narrowing staircase to the very top of the house. The wailing was muffled but still piercing through the closed door ahead of them. Jack could feel it growing, building up to some incomprehensible crescendo. Whatever was making it was getting ready for something big.

His sure fingers opened the latch. Jack stepped out into the cool night air. There was no sign of Grandma X on the widow's walk. They were alone.

Jaide rushed to the rail and looked down.

"I can't see anything big," she said. "Not as big as an elephant, anyway. Can you?"

Jack joined her and searched the shadows for signs of anything — human, animal, or Evil.

"I can't see a monster," he said, frowning. "Uh . . ."

"What?" asked Jaide urgently.

"All I see are a bunch of cats."

"Cats?!"

Jaide strained her eyes until she could just make out a dozen or so feline forms prowling back and forth across the back garden. "Oh, cats! That's what the noise is. I've never heard so many yowling all at once, though."

A sudden thought struck her.

"They're not . . . they're not part of The Evil?"

"They don't have white eyes," said Jack. "Just normal cats, I guess."

Jaide felt a mixture of relief and embarrassment at waking Jack for no reason. Nothing was attacking the house.

"Come on," she said, tugging him away from the rail. "Let's get back to bed."

"Wait," he said, pointing. "I think that's Kleo down there, with Ari. And it looks like a fight is about to start."

Jaide strained again. There was a ginger blob in the center of the lawn that could indeed be Ari, and a gray blob that could be Kleo. But it could equally be a cat-size rock, for all she could tell.

Jack suffered from no such ambiguity. He could see the animals below with perfect clarity. The other cats were a mixture of calicos and Siamese, with one perfectly white fluffball standing out like a patch of snow among them. The white one and Kleo were the ones making most of the noise, with Ari and the others providing dissonant backup vocals.

"I don't recognize any of the others," he said, watching how Ari and Kleo stood firm while the rest slowly circled them. "But it's twelve to two, with Ari and Kleo against everyone else."

The wailing had reached an entirely new pitch. Now Kleo and the white cat stood nose to nose, their backs arched and all their hair standing on end. Ari spat at a fat calico that had dared come too close, and it backed away with tail upright and wide. Two more joined it, and they prowled around Ari, yowling menacingly. Jack could sense that the fight was about to start, any second.

"Jaide, they're outnumbered, and Grandma's not here — we have to help them!"

Jaide couldn't tell what, exactly, was going on, but the sound was so piercing now it felt like the night was going to split in two. If Jack said that Kleo and Ari needed their help, she was ready to believe him.

"How?" she asked. "I mean . . . twelve enemy cats . . . that's a lot."

"We'll have to use our Gifts," said Jack.

"Let's do what we did before," she said. "I'll create a tornado and you can kill the light. That's bound to stop the fight."

"I don't know," said Jack. "Are you sure we can control it?"

"Pretty sure, unless . . . have you got anything belonging to Dad on you?"

"No," Jack said, "but you have."

Jaide had forgotten the dressing gown. "Thank goodness you reminded me. Anything could have happened."

She tugged off the dressing gown and dropped it and was about to lean back over the railing when Jack pulled her back.

"We'd better get closer," Jack said. "Your aim's not the best, particularly when you can't see."

"Okay. But come on! I don't want Kleo and Ari to get hurt."

They ran down the stairs, slowing only to tread quietly as they went past their mother's room. She slumbered on, utterly oblivious to the drama unfolding around her.

Grandma X never locked her front door, as far as the twins had ever noticed. They rushed outside and ran around the house, too worried about their feline friends to feel the cold.

The fighting chorus came to a screeching climax just as they rounded the corner. What had been a tense standoff suddenly became an all-out brawl.

"Stop!" shouted Jaide as Ari and Kleo vanished under

an avalanche of whipping tails, slashing claws, and sharp teeth. "Leave them alone — or we'll make you!"

"No, troubletwisters, don't!" yowled Ari. "We can handle it!"

"Yeah, it really looks like it," muttered Jaide, clenching her fists tight. What she needed to do was very clear in her mind. Already the still night air was circling breezily around her. She was certain she could do this. "Jack?"

Jack was already working on his own side of the plan. His Gift stirred at his command, and he felt himself ease smoothly into the darkness. It was like putting on a cloak, one he could flip and twirl at will. He raised one hand and a shadow fell across the moon. The stars remained, and so did the streetlight at the end of the lane. Cat eyes were as good as his, maybe better, so he reached out another hand and snuffed out that light, too.

The cats didn't need light to fight. They could smell one another and hear one another hissing and spitting. Jaide remembered where the two huddles were, and drawing in a deep breath, she exhaled two skinny whirlwinds that shot straight into the cats, sending half of them twisting and turning through the air before depositing them at random across the garden. The cats immediately tried to get back to the fight, but Jack was ready for that.

"To your left!" he called, and Jaide swept them aside again.

The attacking cats howled and bared their teeth, knowing it was the twins behind this strange new development. Two abandoned the fight and rushed at them, sharp claws drawn, ready to scratch their legs. With Jack's help, Jaide knocked them aside, but other cats instantly followed.

The whirlwinds grew stronger and threatened to get out of control, the cats ducking between the twisted gusts as Jaide flailed them around.

Something ran up Jack's back and sank its teeth into his ear. He flailed his arms wildly about his head but couldn't shake his attacker. His grip on his Gift was slipping. The whole area was flickering between light and dark, as though someone was playing with a light switch.

"Stop this now, Jack," said the cat into his ear, muffled but clear. "It's me — Ari. Listen to me!"

"It's okay," he said. "Just get off me — let me concentrate — I can do this!"

The teeth sank deeper, drawing blood that trickled down his neck.

"No, Jack! Jaide! This is wrong — you must stop!"

The light returned. With it, Jaide was able to get control of her two twisters, calling them back and diminishing their size. Cats leaped and jumped to get out of the way, running back to re-form into a line behind the white cat, who was clearly their leader.

Kleo and the white cat faced off against each other, backs arched and fur standing upright as stiff as a brush. Kleo's snarling seemed especially horrible coming from a cat that Jaide knew could talk like a human.

The white cat feinted to its left and lunged from the right. Jaide reacted without thinking, sending the nearest twister driving straight at it. The white cat easily dodged aside. It looked at Jaide, spat on the ground, and stalked away into the night, with its followers close behind.

With shaking hands, Jaide calmed the twisters, slowing their spinning down until they fell apart and became small drifts of unsteady air that soon dissipated.

Only then did she look at Kleo, who came toward her like an angry mother cat finally locating a lost kitten, her eyes narrowed and tail whipping furiously from side to side. The same hissing noise she had made at the white cat was coming from her throat. She looked like she was going to pounce on Jaide and scratch her eyes out.

"Kleo," Jaide stammered, "wait —"

"Nobody asked you to come," Kleo spat. "This is cat business! *My* business! Stay out of it!"

With that, she ran off, leaving Jaide staring after her, shocked and hurt.

"What was *that* all about?" asked Jack.

Ari released his ear, jumped from his shoulder, and stood between the twins with his legs spread wide and firm. He had lost some hair, but he didn't look bothered. Not by that, anyway.

"I tried to warn you." Ari's voice was missing all of its usual rough friendliness. "But you never listen to me. Do you have any idea what you've done?"

"We've *helped*," said Jaide, feeling tears pricking in her eyes. Just moments ago she had been feeling proud of the way she and Jack had used their Gifts to stop the fight. "Haven't we?"

"No, you haven't!" Ari shouted. "You've made Kleo look as if she needs human help to fight her battles. So now she's going to have to fight them all over again. And it'll be even harder next time, because she'll have lost that much more respect in the pride."

"Like a pride of lions?" said Jack.

Ari turned to him. "The proper name for a group of cats is a *kindle*," he said. "An old word that has been taken over by others in more recent times. But Kleo only ever calls us her *pride*. Does that help you understand what this means to her?"

"I didn't know," said Jaide, feeling awful. "I really didn't."

"How could we?" said Jack. "All we wanted to do was —"

"I know, I know," said Ari. He sat on his haunches and licked a gash on the back of his left front paw. "You meant well. Kleo will understand that eventually. If she'd only told you, like I wanted her to . . ."

He stopped, as though his tongue had suddenly frozen solid.

"Told us what?" asked Jaide.

"Nothing," he said.

"Don't make us go through this again, Ari," said Jack.

Ari grimaced.

"Does this have something to do with the monster?" asked Jaide, quick to pounce on the possibility.

"The . . . err . . . I don't know what you're talking about," Ari said shiftily. "Like Kleo told you, this is cat business. Some of our best cats have been poisoned in unusual circumstances, and that has made Kleo vulnerable to a power grab from outside the town. That's where those other cats came from. They're not locals. No one here would be so disloyal . . . unless there were no alternative."

"How have the cats been poisoned?" asked Jaide, keen to move on from their mistake.

"Through the bodies of dead rats scattered across the town. That's how it's getting into us. It's powerful stuff, and it doesn't smell bad, not when the rats are only recently dead. One taste is all it takes. That's why Kleo's so worried. She's our protector, our queen; it's her job to keep us safe. She's been trying to find out who . . . or what . . . is behind the poisoned rats, but she hasn't had any luck so far."

"That's where you were this afternoon, when we were looking for you," said Jack with sudden understanding. "You should have said something. We might have been able to help! Remember those dead rats we saw by the old sawmill? They looked really weird. I bet they were put there for some poor cat to eat."

"If they looked weird, they were old," said Ari. "The trouble is the fresh ones. What cat can resist just a little taste of a dying rat that smells perfectly fine?"

"If they were old rats, maybe they were like a test, done in secret in the old sawmill," Jaide theorized. "I bet *he's* behind it — that guy, Mr. McAndrew, working for The Evil. . . ."

Even Jack thought she might be stretching a bit with that one. "Why would The Evil care about cats?"

"Because it knows Kleo is one of Grandma's Companions, of course," she said. "Anything that weakens her will weaken the Wardens."

"Oh, yeah, that makes sense."

"But Grandma won't listen to us," Jaide said to Ari. "Will you talk to her for us?"

"We're supposed to listen to her, not the other way around." Ari got up and paced out a small circle on the back garden. "I don't see how it could be The Evil. It was repelled when you fixed the East Ward and the combined protection of all four wards fell back over Portland. It was like a door slamming shut, and now nothing of The Evil can get in. You've got no reason to worry on that score."

"Isn't there any way it could get past the wards?" Jaide asked, frustrated that her theory kept crashing against such a fundamental roadblock.

"Not a chance, unless the wards are damaged again, which they haven't been. I think you should look for a more everyday explanation. Humans are mad enough on their own, believe me. They don't need The Evil to cause trouble for cats."

Jack looked around the back garden, at the tufts of multicolored fur and scratched earth. Now that the action was over, he was beginning to feel cold.

"What about Kleo?" he asked. "Will she forgive us?"

"Give her time. Once the poisonings stop, I expect . . . I hope . . . matters will return to normal. But if I were you, I'd stay out of the reach of Kleo's claws for a while."

Jaide still heard Kleo's voice, cutting through her confidence like a knife. *Nobody asked you to come. This is cat business! My business! Stay out of it!*

Ari came over and head-butted her on the leg. "When

Kleo's herself again, she'll know that you meant well. For now, you'd better go inside and get back into bed."

"All right."

Jaide turned away, hugging herself, and walked briskly around the side of the house.

"Good night, Ari," said Jack.

"Good night, Jack. And remember: That was bravely done, even if it was the wrong thing to do."

"Thanks, I guess."

Jack hoped Jaide had overheard. He could tell that Kleo's words had stung her. Hurrying to catch up, he found her not at the front door, as he had expected, but listening at the blue door, which only the two of them and Grandma X could see. It looked black under the moonlight, and the sign hanging above it was barely legible:

ANTIQUES AND CHOICE ARTICLES FOR THE DISCERNING.

The sign had been there the day they arrived in Portland, and had reappeared when the threat of The Evil had passed. They had yet, however, to see a single customer go through the door and into the basement beyond. If Grandma X was the only Warden in Portland, it was hard to imagine the store ever having any customers.

"She's not there," Jaide said, removing her ear from the wood. "That's good."

"Why is that good?" asked Jack. He was thinking only of getting back into bed.

"I want another look in the *Compendium*."

"What for? We already asked it about the monster and it couldn't tell us anything."

"I think we were asking the wrong question. Come on."

Instead of manipulating the blue door's trick lock, which could be opened only by someone on the other side or by using their Gifts, Jaide hurried through the front door and back up the stairs. Susan was still miraculously asleep, snoring softly. Grandma X's bed remained empty, the covers made up.

"Can't we do this tomorrow? I'm tired," Jack whispered as Jaide opened the next door along and stepped through it. Instead of revealing another empty bedroom, it somehow warped space to lead directly to the basement blue room, where their grandmother conducted her secret activities. The room's two chandeliers flickered into life — illuminated not by electric bulbs but by actual candles that lit themselves and never burned down.

"If we don't do it now, Jack, I'll never get to sleep."

The *Compendium* stood on Grandma X's desk next to two similar files that were labeled CORRESPONDENCE and RECEIPTS. Jaide picked up the thick folder and held it in both hands, closing her eyes briefly.

"What are you asking it?" Jack said, staring at her in puzzlement.

Jaide was concentrating too fiercely to speak. Kleo's anger — combined with something Ari had said — had fueled her determination to get *something* right that night.

Can The Evil survive the reestablishment of all four wards?

The *Compendium* opened, revealing a page of words in fine print under the heading "Extraordinarily Unusual Side Effects of Decerebration: a paper by Professor Saxon J. Chiruta III."

"What does it mean?" asked Jack, peering mystified over his sister's shoulder.

"I'm not sure." She liked to read and was proud of her vocabulary, but half of what she saw before her she didn't understand, and the rest didn't make any discernable sense. That every sentence ran for ten lines on average didn't help.

Jack read out loud: "'. . . *ad hoc termination of bellicose effluxion has been observed to incur a paroxysmal truncation of the resulting extrusions (Type IIIa) . . .*' Is this even English?"

Jaide leaned back and rubbed her eyes. "I asked the *Compendium* what happens when the wards come back on. I mean, everyone says that The Evil can't get back in afterward, but what if they're wrong? What if there's some sneaky way it can get back in and open the door again?"

"And this is the answer?"

Jaide stared at the dense page, wishing the *Compendium* had been more obliging. "Maybe it is."

"Well, we're no wiser, that's for sure."

"No," she said, staring in annoyance at the cryptic text. "Not yet."

Jaide hesitated for a moment, then gripped the corner of the page with her right hand as if she was going to rip it out of the *Compendium*.

Jack gasped. "Jaide! Don't!"

"I need it," Jaide said urgently. "And I can't work out how to open the ring binding —"

She stopped in mid-sentence, the paper in her hand suddenly free of the ancient bronze rings that held all the different pages of the *Compendium* together. They had not opened, but the paper was released.

"Uh . . . thanks," she said to the *Compendium*, folding the paper up and slipping it into her pajama pocket.

"What if Grandma notices it's missing —?"

"Why would she notice?" Jaide tapped the paper. "Anyway, if this page can tell me how The Evil is working through McAndrew despite the wards, Grandma will be pleased."

Then all I'll have to do, she thought to herself, *is make things up to Kleo . . . somehow.*

CHAPTER EIGHT

WEASEL WORDS

Susan woke the twins from deep, exhausted sleep to say good morning and good-bye. This was the third time she had left for her three-day shift at her new job and, while it hadn't become routine, it wasn't so much of a wrench anymore. Jack and Jaide hugged her and followed her downstairs to see her off. Then they walked wearily into the kitchen to make breakfast.

The soup pot was back on the stove again, only this time the stains were blue-gray. Jack opened the lid and took a whiff. He was immensely relieved to smell something sweet and sickly, nothing at all like crushed ants. If Grandma X had been planting poisoned rats to make the cats of Portland sick . . . well, tired or otherwise, he didn't think he could ever make sense of it.

Even to Jaide, the events of the previous night felt dreamlike and confusing. Only the hard reality of the page she had taken from the *Compendium*, now folded up in the pocket of her pajamas, reassured her that it was truly all real.

Grandma X was in a blustery and distracted mood, still in her own dressing gown, with hair wild and crazy about her head. She started talking to the twins long before she had even arrived in the kitchen.

"I'm awfully busy this morning, so you'll have to make your own break — oh, you already have. Well done, troubletwisters. Perhaps you could pop a bit of bread in for me, too?"

She stirred the pot and bustled out again, returning only when Jack had taken her toast out of the toaster, buttered it, and lathered it thickly with jam, just how she liked it.

"Thank you, Jackaran," she said, stuffing an entire slice into her mouth. From one pocket of her dressing gown she produced a handful of herbs and seeds, which she tossed into the pot. From the other came a saltshaker that sprinkled black dust. A powerful metallic smell filled the room as she stirred the pot again.

"What is that, Grandma?" asked Jack, wrinkling his nose.

"Oh, just an herbal concoction, nothing important," she said, devouring another whole piece of toast. "It revitalizes things. Like my garden, for example."

"Can we help?" Jaide asked, thinking that not once in their days in Portland so far had they seen Grandma X show any interest in the garden.

"I'll manage, thank you, Jaidith. Besides, you have to go to school. I'm positive they'll teach you something useful there one day, if only by accident. . . ."

"Are you sure, Grandma?" pressed Jack. "You look tired."

"Me? Nonsense. I always sleep well."

"You didn't hear anything . . . unusual?"

"Like what?" Grandma X's sharp gray eyes were suddenly on Jaide, and the girl felt herself fall back into her seat as though physically pushed.

"Um, cats?"

Grandma X looked around, as though realizing only then that Ari and Kleo were absent. Normally, the cats would be buzzing around at breakfast, looking for early morning treats, particularly Ari, who had an appetite as voracious as Jack's.

"Did you hear fighting?" she asked the twins.

"Yes," said Jaide. "We thought it was the monster."

Grandma X smiled.

"You see how these things begin? If you hear it again, just ignore it. Kleo is being challenged, and we must let her sort it out."

"Isn't there something we can do without her knowing?" asked Jack, wishing she had told them that long before now.

"No, because she *would* know," said Grandma X, turning back to the pot and giving it a vigorous stir. "Unless you were considerably more cunning than I would like you to be. Now, upstairs at once, troubletwisters, or you'll be late!"

Rebuffed, the twins went to get dressed. When they returned downstairs only minutes later, they found the pot gone, and Grandma X with it.

"I guess we'll let ourselves out," said Jaide, hefting her bag higher on her shoulder.

"She's definitely up to something," said Jack. "I'm on to her tricks now. Like, she never really said that the potion was for her garden, only kind of *suggested* it was."

"And she said she always sleeps well, but that doesn't mean she slept well last night, or even went to bed at all," said Jaide.

"There's *something* she's not telling us."

"Secret secrets," muttered Jaide as they wheeled their bikes out of the laundry room and set off to school. Her tone made it sound like the worst curse imaginable.

Mr. Carver was in a subdued mood when they arrived at school that morning, which was unusual. Normally, he greeted them individually with syrupy cheer and started the day with a singalong, accompanied by one of his strange instrumental performances. That day, he asked all his students to take a seat and sit quietly. Tara came in from the playground after Jack and Jaide arrived, and looked at them questioningly. They could only shrug in reply.

When everyone was present, he explained what was going on.

"Today is the memorial service for a valued member of our community," he said. "I'm talking about Renita Daniels, of course. Just last week she was here in this very school, making important repairs, and she will be greatly missed by all of us. Because it's a school day, we cannot attend the service, unless you have a note from your parents, but I thought we would honor her in our own way, by sharing our memories of her and creating a collage. Would anyone like to start?"

There was an awkward silence. Jack and Jaide looked at each other, and said nothing. They couldn't very well explain that the last time they had seen Rennie, she had been possessed by The Evil and trying to kill them.

"Who was she?" asked Kyle with a perplexed frown.

"You know — Rennie," said Miralda. "Always wore overalls, carried a wrench . . ."

"Oh, her. Why's she important?"

"We are the sum of the people around us," Mr. Carver said. "They shape us and make us who we are. And Rennie, poor Rennie — she did her best to carry on, but it was hard, and we all felt it."

"Why 'poor' Rennie?" asked Tara.

"Such a tragic story," said Mr. Carver, wiping a tear from his eye. "She had two young children — too young for school, I never met them. They drowned in a terrible accident, and now she has drowned, too."

"Does that mean they found her body?" asked Jack.

"Poor Rennie nothing," said Miralda. "My dad said she was obviously negligent."

"What does that mean?" asked Kyle.

"You know, it was entirely her fault, what happened. She shouldn't have been on that old jetty when it was *clearly* marked as dangerous. And it wasn't the council's fault the sign had fallen off or that the light had stopped working —"

"Did they find her body?" repeated Jaide.

"Let's not dwell on the negatives," said Mr. Carver, putting his index fingers to his temples and breathing deeply through his nose. "Let us remember her as the vibrant, living soul she once was and seek some fitting way to preserve our memories of her. Miralda, perhaps you could draw her wrench. Kyle, you could draw her van. Jack, Jaide, and Tara — you are probably too new to have known her well, but I'd still like you to participate, if you don't mind. Perhaps you could partner up and come up with something between you. Remember, this is a sensitive time, and we want to be respectful."

He handed out paper to everyone and put on a particularly mournful tune over the school's PA, which he accompanied on a round-bodied guitar that sounded like a depressed banjo.

Tara joined Jack and Jaide at their table and leaned in to whisper, "I guess this beats actually going to the service. Funerals are so boring. Did you ever meet this Jenny or Benny or whoever she was?"

"Uh, yes," said Jaide. "We saw her when she was working here, fixing the equipment."

"What did she look like?"

"She was tall." Jaide repressed her memories of Rennie with wild, white eyes and rats growing out of her, climbing on spiderweb ropes with a cockroach cloak across her shoulders. That image had haunted her dreams for a week.

"And she was sad," said Jack, understanding only now about her kids and why she had seemed so anxious about them not hurting themselves when they had first met. He still remembered the look in her eyes. She had seemed both wounded and very alone.

"I don't know how to draw *sad*," said Tara, "but *tall* I can do. I'm actually quite good at drawing. Can you tell me anything else about her?"

While Jack searched his memory for anything that didn't involve The Evil, Jaide pulled the page she had stolen from the *Compendium* from her pocket and went looking for a dictionary. There was just one, and it had been well thumbed by several generations of children. She brought it back to the table, laid the page out flat, and began to translate.

"*Amidst the matrix of contingencies upon which every Warden is beholden to focalize . . .*"

"So," Tara said, "brown hair, long face, big nose . . . anything else?"

Jack shook his head. He wasn't sure how much he actually remembered and how much he had made up, but he supposed it didn't matter. Rennie had fallen from the lighthouse and drowned. She wasn't going to complain if he got it wrong.

"Your dad," he asked as she got to work drawing. "Is his name Martin?"

"Yes. Oh, yeah, that's right — he said he met you yesterday, at the house. You'll be seeing a lot more of him there. He's going to work on renovating that old place while construction is suspended on Riverview House. He said there have been vandals in there, so he needs to board up the windows himself, at least until he can find another contractor."

"Uh, great," Jack said, glancing nervously at Jaide. She

hadn't heard. Her nose was buried in an old book and her face wore a look of furious concentration. "Was he at the sawmill building site last night?"

She nodded. "I guess so. He didn't come home until late. I had to take the train home."

So it could easily have been Martin McAndrew behind the wheel of the van that had tried to run them down. Jack filed that away for future reference.

"Has he seemed . . . different . . . lately?"

Tara shrugged. "It's hard to tell with Dad. He's always so busy. I only really get to talk to him when we're in the car together. That's the main reason I wanted to come to this school — apart from the fact that it annoys Mom. She wants me to go to a real school, you know, where they make you actually work rather than draw pictures of someone you never met."

Jack could feel the conversation being dragged away from what he wanted to know. He wished Jaide would pay attention and help him. She was better at talking to people they didn't know well.

"Does your dad ever wear dark glasses?"

"All the time. He works outside, remember?" Tara looked up from her half-finished drawing. "You're an odd boy, Jack Shield. Why do you want to know so much about my dad?"

"I'm, uh, interested in buildings," he stammered. "I guess that's it."

"Well, he'd be happy to talk to you about it, I'm sure. It's all he ever talks about at home. Why don't you come over one day and meet him properly?"

Jaide saved Jack by suddenly slamming the book closed and putting her head in her hands. "It's no use. The words are too hard and this dictionary is hopeless! It's for little kids, not —"

She almost said *Wardens*, but then she noticed Tara staring at her.

". . . not older kids like us," she finished rather lamely.

"You're not actually working, are you?" Tara asked her with a playful look in her eye.

"Mom gives us homework," Jaide improvised as she folded up the page. "I'm running behind. Is your full name Tara McAndrew?"

"No," said Tara. "It's Tara Lin. I have my mother's last name."

"But your father is Martin McAndrew?"

"Yes. Jack just asked me that. What's with you two?"

"Maybe Jaide's interested in buildings, too," said Jack, staring at her with a hopeless look.

"I . . . suppose that's it," Jaide said, although nothing could have been further from the truth. Before she'd discovered about Wardens, she had wanted to be a photographer. Her camera being blown up with her house by The Evil had ended that dream. "You know, I think your dad knew Rennie. He said she had something of his."

"Really?" Tara looked genuinely mystified. "I wonder what it was."

"He didn't tell us."

"Well, he'll be annoyed about it, whatever it is, since she's dead now and he has no chance of getting it back."

Mr. Carver chose that moment to lean over Jack's shoulder to see what they had done, and to praise their efforts.

"I like her hair, although I don't believe she ever wore it curled like that. It's quite a good likeness."

Tara beamed. "What color were her eyes, Mr. Carver?"

"Call me *Heath*, please. I'm not sure, Tara. Perhaps you could just leave them as they are for now."

"They were blue," said Jaide, more firmly than she'd intended. She hoped her face wasn't betraying the sudden, terrible memory of the last time she'd seen Rennie's eyes, all white and luminous.

Everyone looked at her.

"That is, I think they were," she said. It was a guess, but anything was better than leaving Rennie's picture the way it was.

"That will do for now," said Mr. Carver, patting Jaide on the shoulder. "Well done, well done."

He wandered off as Tara leaned over the portrait to color the blank white eyes a much more reassuring sky blue.

The lunchtime tune took forever to come, but finally, Mr. Carver played it and they were free to stop drawing.

"Come on," said Jaide to Jack, as Tara went to get her lunch box from her bag. "We're going home to eat. We have bikes now. We can do that."

"Why? We already have a packed lunch."

"They don't know that." She lowered her voice. "I need another dictionary. And it'll look weird if I go alone."

Jack thought it *was* a bit weird, and his stomach agreed, but he decided he could put off his sandwich for a couple of minutes if his sister really thought they should.

"All right."

Jaide told Mr. Carver and he gave them permission to ride home, provided they were back in time for the afternoon session. They assured him they would be, and ran off to their bikes.

As they pedaled up Dock Road, Jack felt an unnerving sensation between his shoulder blades, as though someone was watching him closely. He studied the shops to his right, but could see no one looking at them. The fish market to his left was full of people, but none of them were paying attention to him, either. He told himself he was imagining things and pedaled furiously to catch up to Jaide, who had pulled ahead while he was distracted.

They dropped their bikes on the lawn and ran up the front steps. Jaide grabbed the front door handle and turned it, but instead of bursting into the house as they always did, they crashed headlong into the door. For the first time ever, it was locked.

"Ow!" said Jack, rubbing his elbow. He tried the handle himself, but it wouldn't budge. "Now what?"

Jaide kicked the door as though it had affronted her personally. "We try the back, I guess."

It was the same with the laundry room door. No matter how they wrenched the handle, it wouldn't turn.

"The curtains are closed, too," said Jack, stepping back to stare up at the windows.

"What's she up to in there?" muttered Jaide.

Something rattled in the yard next door, perhaps a brick dropping from the run-down walls, or a careless footfall kicking a stone, and the twins turned as one to stare at the fence.

Both of them expected to see Martin McAndrew there, staring at them with inquisitive eyes and his all-too-brilliant smile. But there was no sign of him.

"Hello?" called Jaide.

Jack didn't say anything. The odd feeling had returned. In one of the empty windows, from the shadows of the house's hollow shell, he was sure that someone or something was watching them. He was also sure it wasn't a vandal.

"Ari? Kleo?"

Jaide tried to sound brave, but she was feeling it, too. The tiny patch of skin between her shoulder blades itched worse than a mosquito bite and the hair of her arms was all standing on end.

"*Grandma?*"

A sliver of broken glass slipped from its frame and smashed, sending a tiny avalanche down the side of the ruined house. The courage of both twins broke at exactly that moment, and they turned and fled around the other side of their grandmother's house. Whatever was lurking next door, they didn't want to face it alone, not when they were barred from the only place in Portland they felt truly safe, Grandma X's home.

"Was it The Evil?" gasped Jack as he leaped onto his bike.

"I don't know, and I'm not going back to ask!"

They pedaled pell-mell down the cobbled lane, glancing over their shoulders to make sure no one was following them.

"Stop right there!" a voice cried.

CHAPTER NINE

WHERE THERE'S FIRE . . .

Jack and Jaide skidded to a halt, very nearly bowling over a woman in a postal uniform standing sturdily in the middle of the lane. She had raised one hand in a commanding gesture, like a traffic cop. All the hounds of Hades could have been on their heels, but nothing would have compelled them to disobey the fierce expression on her broad face.

"Not so fast! Why aren't you at school? Are you Jaidith and Jackaran Shield?"

Jack could only gape at her, stunned by the barrage of questions. The postwoman wasn't large in stature, but what she lacked in height she more than made up for in her barking tone.

"I — I'm Jaide."

"A postcard for you, here." The woman thrust a small stack of mail into her hand. "It is from your father. He wishes you well."

"Thanks. . . ?"

The postwoman turned her attention to Jack. "So you must be Jack. You are too quiet. Why did you not answer my question? I have a postcard for you, too. Your sister has it now. You could have had it first. He tells wild stories, just like he used to."

"It's not . . . I mean . . . that is, we were in a hurry to get back to school."

"No child is ever in a hurry to get to school. You rode as though the monster itself was after you." Her keen green eyes narrowed. "Have you seen it?"

Jack didn't know. He hadn't seen anything so far that could *definitely* have been the monster, for all that he felt and suspected.

"Have *you*?" Jaide asked on an impulse.

The postwoman sucked in air through narrow, wide-spaced teeth. Her eyes lost their focus and her voice some of its harsh tone. "A huge thing it is, with the tail of a dragon and the head of a wolf. A chimera. You are very clever children. They say the monster lived in Portland long before mankind ever did, and ate the first settlers who tried to build here. I haven't seen it myself, but my sister did, and she died of the fright. She said it had six long legs and scales like dinner plates."

"How could she have said that if it frightened her to death?" asked Jack.

The postwoman's focus returned. "It was a slow fright, in her lungs. Some people said she smoked too much, but I knew."

"Okay . . . sure." Jaide shifted restlessly on her feet. "Can we go now?"

"Yes, yes. Back to school with you, and be brisk about it! No dawdling! The clock is ticking!"

The postwoman obeyed her own imperative, turning smartly to march off along the cobbled lane and, turning left, disappear up Parkhill Street.

"Completely bonkers," said Jack. His stomach rumbled as though in agreement. Now that his fright had passed, his hunger had returned with a vengeance. "Can we eat our lunch now?"

"No, we still have to get a dictionary."

"Where from?"

"Wait a second and I'll show you. I don't want to go anywhere until she's long gone. And while we wait . . ."

Jaide leafed through the stack of letters until she came to the card from their father, noticing as she did so that all of the letters were addressed *To the occupant* or *To the proprietor* or even *To the lady of the house*. No one addressed Grandma X by name — something they had observed when first arriving in Portland, but which they'd never gotten to the bottom of. When asked, she always changed the subject or said it was yet another mystery.

At the very bottom of the stack were two postcards from somewhere in Europe, one addressed to Jaide, the other to Jack, just as the postwoman had promised. Jaide's started with *Dear troubletwisters* and ended mid-sentence. Jack's picked up from there, and concluded in the bottom corner with a P.S. The letter in its entirety said:

Dear troubletwisters,

So you found my old soccer ball, did you? I thought I'd lost that long ago! You know, I once kicked a goal in Scarborough from the field in

Portland. Shame you popped it. (I advise against trying anything like that while your mother is present. Or ever. Don't forget your promise.) You can probably tell that I'm not in Venice anymore. Where I've gone is a mystery to me, as the storm I used was contrary and changed direction, but I'm sure I'll work it out soon enough. This is just a quick note to say that I miss you both immensely and wish we were together.

Love always,

Dad xx

P.S. Don't forget your promise!

Jack leaned closely over Jaide's shoulder to read with her.

"How did he know about the soccer ball?" he asked. "That was only yesterday! And how did these cards get here so quickly?"

Jaide had as little idea as he did. "He's a Warden," she said. "I guess he can do things like this."

"Did Grandma X tell him or is he spying on us somehow?"

"I don't know that, either." The matter of the promise bothered her. They were sneaking around behind Grandma X's back, which they knew she wouldn't like — but what else were they supposed to do, when she was keeping secrets from them and ignoring everything they thought was important? If The Evil *had* found a way back into Portland, it was up to them to stop it, and them alone.

She put the mail into her school bag. They had bigger

things to worry about than what their faraway father was up to. "Come on. Let's get that dictionary."

They headed to the bookshop by their house. Its proprietor, Rodeo Dave, was sitting behind the counter, brushing his mustache with a tiny brush, when the twins came in.

"Howdy, neighbors!" He rushed out and shook both their hands, nearly toppling a stack of bargain paperbacks as he went. "What can I do for you this fine day? If you're looking for Kleo, I'm afraid she's elsewhere. Haven't seen much of her lately, come to think of it. Maybe she's got a boyfriend."

His grin was wide and infectious. There was no one else in the bookstore, but that wasn't unusual. In the last week, Jack had seen only two customers browsing the shelves. And no wonder, he thought: The books were stacked right up to the ceiling, in no obvious order. Romances cozied up to fat political biographies, which looked uncomfortable in the company of trashy sci-fi novels and murder mysteries. Rare editions slummed with paperbacks, and encyclopedias warred with condensed novels for control of their shelves. Everywhere was the smell of old paper and glue, and dust, thick with every breath.

"We're looking for a dictionary," said Jaide. "A good one. The one at school is hopeless and Mr. Carver is never going to let us use the computers today."

"Ah!" Rodeo Dave rubbed his hands together. "I have just the thing."

He led them to a deep, dark corner of the shop and proudly showed them a series of thick gray volumes that filled an entire shelf. Jaide pulled one out and cradled it in two hands. It seemed to weigh as much as she did and covered just the letter *E*.

She put it back.

"Have you got anything that would fit in my bag?"

"Hmm." Rodeo Dave looked around and tapped his chin. "What about this one?"

He slid a book that was almost perfectly cubical from an upper shelf and handed it to Jack. The letters on the cover had faded to illegibility, but when he opened it, Jack saw the usual list of words and definitions in tiny print.

"I think that'll do the trick," he said. "Right, Jaide?"

"Perfect. How much is it?"

"For you? Nothing. That book's been sitting there as long as the shop. You're doing me a favor taking it off my hands. I can use the space."

"Really? Thanks."

"Don't mention it. Would you like to join me for lunch? I was just about to eat."

"Well, we should really —"

"That would be great," said Jack, whose stomach would brook no further delay. "We have sandwiches."

"So do I! Pull up a chair and I'll get you a drink. I presume you like lemonade?"

The three of them gathered around the counter and unwrapped their lunches. Susan had packed for the twins before she left, stocking their lunch boxes with extra treats that Grandma X never included. Jack ate the treats first before moving on to his more serious sandwich. Rodeo Dave had a round, brown roll that stank of pickles, which he ate in small, measured bites in order to keep the crumbs out of his mustache.

"I was talking to your grandmother the other day," he said. "She tells me you're settling in fine now, after a bit of a rough start."

"What do you mean?" asked Jaide. Surely, Grandma X wouldn't have told him about The Evil?

"The storm, school being closed — all that. Worse even than the winter of '72, and that's saying something. Quite a welcome Portland has given you." He winked and leaned in closer. "And now there's all this talk of the monster. You must think us completely cracked."

"Well," said Jack, "we did just bump into the postwoman. . . ."

"Did you, now?" Rodeo Dave rocked back in his chair and laughed. "Well, don't let our Hilma bother you. That's Hilma von Klippert, if you please. She's been delivering the mail as long as that dictionary's been on my shelf, and she's seen a thing or two, without a doubt."

"She said she knew Dad."

"She did. They were even an item once," he said, then screwed up an eye and tilted his head to one side. "Or was that Sal Govey? I forget, now."

Jaide couldn't imagine their father ever being interested in anyone like Hilma von Klippert — or vice versa.

"Did her sister really see the monster?" Jaide asked.

"What do you think?"

She shook her head.

"Right. And no one else around here seems to have seen it, either. If it's not their sister, it's their father or their best friend or a cousin." He grinned, exposing yellow-tinged teeth. "I have a friend in Camfferman Crescent who says it's a giant snake, a boa constrictor that escaped from the Rourke Estate menagerie, which has grown long and fat on missing pets and sheep. He's never seen it himself. He just knows someone who swears *she* did, and barely escaped with her life. See what I mean?"

"Couldn't there be something to it, though?" asked Jaide. "If everyone says the same thing, maybe there's a little bit of truth behind it."

"Where there's smoke there's fire?" Rodeo Dave shrugged. "If that's the case, why does the monster always look different? Maybe it's the other way around."

"Where there's fire there's smoke?" Jack scratched his head. "What does *that* mean?"

"Beats me, but it's worth thinking about." Rodeo Dave folded up the grease paper his sandwich had been wrapped in and wiped the crumbs off his desk. "I suppose I'd better be getting back to work. . . ."

Jaide looked around her. The store was as empty as it had been when they walked in.

"Give Kleo a pat for us," said Jack, who still felt bad about making her look small in the eyes of the other cats.

"I will, whenever she turns up."

They hurried back to school, the dictionary a dead weight in Jaide's backpack. The end-of-lunch tune sounded just as they propped their bikes up in the rack and fastened the locks. Tara was waiting for them at their table.

"Where did you go?" she asked. "It's really boring here without you."

Jack explained about going home for lunch, while Jaide got stuck into deciphering the article.

"It must be great living so close to school," Tara said, propping her chin on one hand and sighing dramatically. "You can be home in no time at all. I have to wait around for Dad, and then drive all the way to Scarborough. Or get the train, if it's running."

Jack felt uncomfortable, sensing that she was fishing for an invitation. That would be impossible, he knew, until the business with the monster was sorted out. Not to mention her father.

"It's pretty bad, actually," he said. "Every time we go anywhere, we pass the school. It's like it's following us."

"Now, that would be weird." Tara smiled. "Ringing its prayer bells and playing its crazy tunes . . ."

Tara finished the portrait of Rennie and together they worked on the background, before finally all the pictures were gathered up by Mr. Carver and put in an envelope.

"I'll make sure her family gets these later," he said with one hand on his heart. "They'll be thrilled."

"She doesn't *have* any family," Miralda said. "Don't you know that? She was an only child and her ex-husband left ages ago. That's why her story was so tragic, apparently."

"Her parents, then —"

"Dead for years."

"Oh."

"What a waste of time!" groaned Kyle. "I used my best black marker, too."

"Well, it's the thought that counts," said Mr. Carver, rather unconvincingly. "And it doesn't hurt for you to be reminded that everyone is important, even if they live alone —"

"And no one knows anything about them." Miralda smirked.

"I think it's sad," said Tara. "And you should, too. I can't think of anything worse than being forgotten."

Every head turned to face her.

"What's your name, again?" asked Kyle.

"Har har." Tara wasn't fazed at all. "Remind me not to forget your amazing sense of humor."

"Students, students." Mr. Carver raised his hands for calm. "Let's observe a minute's silence for Rennie, and then we'll get on with your education."

"Do we have to?" asked Kyle.

"What's one minute out of your life, Kyle? You'll have plenty left over."

"I meant getting on with my education."

Mr. Carver looked weary, but he did eventually manage to calm the class down. A fragile silence fell, in which Jack clearly heard cars driving by down Main Street, the whoosh of a fishing boat's bilge pump, and the barking of a distant dog. He thought about Rennie and wondered what happened to someone who died while possessed by The Evil. Were they themselves at the end, or were they so completely absorbed that they never knew what happened? Rennie had gone back to herself at least once; he had seen her eyes change back to normal when Jaide had whacked her over the head with a silver tray. Could she have gone permanently back to normal if she hadn't fallen off the lighthouse and drowned?

He snuck a quick glance at his watch. Surely, it had been a minute already. It felt like more than five. . . .

"Got it!"

The sudden cry made the entire classroom jump.

"Jaide — shhhh!"

She looked up from the dictionary with innocent alarm. She'd been so engrossed in the puzzle of the *Compendium* article that she hadn't noticed how quiet it had become.

"Sorry, Mr. Carver. What are we doing?"

"That's *Heath*, and . . . oh, never mind. The moment has passed. Free drawing for an hour, children. Try creating something your parents would like to see, in appreciation for everything they've done for you. Remember, they won't be here forever."

Mr. Carver glanced at Kyle.

"No more monsters, please. I think we've had enough of them for two lifetimes."

"What is it?" whispered Jack to Jaide as the noise of the classroom returned to its usual high level. "What have you found?"

Jaide glanced at Tara. She was getting up to talk to Mr. Carver, and the troubletwisters were free to converse in private.

"This paper," she whispered, tapping the sheet she had stolen from the *Compendium*, "is all about what happens when wards are suddenly restored. 'Decerebration' means to cut off something's head, and that's what happens to The Evil — or some of it, at least. Most of it's pushed back out of the world, back wherever it came from, but some of it is cut off — like the tip of a finger caught in a door."

"Or bitten by the Oracular Crocodile," Jack muttered.

"Exactly. But a bit of The Evil isn't like a bit of us. The Evil is Evil all the way through, and it can still control things. So if a bit of it was cut off when we fixed the East Ward —"

"It could still be here!" said Jack, gripping the edge of the table. "It could be in Tara's dad, or it could be the monster. . . ."

"Professor Chiruta says that these leftover bits of The Evil — he calls them *excisions* — are usually very small and weak, so it's probably in something tiny and unnoticed."

"It could be a rat, which would explain why it's targeting the cats. They're natural enemies."

"That's true. But what do we do about it?"

"You mean you haven't worked that out yet?"

Despite this friendly sneer, Jack was mightily impressed with Jaide for deciphering the article. He doubted even Grandma X had ever heard of these excision things. When she found out, maybe then she would believe them. "Straight after school, we'll —"

"You two are whispering again," said Tara, plonking herself down between them. "It's very irritating. Anyone would think you didn't want me around."

Jaide sympathized. She and Jack had also been picked on by the locals in their first few days, and would dearly have loved a friend. It wasn't Tara's fault her timing was terrible, or that her father was probably in league with The Evil.

The excision in Portland didn't have to be controlling Martin McAndrew to get its work done. All it had to do was offer him something he wanted badly enough, for which he might betray Grandma X — something like her house, for example. . . .

Tara put a thick envelope down on the table in front of them.

"Are they the pictures of Rennie?" Jaide asked, knowing she had to make the effort.

"Mr. Carver said I could have them."

"What are you going to do with them?"

"I don't know, but we can't just throw them out. Someone will want them."

"If her parents died in Portland," Jack said, "they might be in the graveyard."

"Good thinking, Jack. I'll look into that." Tara stuffed the pictures into her bag, and then turned brightly back to the table. "So, what are we going to draw now? Miralda and Kyle as a two-headed ogre?"

"With a bad attitude," added Jack with a grin.

"How do I draw that?"

"Like sad," said Jaide, "but *meaner.*"

CHAPTER TEN

HEART OF DARKNESS

Once again, Jack and Jaide were out the door the second the farewell tune finished, but this time they paused just long enough to say good-bye to Tara.

"See you on Monday!" she called after them as they rode away, and that startled both of them. The trouble-twisters had been so wrapped up in their research that they had forgotten it was Friday.

They waved back, then put their heads down and pedaled as hard as they could.

At the house, they found the blinds up again, the front door unlocked, and no creepy sensations of being watched from the house next door.

"Grandma? Grandma?"

There was no answer.

"She's done it again," said Jaide, putting her hands on her hips and glaring at Jack as though it was entirely his fault.

Jack was shocked by how much Jaide looked like their mother when she was mad. "Maybe she left a note."

"Not a note *exactly*," said a voice from the stairs.

It was Ari, padding lightly down from the second floor to join them in the hallway.

"Where is she?" asked Jaide.

"Busy. She asked Kleo and me to look after you."

"Kleo's here?" Jack craned to look up the stairwell.

"I am."

The voice came from the kitchen, where Kleo was sitting on the table, looking regal.

The twins rushed to her. The cat narrowed her eyes.

"Kleo, we're sorry. We didn't mean to interfere."

"If there's anything we can do to make it up to you . . ."

Kleo sniffed, rejecting all forms of apology. "Your grandmother asked me to remind you to do your exercises. She promised me that she would be back as soon as she can."

Jaide's hopes fell. There was no mistaking the cat's frosty tone.

"All right, but please . . . can you help us with something?" Jaide asked. "We think there's a piece of The Evil left in Portland, an *excision*, and it's behind the poisonings —"

"Or the monster," added Jack.

"Or both!"

Kleo deigned to look at them.

"Exercises first, talk later."

"But, Kleo!"

"Exercises first," said Kleo, very coolly. "Talk *later*. If at all."

"Yes, but what's Grandma X *doing* and why won't she tell us exactly what's going on?"

"That's her business, and her business it will remain."

Jaide bit her tongue and tried her best to swallow the urge to argue. Kleo was wrong, but it was clear she wasn't going to change her mind. They would have to wait until Grandma X came home, and hope it wouldn't be too late to convince her then.

"All right," she said. "We'll do our exercises. In the blue room, as usual?"

"That is correct."

Kleo hopped down from the table and loped out of the kitchen. The twins followed her, and Ari followed them. They made a tense, silent progression up the stairs to the house's second floor, passing through the secret door to the basement and closing the elephant tapestry shut behind them.

The blue room looked much the same as it had the previous night, apart from a pile of herbs and multicolored powders in the center of the desk. Jack eyed them curiously, wondering if they would be part of their training, but Kleo didn't mention them once.

"Your grandmother wants you to practice the skills you have already been using," Kleo said, taking a position on the back of a princely leather chair that looked as though it had been made from the skin of a dinosaur. "Jaide, you will concentrate on keeping this candle burning while Jack does his best to put it out."

In the center of the room was a small, circular table on which stood an elaborate, wax-covered candelabra containing one single yellow candle. Beside it was a box of matches.

"That's all?" asked Jaide.

"That's all," Kleo said, meeting her gaze with feline immovability.

"I think," said Ari, curling up on a gold-threaded cushion and closing one eye, "doing *only* that is the point, troubletwisters."

"All right," said Jack, resigning himself to doing nothing new or interesting that afternoon. He lit the candle with a match. It burned with a clear, yellow light. Above him, the chandeliers went out, and strange shadows stretched across the crowded, antique-filled room. Kleo's eyes shone back at him like glass coins.

"Begin," she said.

Jack pursed his lips and blew the candle out.

"Not like that," Kleo said in a weary tone. "Using your Gift."

"But why use my Gift when doing it the ordinary way is easier?"

"Because this is an *exercise* for your Gift."

A match flared. Jaide had found the box by feel in the darkness. "Let's not mess around. Let's just get on with it."

"But I wasn't messing around! It really does seem that Wardens do things the hard way for no good reason. I mean, why did Dad send us that postcard when he could have just called us? Why fight The Evil with magic when a machine gun might work better?"

"What if The Evil took over the machine gun and turned it against you?" Kleo said. "What if your father's voice on the telephone line woke your Gifts unexpectedly? Do not be so glib when it comes to the wisdom of your grandmother. She nearly always knows better than anyone."

"Just nearly?" asked Jaide.

Kleo's cold, blue eyes said it as clearly as words: *She invited you here, didn't she?*

"Try again," the cat instructed, "using only your Gifts."

Jack sighed and did his best to draw the shadows in around the bright flame, making it gutter and fade.

Then Jaide blew it with a gentle but recuperating breeze, bringing it back to its former strength.

"Good," said Kleo. "Try harder."

Jaide got in first, this time. A rush of oxygen sent the flame shooting toward the ceiling in a thin, wavering line.

Jack gathered his concentration and wrapped the flame in ribbons of darkness, drawing it back down. He could feel his sister fighting him, and he managed to outdo her only with a mighty effort.

"Better. Try harder still."

Jack gritted his teeth and poured an avalanche of shadow onto the feeble flame. If he could blow it out with a single breath, he told himself, why couldn't he do the same with his Gift?

The flame shrank down to a single glowing point, as faint as a distant star, and it looked for a second that he might have put it out.

Jaide refused to let her brother beat her. Calling on all the energy inside her, all the energy of the sun that fueled her Gift, she held the spark on the brink of going out, then both swelled it and brightened it. This new flame didn't burn as it had before. It was spherical and white, and shrank and grew in time with the beating of her heart.

"This is a duel — a competition," Kleo informed them. "The winner will save the other from The Evil, one day."

Jack didn't really hear what she was saying. He just heard the word *competition* and found a reserve of strength he hadn't known was there.

Flame and darkness warred in a vivid column, spiraling ribbons rippling up and down its side, like a barber's pole but in black and white. Shadows danced wildly as light flashed and darkness crashed back in. The twins each glared at the candelabra and willed with all their might.

Ari uncurled and crouched on all fours on the cushion, with his head down low and ears twitching.

I'm going to win, Jack thought as he pressed the flame back down to a tiny flicker. Jaide felt her brother's confidence and renewed her determination to keep the flame alive at all costs. The flame roared up to fill the room, driving every last shadow into retreat.

Jaide whooped in triumph, her face glowing in the brilliance.

"Enough," said Kleo. "Jaide is the victor. Well done."

"She only beat me because I was distracted," said Jack disappointedly as the candle flame returned to normal.

"Regardless, she won. There will be many distractions next time you come face-to-face with The Evil. It will show you no forgiveness." The tips of her sharp teeth showed. "Again."

Ari looked sharply at her. "Kleo, perhaps this is a little too fast. Grandma X did say —"

Kleo looked at him, and Ari fell silent.

"Again," she repeated. "This time with two candles."

Jaide found a box under the table and lit a new candle with the flame of the first. She stuck it firmly in the candelabra and stepped back.

"Winner goes first?" she said to Jack.

"Not likely."

While she had been busy with the second candle, he had been working out a different strategy. Instead of trying to smother the flames with darkness, his new plan was to snuff them out from the inside. Unnoticed by Jaide, he had moved slightly to his right so that the tip of his toe overlapped the flickering shadow of the table cast by the candles. The moment the contest began, he sent himself down into the shadow and from there moved up the table legs, under the candelabra, and to the base of the first candle. From there it was much harder, because the shadows cast by both flames were so unreliable, particularly with Jaide whipping them up into a frenzy, but with one wild leap he made it to where he wanted to be.

At the heart of every flame was a patch of darkness. Jack had often stared into gas flames and birthday candles and seen it for himself. It looked as though the brightness of the flame was floating in thin air, created out of nothing. He knew there was some kind of scientific explanation for why that should be the case, but it looked magical to him regardless.

And now he was inside that dark heart, and he could speak to it as he spoke to ordinary shadows. He found it was much easier to smother a flame from within than to overwhelm it from without.

Jaide gasped as one of her twin towers of light suddenly went out. It felt as though Jack had reached inside of her and ripped something out. The shock of it almost physically hurt her, even though it was the flame Jack had attacked, not her. She didn't know exactly what he had done, but she turned her Gift to strengthening the second flame before he could do it a second time.

Jack felt her fighting back. It was hard getting into the second flame's heart because she was swirling it around like a corkscrew, keeping the shadows moving. Short of setting the actual candle wax on fire, however, there was no way she could stop him forever. He saw an opening and took it, and once there, he reached out to do exactly what he had done before.

"No!" Jaide cried, sensing victory about to be snatched from her. The remaining candle flame feathered and branched into thousands of individual flames, fueled by dozens of tiny twisters, each with a life of its own.

Jack became confused by all the dark hearts forming around him. He couldn't kill them all at once — and to make matters worse, it was getting hard to tell light from dark in the first place. He could feel the flame wrapping him up and drawing him out of the shadow, into itself. He fought that feeling, not knowing what would happen if he gave in to it.

"Jack?" said Jaide, feeling that she, too, was losing control of the duel. Long, thin shadows were reaching out from the candle's wick. It looked as though a flame made of darkness was eating into the ordinary fire and threatening to devour it.

She tried to tell her Gift to stop, but it was as caught up in the duel as she had been and didn't want to let go.

The shadow-flame grew higher and wider until it licked at the ceiling of the blue room.

"Stop," commanded Kleo.

Both Jaide and Jack were too embroiled in the duel to hear.

"Stop, I said — *I am trying to listen to something!*"

The oddness of her comment — why wasn't she worried about burning down the house? — was what caught the twins' attention. Jack snapped instantly back into his body, staggering a little. Jaide pressed a hand to her aching forehead as the allure of the dark flame ebbed. It was a relief to let it go, even though that meant neither of them won.

Blinking, they turned to look at Kleo.

She was poised oddly, with three legs on the back of the chair and the fourth crooked as though about to knock on an invisible door. Her head was cocked.

"I hear them," she said. "I must go to them."

"But your oath!" Ari protested, hopping from perch to perch until he stood next to her, looking worried. "She'll be angry."

"I am a Warden Companion," she snapped at him, "not a babysitter. *You* stay with them."

Kleo broke her pose and ran for the exit from the blue room. Ari followed her, with the twins doing their best to keep up.

Jack reached the front door first, but by then Kleo was long gone. There was just Ari pacing back and forth, peering out into the town with his tail whipping like a snake. It was surprisingly dark; more time had passed in the blue room than Jack had guessed.

"What's wrong?" he asked the cat.

"Can't you hear it?" Ari said. "Her people are fighting."

Jack couldn't hear anything over Jaide's belated arrival.

"If that's the case, then of course Kleo should go help them," Jaide said. "And we should help her!"

"It doesn't work like that," said Ari, with heartfelt weariness.

"Then what should we do?" asked Jack.

"Return to your exercises. That's what she and your grandmother would want."

It was Jaide's turn to pace. "This is ridiculous. What's the point of having a Gift if we can't use it?"

"Using it wisely," said Ari, "that's the trick of it. . . ."

"So people keep saying, but who's going to teach us to be wise? You?"

Ari's tail drooped disconsolately, and that took some of the wind out of Jaide's sails.

"Sorry, Ari," she said, crouching down to give him a tight hug. "Please don't hate me, too. I'm just frustrated."

"We're all frustrated," said Ari, muffled by her shoulder, "and caught in the middle, and suffocating —"

"Oh, sorry." Jaide let him go, and he shook himself all over to unflatten his fur.

"Why don't we ask the Oracular Crocodile what to do?" Jack suggested.

Jaide's bitten fingertip gave an involuntary twitch. "I don't think so. Not after last time."

"We won't need to give it any more blood. Let's try."

Before she could argue, he was off, trailing Ari like a shadow. When Jaide caught up with them, they had the animated crocodile skull in front of them, and were deep in argument with it.

"But you owe us," Jack was saying.

"Num num num."

"You took more than your fair share last time, and you won't get anything ever again until you come good on it. Tell us how to find the excision!"

Its red eyes flashed. "Num num!"

"No. You can just sit there and starve for all I care. Maybe we'll put you in a box and lock it in a drawer!"

Jack folded his arms and turned away.

"Mmmmmmmm." The skull sounded as though it were full of wasps. "Mmmmmmmm." Then it stopped and said, "Cast-iron wind detection instrument incorporating astronomical details above the cardinal points."

"What?" said Jaide.

With a slightly malicious tone, the skull repeated what it had told them. "Cast-iron wind detection instrument incorporating astronomical details above the cardinal points."

"It sounds as bad as Professor Saxon J. Chiruta III," Jaide commented, scratching her head.

"What's a cardinal point?" asked Jack.

"They're what a compass points to," said Ari. "East, west, north, south."

"And what does it mean by astronomical details?"

"I don't know. The sun? A comet?"

Jaide snapped her fingers. "Moon and stars — it's talking about the weather vane!"

They ran outside and stared up at the night sky. The weather vane's trusty arrow was barely visible; only Jack could make out which way it was facing, and even with his night vision he had to stare at it for quite a while.

"We should have thought of this earlier," said Jaide. "Or you should have told us," she added to Ari.

"Don't look at me," he said innocently. "I'm a cat."

"Exactly."

"It's pointing west," declared Jack, finally.

"Are you sure?"

"Positive. And the wind is from the south."

"So the excision is to the west."

Jaide shivered, thinking of the monster and all the white-eyed creatures the last time The Evil had directly attacked them.

"You mustn't do anything about this," said Ari. "You know what Kleo would say. You know what your grandmother would say."

"They're not here," said Jack. "We are."

"And here's where you should stay. You can't get yourselves overexcited or you never know what might happen."

"But what will happen if we don't do something?" Jaide was staring out into the night, following with her mind the direction the arrow was indicating.

"You know where it's pointing, don't you?" she asked Jack.

He nodded. "The old sawmill. The building site."

"Let's go."

Ari protested as they went to get a flashlight and then their bikes, but once they were under way, they left him far behind.

There was nothing he could do to stop them.

CHAPTER ELEVEN

NIGHT OF THE MOTHS

The building site was as dark and gloomy as it had been the previous night. The only difference was a white van parked out in front, with the MMM Holdings logo on it.

BUILDINGS TO LIVE IN.

Someone was there.

Jack and Jaide cycled to the back of the site and tiptoed through the hastily and rather poorly repaired hole in the fence.

"Do you feel that?" Jaide whispered to Jack. She couldn't explain it, exactly, because it wasn't anything she could hear or see. But the hair on the back of her neck was prickling, and she was acutely aware of the way the wind was nervously circling about her. Not like a twister. Just not at all normal.

Jack nodded. The feeling was the same as it had been earlier that day, from the house next door. He felt like something was watching them, and watching them closely. The moon hadn't risen yet, so the shadows were dark even to his night-sensitive eyes. There were dozens of hiding spots.

"Careful," he said, warning Jaide away from the trench they had skirted the night before. The squelchy patch of poisoned rats had been cleaned up, and the smell of crushed ants was gone.

"How about a little light?" she whispered.

"All right." He flicked on the flashlight and swept it around them.

The light only made it worse. Now the shadows were moving.

"Look!" said Jaide, grabbing his arm and pointing down into the trench.

There was something odd lying on the bottom.

Jack edged closer, playing the light across it. It looked like a long tube of plastic wrapping, until he got even closer and saw that the texture was more like paper. It was kind of olive-gray and there were odd ridges and scaly patches. It was at least five yards long and perhaps six feet in diameter.

"Is that . . . a *snake skin*?" he said, remembering Rodeo Dave's account of the escaped boa constrictor. "It's huge!"

Jaide was thinking exactly the same thing. She looked around them, imagining a giant serpent about to strike at any moment.

"You know," she said slowly, "maybe we *should* go home. . . ."

"In a minute," said Jack, sweeping the flashlight around them again. "The answers are here. When we find them we can tell Grandma and —"

He froze. The light had picked out a figure peering at them from behind a stack of corrugated iron. Definitely a person, with a head and shoulders and some kind of hood obscuring his or her face.

As soon as the light struck their dark observer, the hood boiled into a cloud of heavy gray moths that swarmed straight for them, their eyes gleaming pure white.

The twins acted instinctively, the lessons they had learned that afternoon fresh in their minds. Jaide called her Gift up and out in a series of tiny twisters, while Jack reached for the shadows in order to draw them about him and his sister, obscuring them from view.

But something went wrong. The twisters roared away from Jaide and whistled off into the distance. Instead of shadow, Jack found he had wrapped Jaide and himself in an intense white light that, rather than shielding them, attracted even more moths, some of them not even the white-eyed ones under the control of The Evil.

The moths swarmed in on them, their fat bodies and scratchy antennae crawling over every bit of exposed skin, more and more flying in as the first wave tried to get under their clothes, into their ears and noses and eyes.

With the physical assault of the moths came a terrible, silent wave of pressure on their minds. This time, The Evil said nothing to them — but somehow this was almost worse than if it had. There was just a blind, groping *thing* reaching into their heads, trying to swallow up their minds and take them out of themselves forever.

"Who's there?" called a girl's voice. "What's going on?" Jaide recognized Tara's voice.

"Keep back!" Jaide shouted, but further words were smothered by an avalanche of moths that filled her mouth. Jaide spat them out and bent over double, slapping herself in a desperate attempt to escape the smothering insects.

"Jaide? Is that — ahhh!"

Tara disappeared under another vast wave of moths. Shrieking, she turned to run, tripped over a piece of timber, and fell to the ground under a ten-inch-deep blanket of insects.

Jack ran in a circle, windmilling his arms across his face to keep it clear enough to see through slitted eyes. He was still trying to shield himself with shadow, but his Gift just kept fueling the intense light — doing the exact opposite of what he was asking it to do.

The exact opposite, thought Jack.

"Opposite!" he shouted to Jaide, spitting out a moth. "Tell your twisters to go away!"

Jaide's whole head was covered in moths, and they'd gotten into her ears as well. She heard Jack's voice as if it came from very far away. Too afraid to open her eyes, she concentrated on the whirlwinds, imagining them leaving the sawmill, flying out across the town, and then over the sea, going far, far, far away. . . .

A fierce, cold breeze hit the side of her head, followed by another wind that picked her up and spun her around. Jaide opened her eyes, moths peeling off her in all directions as two small twisters spun in an eccentric dance around her and Jack.

"Light!" said Jack, holding up his hands. "Give me light!"

The brilliant white light around him faded, till there was only the familiar yellow beam of the flashlight.

"Come to me, twisters," said Jaide quietly, reaching out for the whirlwinds. They spun away instead, carrying off a great cargo of moths.

The twins ran over to Tara, who now had only a light coverlet of insects. Brushing them aside, they helped her up.

Distantly, on the street outside the building site, they heard the screech of tires and a car pulling away.

"Oh," said Tara, uncovering her head and blinking up at them. "Oh! What was that all about?"

"I guess they were attracted by the light," said Jack, turning off the flashlight. "What are you doing here?"

"I . . . I was at the cinema," said Tara shakily. "I'm supposed to meet my father here. Have you seen him?"

Jaide thought of the silhouette they had spotted just before the moths had attacked them. She hadn't gotten a look at its face at all.

"We saw someone. . . ."

"I'm sure . . . at least I think I saw his van out front," Tara said, still looking a little dazed. "He must be here somewhere."

Tara headed off to the gate, confidently avoiding the perils of the unlit building site. Jack and Jaide exchanged a look, then followed. While they didn't want to bump into Martin McAndrew in the dark, they didn't want to leave Tara alone, either, not when The Evil was about.

They came around the sawmill and saw Tara's father getting out of the MMM Holdings van.

"*There* he is," Tara said, hurrying to meet him

Pretending to arrive, Jack thought, as they trailed her.

"Sorry, darling," Mr. McAndrew said as he and his daughter embraced. "The council meeting is running much later than I expected. You'll have to come back with me and —" He spotted the twins and smiled broadly. "Oh, hello . . . Jack and Jaide, isn't it? This is a surprise. Is Tara giving you a tour of the site?"

"Not exactly," Jaide said, trying to get a good look at his eyes. By the streetlights, they looked normal, with no sign of luminous white. "We were just riding past and saw Tara here."

"There were these moths!" exclaimed Tara. "Thousands of them! They swarmed all over us from out of nowhere, and then they disappeared. It was amazing! Actually, it was more creepy than amazing but —"

"Moths, did you say?"

Grandma X's voice came out of the gloom behind them, and the twins turned to face her with relief.

"Finally!" Jack cried out.

"Where have you *been*?" Jaide asked.

"I have been out looking for you two, of course." She took in Tara and her father in a glance, shooting the latter a particularly sharp glance. "This is an odd place for an evening rendezvous."

Jaide stood on tiptoes in order to whisper into her ear, "*We've got so much to tell you.*"

Grandma X shook her head minutely. *Not now.*

"Yes, it is a bit extraordinary," said Mr. McAndrew, looking uneasy. "But I'm learning fast that nothing in Portland is *ever* merely ordinary. Well, come on, Tara. The meeting is waiting for me, and I'd better not keep them much longer if I expect to get this approval through."

"Do I have to go?" she asked in tortured tones. "It's so boring . . . just a bunch of old people sitting around arguing in circles all night."

"Now, now, dear. I'm afraid we don't have any choice." Mr. McAndrew patted his daughter on the head, or tried to. She squirmed out of his way and folded her arms. "Believe me, I'll be just as happy as you when it's over."

"But, *Dad* —"

"She could come with us," Grandma X unexpectedly volunteered. "Until your meeting is over. We're about to have dinner, and she would be very welcome."

The twins stared at her in surprise. What was she thinking? With Tara around, there was no way they could talk about the monster or the excision.

Tara practically bounced in delight. "Please, Dad, can I?"

"Well, if you're sure it's no trouble."

"No trouble at all, Martin. I find these two a handful at the quietest of times. It'll be good for them to have someone to play with before bed."

"Well, great!" He clapped his hands together. "That's settled, then. I'd best be off. As soon as the meeting is over, I'll come by and pick Tara up. I know where the house is, of course."

His eagerness to get away was obvious to the twins as he hurried across the site, through the open gate, and into the van. It started with a roar and accelerated off into the night.

"You've got a moth caught in your hair," Tara told Jaide.

"Yuck. Where?"

"Here." Tara plucked the insect from her and held it up between thumb and forefinger. It looked quite dead. "Hey, let's see if we can find out what species it is!"

"How?"

"On the Web. Do you have the Internet?" Tara asked Grandma X.

"I can let you use my computer," she said, "so long as you only download information on moths, not viruses."

"Excellent! Maybe we'll find out what made them swarm like that."

Her excitement was contagious, but neither twin had forgotten the real reason for the swarming. Jack peered closely at the dead bug, looking for any sign of whiteness in its eyes.

"Are you sure it's dead?" he asked.

"I'm pretty sure there's no such thing as a zombie moth, Jackaran," said Grandma X. "This way, children. I'm parked at the back of the block, where I saw your bikes."

She led the way back around the sawmill while Jaide explained to Tara that Jackaran was Jack's full name, and Jaidith was Jaide's. Jack took the opportunity to walk close to Grandma X.

"There's something you have to see," he whispered.

"What kind of something?"

"I don't know. It's over here."

He guided her past the trench where they'd seen the giant snake skin, but when he shone the flashlight beam down into the trench, it was gone.

"Where did it go?" he asked, sweeping the light from one end of the trench to the other. There was definitely nothing there.

"Where did what go?" asked Tara, coming to look, too.

"Uh, I thought I saw a frog," said Jack, the first thing that came into his mind. "But it must have hopped out."

"I suppose it must have," said Grandma X, heading on to the fence and ushering the two puzzled trouble-twisters and one oblivious Tara through the hole. "Now, Jackaran and Jaidith, you ride your bikes straight home. Tara, you come with me."

"Okay," she said. "Hey, cool car! How old is it?"

"Old enough to have a personality," Grandma X said, getting inside, "and an intense dislike of waking up on cold mornings."

"Sounds like my mom."

The car doors slammed, and Jack and Jaide rode off through the beam of its headlights.

"How did he *do* that?" asked Jaide, pedaling harder to take out her frustration.

"Who? Do what?"

"Tara's dad, of course. He must have hidden the skin while we were distracted."

"Could the moths have carried it away?"

"Maybe."

"Or maybe it was more than empty skin after all?"

"I don't know, Jack. If it was the monster, what was it doing pretending to be dead? Or deflated? Why didn't it just eat us there and then?"

Jack had no good answer for that, and he doubted they were going to get any closer to an answer that night.

When they got home, the weather vane was pointing out the proper wind direction, and Ari was waiting impatiently on the veranda. He glared at them, then ran off into the garden, so the twins could tell that he was both relieved and annoyed. They wondered if he was going to get into trouble from both Kleo and Grandma X for letting them out of his sight.

They searched moths and other Lepidoptera while Grandma X prepared dinner. They could tell she was distracted by something, because that night they had one of her busy meals, where she rummaged through the fridge and the pantry and put together whatever she could find in odd combinations. So they had baked beans, rice, and steamed vegetables, followed by raspberry jelly with chocolate on the side. Tara didn't seem to mind, not even when Grandma X got out the mysterious soup pot again and began cooking up a particularly noxious brew.

"My mother only cooks healthy stuff," she said, "and the same things, over and over again. Dad only ever gets take-out, from the same place, which I don't like. We never have anything different. Sometimes my grandpa comes and stays with us, and we have fantastic stir-fries, but he only visits when my grandmother is mad at him and kicks him out for a while."

The moth was proving tough to identify, and even the twins were distracted by the search. They'd never realized just how many moths and butterflies existed in the world, or how hideous they were when magnified. Weirdly, butterflies, which looked so beautiful from afar, were much uglier up close than moths. Moths looked practically beautiful in comparison.

In the end, they decided that it was probably an imperial silk moth, and found a jar to seal its remains in, so Tara could take it home. Jack wanted to sticky-tape it shut, but even Jaide thought that was going too far. They had been alone with it for an hour and it hadn't even twitched.

They'd only just got out a board game when a horn's sharp tooting came from outside the house.

"That'll be Dad," said Tara, jumping up. "He'll be in a hurry. He always is."

They rushed to the door, and sure enough, there was the MMM Holdings van parked in the driveway, with Martin McAndrew tapping his fingers on the wheel.

"Come along, Tara!" he called. "Did you have a good time?"

"Excellent, Dad," she said, only reluctantly walking out to meet him. "Do I have to go home now?"

"Well, it's been a long day, and you have to feed Fi-Fi. . . ."

"I'm sure the kids would love to see each other another time," said Grandma X, appearing suddenly behind them with a pink-tinged wooden spoon in one hand.

The twins shot her a dirty look, which Grandma X completely ignored.

"What about tomorrow?" Tara said. "Could they come over to our house, Dad?"

"I'm afraid they're busy during the day," Grandma X said. "But tomorrow night they're available."

Jaide felt a rising sense of panic. They couldn't leave Portland when The Evil was running loose!

"Can the twins stay over?" asked Tara. "Please, Daddy, say yes."

Mr. McAndrew looked from his anxious daughter to the tense trio on the steps. He smiled. "Of course, my love. Jack, Jaide — you are very welcome."

Jaide and Jack nudged their grandmother from both sides, but it was too late.

"I think that's a wonderful idea," she said. "I'll put them on the train in the afternoon, then they can catch the train home the next morning. Shall I call you to confirm the times?"

"That would be perfect." Mr. McAndrew's white teeth gleamed at them as he told Grandma X the phone number. "We'll be waiting for them at the station."

"You can meet Fi-Fi," said Tara, climbing into the van. "She's my puppy. You'll just adore her!"

The twins waved listlessly as the van trundled forward, kicking up gravel in its driver's haste. As its glowing taillights vanished up the lane, the twins turned on Grandma X, who was already retreating inside.

"What did you do that for?" asked Jaide.

"What do you mean? She's your friend, isn't she?"

"Yes, but we don't want to go to her house!"

"Why not?" Grandma X called over her shoulder. "I thought you'd relish the chance to see what Martin McAndrew's home is like. I mean, if he's an agent of The Evil, like you think, won't there be some kind of sign?"

"But what if it's dangerous?" said Jack.

"That didn't seem to bother you tonight."

"You don't believe us," said Jaide. "You're just trying to get us out of your hair!"

Grandma X didn't deny that. She vanished into the kitchen to tend to her new concoction.

In the hallway, the twins conferred.

"She's right," said Jack. "This is a good chance to check him out."

"But what if we don't find anything?"

"Then maybe she's right about that too."

"But she can't be! Did you see the way he stayed in his car — like he was afraid of setting foot in the garden? That's because it's protected, and he's in league with The Evil!"

"So we prove her wrong," said Jack.

Jaide could accept that angle. "All right. We prove her wrong."

"When you've finished whispering out there," called Grandma X from the kitchen, "you can brush your teeth and go to your rooms to read for a while before turning out the light."

The twins leaned their heads around the kitchen door. Grandma X was still at the pot, stirring and tipping in bowls of mysterious ingredients.

"What's going on tomorrow during the day?" asked Jaide.

"It's Saturday," said Jack, worried that it might be more homework that Mr. Carver hadn't set.

"I have a treat in store for you," Grandma X said

without looking up from the concoction. "A special teacher, and a very special lesson."

"Who?" asked Jack.

"What?" asked Jaide.

Both their interests were piqued, but Grandma X would tell them nothing more.

CHAPTER TWELVE
THE SHAPE-SHIFTER

The twins woke to find the only Warden they had ever met, apart from their father and grandmother, sitting at the kitchen table eating a perfectly ordinary bowl of porridge.

"Good morning, Jack and Jaide," said Custer. "It's nice to meet you under more congenial circumstances."

Custer was an odd-looking man with close-set yellow eyes, sharp cheekbones, and long blond hair — but that wasn't remotely the oddest thing about him. They had met him briefly after the fixing of the East Ward, when the threat of The Evil had abated and the storm gripping Portland had begun to ebb. He and their father were trusted friends, and they both traveled by unusual means: Hector by lightning, Custer in the form of a saber-toothed tiger. Custer had assumed that Hector was the one who had fixed the ward, and nothing the twins had said would convince him otherwise.

"It's good of you to come, Nate," said Grandma X, handing him a mug of hot chocolate and pouring one each for the twins. "The moon is growing old and my Gift is therefore on the wane. While I'm busy, our troubletwisters here could use a firm, guiding hand."

Custer's odd eyes drilled into the twins, one after the other. "Not to worry," he said. "Happy to help out."

"How do you know Dad?" asked Jack, sniffing at his hot chocolate and deciding it was probably safe to drink.

"We fought together, a long time ago."

"Dad was in the army?" Jaide was surprised. She couldn't imagine her floppy-haired, eccentric father dressed in a uniform and holding a gun.

"Not in the army," Custer clarified. "Against The Evil. We lost our — that is, when the battle was won, both our families had reason to mourn. That kind of bond can never be broken."

"This was before you were born," said Grandma X to the twins. "Your father was barely a teenager. Toast?"

Jack nodded eagerly, but he wasn't done with learning about his father, and the life he had led that until recently they had known nothing about.

"Was Dad brave?" he asked Custer.

"Very." Custer leaned forward and rested his hands on the table. "This was in the Pacific. A new island had appeared out of the ocean floor and The Evil had found a way into our world through it. The enemy was well established by the time we arrived, inhabiting albatrosses and sharks, even the stones of the island, which rose up against us in the form of granite giants. We had less than twenty-four hours to establish the wards before it found a way to reach civilization. We lost many good Wardens that day."

"Custer," said Grandma X softly, "the table."

Long, yellowish claws had emerged from the end of Custer's fingers and were in danger of scouring the wood.

He folded his hands into fists and straightened.

"Enough old news," he said. "Let's talk of you two. Your grandmother tells me you've advanced quickly, but that your Gifts remain unsettled. She also tells me that you're seeing The Evil everywhere, thanks to your reading of the *Compendium*. It's only natural for you to be excited about everything at this point in your development, but control is more important than excitement, and that's what I'm here to teach you."

"We *have* control," said Jaide. "We dueled yesterday, and I won —"

"An illusion," said Custer firmly. "Fighting your brother is a far cry from fighting The Evil. No matter how mean or treacherous you might think Jack to be sometimes, our enemy is a thousand times worse. We must be certain of your capabilities before you can be trusted with the responsibilities of being a Warden."

The long-term promise of being a Warden stilled Jaide's tongue. That was what she wanted more than anything.

"Is there a special ceremony to become a Warden?" asked Jack around a mouthful of toast and peanut butter. "Like graduation?"

"You mean, do we wear robes and put on funny hats and get a certificate to put on the wall?" Custer sniffed. "No. We don't go in for that, any more than we use wands when we use our Gifts. It's all in our heads." He tapped his temple with one perfectly ordinary fingernail. "That's where the real battle is fought."

"Who else is a Warden?" asked Jaide. "Anyone famous?"

"Wardens work in the background, where no one can see them. It has to be that way, because otherwise the distractions of the world will hamper our fight against the enemy. The Evil is always willing to use everyday confusions against us. We must be careful when we choose our friends, for instance. Even a small kindness can turn to harm."

Jack thought of Tara, but couldn't see how anything they did could be bad for her — particularly if her father was already on the side of The Evil. Surely, having them around could only do her good.

"What's stopping a Warden from using his Gift to make money?" he asked.

"Nothing," said Custer, "but his conscience. And in some situations, it might well be justified."

"I'll leave you three to it," said Grandma X. "You can practice in the garden. Try not to destroy anything, particularly yourselves."

She kissed both troubletwisters on the head, then hurried out of the kitchen. Moments later, they heard the firing up of the Hillman Minx, and the twins were alone with their temporary tutor.

"Finished your breakfast?" he asked. "Let's do as she says and go outside."

They went to stand under the Douglas fir, which, despite the battering it had received in recent times, was still standing tall and true. The morning was both sunny and cool at the same time. A thin breeze wound around the house, whistling in the eaves.

They stood in a triangle. Custer faced the twins with

his hands in the pockets of his brown suede trousers. Gray hairs poked out of the V of his open collar.

"You have seen my other face," he said in a solemn voice. "You know that I can change my shape."

They nodded.

"You're a . . . were-cat?" said Jack.

"A shape-shifter," Custer corrected him. "There are many different kinds of shape-shifters, and some of them you will have heard of, such as vampires, lycanthropes, berserkers, selkies, naga, kitsune. Although the stories told about them are mostly false, all these legendary beings have a basis in fact."

"Where there's smoke, there's fire," said Jaide.

"Exactly. The fire in this case is us, the Wardens. We use our shape-shifting abilities only for good, and only to fight The Evil."

"The Evil can change its shape, too," said Jack, who had seen it adopt the appearance of a person at least once.

Custer shook his head. "The Evil can only pretend. It takes the creatures it possesses and blends them in unnatural ways in order to create the appearance of another being. But it's just an act. It has no true shape. Only humans can be shape-shifters."

An idea occurred to Jaide in a sudden flash. "Could the Monster of Portland be a shape-shifter?"

"The what?" asked Custer.

"The Monster of Portland," repeated Jaide. "Uh, this creature people see around here, and we saw its skin . . . at least we think it was its skin."

Custer frowned, as if he didn't know what the trouble-twisters were talking about. But it was not an entirely convincing frown.

"Only Wardens can be shape-shifters," said Custer. "And . . . sometimes if The Evil captures a troubletwister with that Gift, then that part of The Evil will retain the ability. Until the Warden is fully subsumed, and forgets he or she was ever human. Now please, troubletwisters, let's stick to the subject."

The twins exchanged a glance. Custer was hiding some-thing, too — that was very clear. His protestation that the monster didn't exist only made them more certain than ever that it did.

But they didn't want to make Custer mad. His claws were showing again, and his teeth looked longer than they had before.

"All right," said Jaide.

"Sorry," added Jack.

"Thank you. Now, why should we be able to do what The Evil cannot? The answer is simple. We all possess something that our enemy lacks, something it desires greatly but cannot ever have. That is our inner nature, our selves, our *souls*. Where The Evil is a being of hunger and appetite that can never be filled — empty, heartless, cold — we are filled to the brim with life, and it is this life that gives us the edge. You see, shape-shifting isn't only about shape. It's about understanding one's nature, which one must do before appearing as anything else — and one must first *have* a nature before one can understand it."

Here Custer lost the twins, who were less interested in the theory than what they could do with it.

"So does that mean we could be shape-shifters, too?" asked Jack.

"Maybe, if your Gift allows it."

"How will we know?" asked Jaide.

"That's partly why I'm here," he told them. "I will test you, and hopefully teach you a thing or two about yourselves in the process."

He reached into the pocket of his coat and brought out a familiar deck of cards. Familiar to the troubletwisters, anyway, though they would have puzzled anyone else. They were made of gold, were very heavy, and did not have any of the usual illustrations.

"Grandma's cards," said Jaide.

"No," replied Custer. "This is my own deck. The cards are essentially the same, though I do not use them in exactly the same way. Your grandmother's Gifts are primarily governed by the moon and stars — she is a strong diviner, among other things. My Gifts are primarily of the water and the air, of living things and movement — I do not have the deep skills of divination. But the cards may answer to either of you in different ways, and that will . . . perhaps . . . tell me something about your Gifts and how they are developing."

Custer placed the cards on one of the exposed roots of the tree. There was a flat section of the root, almost like a small table, that might have been made for the cards. It had space for the deck, with room next to it to lay cards out flat, faceup.

"Jaide," he said. "Take the five topmost cards and place them in a cross, like a compass, with the last card at the center."

Jaide picked up the first card. It was cool, and even heavier than she remembered. It was also blank, showing only the sheen of hammered gold.

"It's blank," she said, showing it to the others.

"Put it down next to the deck," said Custer. "Now the others. No . . . wait a moment, Jack. I'll tell you when it's your turn."

Jaide put down her cards. As her fingers left the last one, something moved across the gold, so swiftly she couldn't be sure what she'd seen. It might have been a cloud, or a wave, or just some irregular shape. . . .

"Good," said Custer, who had been watching intently. With a swift motion, he scooped up the five cards and placed them to one side, facedown. "Jack, you can try now."

Jack took his first card. It didn't show a symbol or the even sheen of blank gold. Instead, it was completely shadowed and dark, staying that way for at least a second before the gold came shining through, like the sun banishing the night. The next four cards he dealt were completely blank.

"What does this mean?" asked Jack, sitting back and scratching his head.

"It is a divination technique," Custer explained. "The Fivefold Path reveals certain things about your Gifts — specifically, the Gift you might have, the Gift you want to have, the Gift you shouldn't have, the Gift you need to have, and the Gift you can't ever have."

"But the cards didn't show anything," said Jaide.

"Because your natures are still not set. Which means anything might happen to your Gifts, depending on the influences that come to bear."

"What kind of influences?" asked Jack.

Custer waved the question away. "I think we'll leave the cards for now. Please, both of you sit down with your backs against this wonderful tree. No, on opposite sides."

The twins had automatically sat down together. But Custer moved them apart. To Jaide he gave the exercise of imagining herself floating, like in an endless sky, alone and weightless, while Jack was to picture himself in cool, comfortable darkness.

"Let your true self step forward," he told them, touching them lightly on the crowns of their heads. "You might be surprised who you see."

Nothing happened for a good long while, except that the ground got far less comfortable and the supposedly soft needles that grew straight out of the trunk of the tree weren't all that soft when you were leaning against them.

Jack wondered if Jaide was as distracted as he was. He couldn't see what sitting around doing nothing at all was going to accomplish. Perhaps if he *could* change into a tiger or something by the end of the day, it might be worth it, but he couldn't imagine that happening. Custer wasn't actually teaching them anything. He figured that all the talk of selves and souls and Gifts was just mumbo jumbo designed to keep them out of Grandma X's hair.

You were foolish to try to resist us, said a ghostly voice from his memory. *Your inner self wants to join us. . . .*

Be quiet, Jack told the voice, but it kept on talking.

Surrender. We know you want to give in.

He hugged himself and squeezed his eyes tightly shut.

Please don't let that be my inner self, he thought fearfully, all his criticisms of Custer forgotten.

Jaide was having no less trying a time. Her imaginary skies were full of odd currents of thought that unbalanced her. She couldn't stop thinking about things no matter how she tried. First of all, she blamed her mother for leaving them alone in Portland, then Grandma X for not believing them, then Kleo, again, for not letting them help.

She kept hearing that hissing voice in her mind.

Nobody asked you to come. This is cat business! My business! Stay out of it!

No one wanted her help, Jaide thought bitterly. Grandma X, Kleo, their own father . . . no one realized that she could be very helpful, that she could do great things if only they'd let her.

Hot, moist air blew in her face. She blinked, startled, and opened her eyes.

She was face-to-face with a saber-toothed tiger, Custer in his animal form. His eyes stared at her unblinkingly, but she could barely take her eyes off his massive fangs. They were just an inch or two from her. With one bite, he could snap her head clean off.

Instead of biting her, he sniffed once, nodded, then turned and padded around the tree to where Jack was sitting with his hands clenched tightly in his lap.

Jaide followed, suddenly afraid for her brother, although she didn't know why.

Custer sniffed him, too, then bent and nudged him in the chest, like a giant version of Ari.

"What —?" Jack's eyes flickered open. He stared in confusion at Custer, then Jaide. "Why are you interrupting me? I thought this was the exercise."

"It was," said Custer. His voice came out deep and resonant from his tiger's barrel chest. "And you have seen your doubts. You know yourself better now, and it's up to you whether you reveal that knowledge or keep it to yourself. What matters is how you use this knowledge to make yourself stronger."

The twins studied each other, wondering what the other had experienced during the meditation. Neither volunteered anything.

After a short silence, Custer said, "All right, time to show me what you have learned already."

He bade them sit on either side of him and do as he commanded. They started small: Jaide conjured a breeze barely strong enough to tip over a fallen leaf; Jack made his hand vanish into the tree's shadow. Slowly, the tasks became more complex and the commands more frequent, until the garden was awash with whirling winds and shadows, and the twins no longer had time to think about what, precisely, they were doing. As a result, more and more frequently, their attempts to obey Custer went awry.

"Eddy — here! Shade — there!"

Custer prowled back and forth between them, pointing and snapping orders. They hadn't noticed him change back into human form. They heard only his voice — and it was a voice that brooked no disagreement. Under the gaze of those odd, yellow eyes, they tried their best to do everything he said.

Inevitably, perhaps, it all went wrong.

In the middle of calling up a pair of tiny twisters, Jaide felt something inside her snap like a rubber band. The twisters reared up like snakes, coiling around each other and tying themselves into a tight knot. Then they vanished, and nothing Jaide could do would bring them back.

Jack fared no better. His shadows suddenly took on a life of their own, as though they had become twisters of air, just like his sister could create. He struggled to bring them back under his command, but they danced around him like mad dervishes, straining to be set free.

Then he, too, felt an odd breaking sensation inside him. As his Gift dissolved and fell away, he cried out in dismay.

Jaide was too deep in her own crisis to hear him. She waved her hands, commanded under her breath, did everything she had done before — but nothing she did would bring her Gift back.

Then, without warning, it all returned, and more. Wind swirled around her, kicking up dust and pine needles — and shadows, too, as though she had inherited Jack's Gift along with hers, in one wild, untamable mix.

"Cease!" barked Custer.

Instantly, the mad tangle of shadows and air fell away.

The twins stared at each other, confused and distraught, awaiting an explanation for what had just happened.

All Custer said, however, was, "It is time for lunch."

They went inside, where they found all the ingredients required for sandwiches laid out on the table. Jaide's appetite was as disturbed as the rest of her. She didn't immediately dig in like Jack, who felt hungry enough to eat all of it, and the table as well. She hung back until Jack had made his usual teetering tower of food, and only decided that she would eat at all because Custer insisted.

"Using your Gift is no different from working any other part of your mind or body," he said. "It takes energy, and that energy must be restored. Fail to take sustenance, and your Gift will either wither — or it will consume *you* by degrees, until there is nothing left."

The latter thought was so horrible that Jaide forced herself to make a ham and cheese sandwich and eat it all down.

Custer ate only greens and a tomato, with half a piece of buttered bread. Still he said nothing about what had happened to them in the garden. Jack and Jaide didn't ask, either, until Jack was halfway through his sandwich and able to think about something other than food.

"My Gifts aren't gone for good, are they?" he asked.

"Most likely they will return," said Custer, not very reassuringly. "How long that will take, though, I cannot tell you."

"I think I have Jack's Gift as well as mine now," Jaide confessed. "And I think for a while he had mine. How is that possible? How can our Gifts move like that?"

"You are twins," Custer said. "You are connected. Furthermore, you are still unsure of who you are. You think you understand your Gifts, but in truth you have barely been introduced to them. They are changeable and fickle. Until you understand yourselves, you cannot understand them."

"You did this to us," said Jack, feeling a flash of sudden resentment. "You made us doubt ourselves, and now our Gifts have gone mad."

"Is this the first time you have felt like this?" he asked them.

The twins lowered their eyes, remembering the attack of the moths, when their Gifts had seemed to reverse their effects, and the duel with the candles, when they had become weirdly entangled. Their Gifts had been acting up already, and they hadn't realized what was going on.

"Doubt is one of the many weapons The Evil will use against you," said Custer. "You can be sure of that. Learn to resist now, or fall later."

Jaide's appetite had gone again, but she forced herself to keep eating. If what Custer said was true, their Gifts might not settle for ages, and she might end up being a Shadow Walker instead of Jack. She didn't like that thought. Her brief experiences of flying in the embrace of the wind had been so exhilarating, and at the same time so terrifying, that she had never felt quite so alive. She couldn't imagine never doing it again.

The thought was too dismaying. She had to change the subject.

"Do you know what an excision is, Custer?"

Custer frowned again, this time genuinely.

"I recall that it is a bit of . . . leftover Evil," he said slowly. "A remnant or relict that remains when wards are reestablished. Why do you ask?"

"We think there's one loose in Portland," said Jaide eagerly. "We have to —"

"Do nothing!" instructed Custer firmly. "Such things are weak and fade of their own accord. They cannot survive without a connection to the greater mass of The Evil."

"But it *wasn't* weak, not last night at the sawmill," said Jaide. "The Evil took over thousands of moths. Thousands!"

Custer did not answer immediately. He simply looked at them, shifting his gaze from Jaide to Jack and back again, as if he was searching for something that was not immediately obvious.

"Moths have simple minds," he said finally. "Even a fading excision of The Evil could probably manage a few thousand moths. Nevertheless, I will mention the matter to your grandmother. But you need to keep out of it. Your Gifts are in a perilous state. Control is the most important thing for you to learn now. When you have mastered yourselves and your Gifts, then you can begin the great work ahead of you, and go forth against The Evil."

Jack thought of his father with Custer on a brand-new island in the Pacific, fighting sharks and giant birds possessed by The Evil. That made their fears about Portland and the excision seem very small, even if it didn't dispel them entirely. It wasn't just the moths; there was also the strange feeling they'd had of being watched, and the mysterious skin they had found on the building site.

"But what about the giant snake skin or whatever it was we found?" Jaide asked. "It isn't just moths!"

"I said you should stay out of it," instructed Custer firmly. "If your assistance is required, I am sure you will be asked for it."

Jaide went white, and felt tears starting in her eyes. Jack shifted uneasily next to her, wanting to help, but unsure of what he could do.

Deep inside Jaide, humiliation fought against anger. This was the second time her help had been refused, her good deeds repudiated. First Kleo hissed at her to go away, and now Custer was telling her much the same thing.

Stupid cats! thought Jaide. Anger had won over the feelings of humiliation and hurt. *Big and little! They don't know when they need help! Well, they're going to get it anyway.*

"If you've finished," said Custer, indicating their empty plates, "I suggest we resume."

Without argument, but without much enthusiasm, either, the twins followed him back out into the yard.

CHAPTER THIRTEEN
ALL ABOARD THE RED ROCKET!

Custer worked with them for another two hours, but wasn't able to return their Gifts to their former state. Jaide had both Jack's and her own tangled up in an unruly mess, while Jack had nothing. Both found it frustrating, and behind his bluff, impassive manner they sensed Custer felt the same. Of course, *he* wasn't the one whose Gifts were in revolt, so they reserved their sympathy entirely for themselves.

In the course of their travails, they witnessed his transformation from human to saber-tooth and back more than once. It was both fascinating and unnerving, the way his teeth and bones stretched, warping his muscles and twisting his skin into new patterns and shapes, and he absorbed his clothes and shoes and everything into his body, too, to become tiger hide. It was clearly something that required a great deal of skill and exertion, for Custer was invariably out of breath when he finished each transformation.

"Will we ever learn to do that?" Jack asked the last time Custer turned back into his human form.

"I don't know. Your Gifts are in a state of flux and your journey to self-discovery has hardly begun. It is sometimes possible to turn incipient Gifts in a particular direction, given hard work and the right influences."

Jack decided to take that as a yes. He would give anything to change into something as powerful as a tiger — a panther, perhaps, or a wolf. . . .

Jaide imagined flying high over the world on the broad wings of an eagle, and wished she didn't have to wait. Why was everything to do with being a Warden hard? Even when their Gifts were working, nothing went as planned.

She was so deep in thought that she didn't notice the miniature vortex that skidded through the shadow of the fir, disappeared behind the trunk, then returned with a ginger tom tangled up in its heart.

"Take it off me!" Ari yelled. "I was just about to come out — honest!"

Custer clapped his hands together, once, and the vortex collapsed, depositing Ari on the ground.

"Uh, I didn't mean to do that!" said Jaide. "I mean, I didn't even know —"

"You didn't," said Custer. "I did. You have my apologies, Aristotle. I thought you were . . . another cat."

Ari sniffed and licked his paws.

"Apology accepted. I was coming to give you a message. *She* says it's time to go, and I am to escort you to the train station."

Custer pulled a gold fob watch from his pocket, flicked the cover open, and looked at it.

"Indeed. The hour has come for me to conclude my tuition. My thanks, Jack and Jaide, for your hard work today."

"Wait!" said Jack in a panic. "You can't leave now. I haven't gotten my Gifts back!"

"I sympathize," said the Warden, "but it's not for me to return them to you. They will come, or not, in their own time."

"But — but —"

Custer put a hand on each of Jack's shoulders and looked deep into his eyes. "Troubletwister, know thyself. Only then will you know your enemy."

He turned to Jaide, bowed, and left on foot as a human, not as a saber-tooth, as she had half expected he would.

That suddenly, their lesson was over.

"Do we really have to go to see Tara?" Jaide asked Ari.

"I was instructed to give you no choice in the matter, but what I should do if you refuse, your grandmother didn't say. She did tell me that she has packed your bags, and that they're sitting on your beds, ready to go."

They went inside and, sure enough, their backpacks were exactly as Ari described.

"Where is Grandma?" Jack asked, still stinging at the fact that Custer had left him powerless against the many threats that seemed to be inhabiting Portland at the moment.

"I have no idea." Ari hopped onto the bed, circled a particular spot three times, and sat down, resting his head on his paws.

"What do you know, then?" asked Jack in exasperation.

"The good news is that the rat-poisonings have stopped."

"Does that mean Kleo is okay now?" asked Jaide. "She won't be challenged?"

Ari tilted his head over, considering.

"No. Although the poisonings have stopped, we lost some good friends, and the balance of power has shifted. There are even more cats from outside to worry about now. There's a rumor of a battle this weekend. If enough outside cats move in, Kleo could be ousted, possibly even run right out of Portland. . . ."

Ari's ears drooped as he said this. Jaide sat next to him and scritched him under the collar.

"Do you know where they're coming from? If we could head them off somehow, maybe —"

Ari butted his head up against her hand, slid between her arm and body, and jumped to the floor, where he paced back and forth angrily.

"Don't even think it! If Kleo knew I'd told you this much, she'd have kittens with cod tails. Now, if you're ready, put on your charms and let's get moving."

"Our what?"

"Charms," said Ari, pointing with his pink nose. "On your bags. Your tickets are there, too."

Jaide picked up an antique locket from the top of her bag. It was a plain silver disc you could open with a thumbnail and it had a pale green ribbon to hang around her throat. When she opened the locket, all it contained was some dry leaves, seeds, and grit.

Jack found a similarly ancient pillbox on his bag. Its contents were the same.

"You're to wear these charms or carry them with you at all times," said Ari. "They'll help hide you from The Evil should it come looking for you."

"But how could it do that?" asked Jaide. "We're protected by the . . . oh, right."

For the first time it occurred to her that they would be leaving Portland, and therefore leaving the protection of the wards behind.

"Is this safe?" asked Jack. "I mean, is it really all right for us to go?"

"I guess it must be," she said, "or Grandma would never let us."

"You know, if you think about it, we should be safer *outside* Portland, because this is where The Evil comes through. If the wards don't work, I mean."

"It's only one of the places," replied Jaide. "I wonder where the next nearest one is? And if The Evil came through there, how far it could go? I mean, could it travel all the way here?"

Ari opened his mouth, but before he could say a word, Jaide continued.

"I know you don't know, Ari. I was just wondering. More things to ask Grandma."

"Exactly," said Ari. "And now we really must go or you'll miss the train, and then I'll be in trouble, too."

"All right," said Jack, resigning himself to leaving the safety of Grandma X's house and, perhaps even more horrifyingly, to having a sleepover with a pair of girls. "Are we supposed to walk there?"

"Take your bikes," Ari said. "You can leave them up at the station. No one would dare steal them — or if they did, they'd never do it a second time."

They shut the door behind them without bothering to turn the lock, like Grandma X did. Ari hopped into the basket on Jaide's bike and braced himself for sudden acceleration.

The route to the station took them right past the old sawmill and the construction site. They saw no signs of moths or of anything to do with The Evil. The hole in the fence had been securely sealed. As they zoomed past, however, Jaide saw something that she hadn't noticed before, partly because it had been shrouded in the gloom, but also because she hadn't thought to look.

Along the southern edge of the building site, just over the fence, was a narrow creek bed, the sides of which had been concreted over so it was more like a drain. Its eastern end vanished under the road and the businesses that ran along the seaward side of the street. The western end opened into a large pipe that led into the rising hillside that hid the railway line from the street, the hillside that to the south became Little Rock.

Jaide slowed as she went past, then put on the brakes, hard.

"Hey!" said Jack, almost crashing into her from behind. "What're you doing?"

"We can't stop," said Ari. "The train is due to leave in five minutes!"

"Hold on," she said, dismounting and giving the handlebars to Jack so the bike wouldn't tip over. "I just want to check something."

She ran off the road and down to the side of the creek

bed. A thin trickle of clear water ran along the green-scummed bottom. There was surprisingly little of the junk she had seen built up in similar drains in the city. Maybe, she thought, it had all been swept clean by the floods of the previous week.

Maybe something more than rubbish had been swept out, too. . . .

She hopped down the sloping concrete wall, being very careful where she put her hands and feet, and making certain that she would be able to get out again afterward. The mouth leading into the hillside would once have seemed impenetrably dark to her eyes, but now that she had Jack's Gift as well as her own, she could see quite clearly the way the concrete walls gave way to natural stone, as though the drain connected to a series of caves that went much deeper underground.

She stepped right up to the opening and put her head into the shadow.

If she were a monster and needed somewhere to hide, she thought, this would be the perfect place. It didn't matter how dark or dank it was. She had seen seaweed turn into a giant sea monster and climb out of the ocean with her very own eyes. If The Evil could do that, a little damp wasn't going to be a problem.

Was there something lurking inside now, in the depths of the tunnel . . . something black and inhuman hanging from the ceiling . . . perhaps something monstrous?

Jaide's foot slipped on a patch of bright green slime, her ankle turned, and she almost fell over. Her gasp of alarm prompted an answering chirrup from many nearby mouths, and the dark mass she had seen suddenly boiled into motion.

Leathery wings batted at her head. Wild, ugly faces glared. She covered her face with her arms and tried not to scream.

Then they were gone, and she could hear Jack and Ari calling for her.

Feeling embarrassed and slightly foolish, she came out of the drain and clambered back up the slope.

"Sorry," she said. "I had to check."

"Bats!" exclaimed Jack. "I bet they gave you a fright."

"We really must get moving," said Ari, tail lashing. "*Really* really."

"All right."

"Did you check their eyes?" asked Jack as Jaide mounted up again.

She nodded. "They were clear."

The twins made it to the platform with bare seconds to spare, chaining their bikes to the rack by the tiny station and running to where the bright red steam train sat, hissing and smoking on the tracks. Behind the locomotive and its coal tender, there was just one carriage. It was half full, mainly with families and groups of children out enjoying a Saturday trip. Jack and Jaide took a seat on the eastern side, so they could wave at Ari as the train pulled out.

Jack was glad to sit down. He still felt shaky after the incident with the tunnel. What had Jaide been thinking going inside? Didn't she know how awful it had been for him in the sewers? First The Evil had almost overwhelmed him with a mass of rats and ants. Then the rising tide had almost drowned him. He still had nightmares about it, and woke shaking, with the voice that had spoken to him down there once again echoing inside his head.

He shook himself all over, telling himself to snap out of it. He wasn't in the tunnels now, and Jaide probably *didn't* know what it had been like for him, because he had never told her. Jaide had simply been doing what she thought right. The drain was next to the old sawmill, where they had found the mystery skin. It made sense that something horrible might be hiding in there, something that occasionally came out at night on its dark and deadly missions —

"Tickets?"

Jack snapped out of his thoughts to see a short, round man in a nineteenth-century conductor's uniform standing next to their seats. His chubby hand was held open toward them as though waiting for a low five.

"Oh, yes." Jack pulled his ticket out of his pocket and gave it to the conductor, who clipped it with a tiny metal punch and gave it back.

Jaide did the same, thinking how odd this was compared to the automated ticketing systems of the city. But Portland was a weird place even without taking into account Grandma X and The Evil and all. They seemed to like old stuff in Portland.

"How long does the train take to Scarborough?" she asked.

"As long as it takes, lass, and not a second more."

With that helpful reply, the conductor moved on to the next row of seats and left the twins to stare out the window.

The train moved much more slowly than the trains they were used to, with much huffing and puffing, so they were still only just passing through the southern outreaches of Portland. Soon, though, they had built up speed and were moving steadily along the coast. The sea to their left was a brilliant, white-flecked blue. Several fishing boats were visible, far out toward the horizon, while closer in, sailboats tilted and turned in the changeable wind. It was all very picturesque, with no sign at all of the great battle being fought behind the scenes, between the Wardens and The Evil, in this troubled place.

A sign on the front wall of the carriage explained the history of the train. Originally called the Coast Flyer, then the Coast Classic Flyer after a refurbishment, it was best known locally as the Red Rocket — due to its color rather than its speed, Jaide assumed. It had been running continuously for over a hundred and sixty years, connecting small coastal towns like Portland and Scarborough that were ignored by modern rail. Originally, the plan had been to connect to the main coastal line, hence the investment in a tunnel through Little Rock, but the collapse of the local whaling industry had seen those dreams come to nothing. Now the Red Rocket was really only a tourist train, and freight was left to other trains and trucks.

Underneath the information poster was a notice of changes to upcoming schedules thanks to damage caused by recent flooding. The Red Rocket would go no farther north than Portland for a month while the Little Rock tunnel was repaired. Idly, Jack wondered how many people that would really inconvenience or disappoint. It was much quicker to drive to Scarborough, and thus far the steam-train experience was decidedly underwhelming.

Finally, the train chuff-chuffed around a bend and there was the mini-metropolis of Scarborough. After Portland, it seemed huge to the twins' eyes, though they would have scorned it as a hick town when they'd lived in the city. Now they knew better. Scarborough boasted a large town hall, a clock tower, a high school, no less than three proper movie theaters, and a mall.

The station was crowded with people, and the air was full of traffic noise and seagulls. As the train squeaked and clanked to a halt, the twins smelled hot French fries, and saw Tara waiting for them, waving, with her father at her side.

Jaide waved back, and even Jack managed to muster some enthusiasm. Maybe it wouldn't be so bad, being away from Portland and all their concerns there. The antique pillbox was safely tucked away in his pocket, so The Evil couldn't find them, even if the leftover bit Jaide called an excision *could* get out through the wards.

On the other hand, there was Tara's father and his possible connection to The Evil, though Jack had always had his doubts about that.

"Hello, Jack! Hello, Jaide!" Tara came bounding up to them the moment they stepped from the carriage. "I'm so relieved you're here. It's been totally boring today, waiting for the train to come. I wish you could have come earlier. Do you want donuts? We can get some over here."

Mr. McAndrew greeted them more soberly, with none of his daughter's wild enthusiasm. His intensely white teeth stayed hidden; obviously, he didn't feel the twins needed to be subjected to his blinding smile.

His eyes were completely normal, Jaide noted, which was encouraging. And when the twins said yes to donuts, he immediately fished out his wallet and gave Tara ten dollars.

"Meet me at the car when you're ready, Tara. I have to make some calls, do some e-mails. You know."

He hardly looked at the twins, giving all his attention to his phone.

Jaide tapped her locket and gave Jack a significant glance. Even though he was usually very attuned to Jaide's thoughts, it took him a moment to work out that she was suggesting that their charms had bamboozled Mr. McAndrew.

Which meant that she *still* thought he had something to do with The Evil.

"I can't wait for you to try the donuts," Tara said brightly while they were waiting in the queue. "They're just awesome! I'll show you around, and then we'll go home so you can meet Fi-Fi. This will be so much fun!"

People turned to look at her, and she seemed to realize how loud she sounded.

"Sorry," she said to Jack and Jaide in a more conspiratorial tone. "I've just been so bored since we moved here. You must know what I mean — Portland is even smaller than here! I love your house, though. I bet there are all sorts of attics and secret passages to explore. We've only ever lived in new houses, and they're all the same after a while."

"How many houses have you lived in?" asked Jack.

"Oh, dozens. I don't know. Dad always has a house to fix up as well as a big project. We move so much." She rolled her eyes. "My mom calls us nomads because we never stop anywhere for long."

"How many schools have you been to?" asked Jaide.

"Five so far. It'll be six soon if Dad can't get that sawmill project started again."

She brightened when the donut seller called them forward.

The twins tried a little harder to be enthusiastic about the visit, for Tara's sake. They'd thought they had it rough, being wrenched from the one home they'd ever lived in, and the same school they'd always attended, to come to far-off Portland. They couldn't imagine what it must be like to go through that process over and over again.

And when Tara returned with the donuts, which *were* awesome, they began to enjoy the day for themselves, too.

Scarborough seemed much more full of life than Portland, which was always pretty quiet. There was music playing in the public thoroughfare, and modern cars were constantly gliding by. It was like coming back to the present after a long trip to the past. Jack and Jaide even began to forget about why they were there, as they explored the shops, licking cinnamon from their fingertips and trying not to get in the way of other people.

"Here's my favorite shop," said Tara, guiding them to a small establishment full of handmade jewelry called Zena's Palace. When they walked in, a tall, very attractive, and beautifully dressed woman came out from behind the counter.

"Hello, dear," she said to Tara, giving her a kiss on the cheek. Then she turned, beaming, to Jack and Jaide, and said hello.

"This is my mom," Tara explained.

"It's nice to meet you," she said to both of them. "I'm Zena Lin. I see from the donuts that Martin must have met you long enough to hand over some money, at least, even if he couldn't tear himself away from work long enough to actually stay with you. I hope Tara has made you feel very welcome. Jaide, I really like that locket. It's exquisitely simple, and obviously very old. Where did you get it?"

The twins immediately warmed to her, even though the attention she paid to the charm Grandma X had given Jaide made her feel momentarily uncomfortable, forcing her to lie about it, saying it was from her mother and that was all she knew.

But she was comforted that Zena dropped her inquiry immediately, seeing that it made her uneasy. She was clearly much more perceptive than her husband. Or maybe just kinder.

Zena was different all around, in fact. Where Martin McAndrew's smile felt forced, Zena Lin's was warm and natural. She was tall and he was almost short. Her hair was thick and styled; his was thin and carelessly parted over a slight bald spot. She seemed at least ten years younger. How they had ever gotten together, Jack couldn't guess, unless perhaps it was The Evil at work again.

"Are you sure it's okay for both of us to stay over?" asked Jaide.

"Of course. We have more beds than we know what to do with. Martin's always wanted a room for a gym, but of course he never exercises and didn't have time to buy the equipment, so we've turned it into a playroom. You'll be able to run amok all you want, as late as you want."

"Great!" said Jack with heartfelt enthusiasm. Grandma X was always making them go to bed early, even earlier than their mother did.

A customer came into the store. "Excuse me," said Zena. "Work beckons! You'd better not keep your father waiting too long. And don't eat too many donuts — we've got roast chicken for dinner!"

Tara and the twins walked back to the parking lot, where Tara's father was leaning against a van, texting or e-mailing away, his fingers flying across his phone.

"Your mother seems really nice," Jaide told Tara.

"She's all right," admitted Tara. "They're both so busy. I barely ever see them."

Jack and Jaide hardly heard her. They were staring at the van. It was definitely the same one that had almost run them over two nights ago — a white van with the MMM logo on the side.

"Sorry we're late, Dad," said Tara before he could say anything. "We went to see Mom."

Mr. McAndrew didn't look up.

"Was she busy?"

"Doing okay. Can we go?"

"Yes. Hop in. I'll only be a couple of seconds."

Tara opened the side door and ushered them inside. Behind the rear seats, the van was full of promotional posters, flyers, and stickers, all featuring MMM Holdings' ominous slogan.

BUILDINGS TO LIVE IN.

McAndrew took more like five minutes to finish his e-mail, but eventually, the twins were on their way to Tara's home. Their new friend chattered as they drove, pointing out landmarks as they flew by, but Jack and Jaide were more interested in the van itself. As casually as possible, they looked over every inch of its interior for any sign of The Evil, without really knowing what to look for. If there had been dead rats, moths, or cockroaches, maybe that would have been a sign, but there was nothing like that at all.

The drive was short, just three corners and two short stretches of paved road from the station. Ahead of them they could see the roof of the mall that Tara's father had helped build, and then, at the end of a winding driveway, a large white blocky house that looked as if it was made out of wedding-cake frosting. The windows were narrow rectangles; the garden was as tidy as a supermodel's hairdo. It looked ostentatious and modern — exactly the sort of thing Grandma X hated — but again there was nothing about it that said The Evil was involved.

Jaide felt her first real twinge of uncertainty. Maybe Grandma X had been right. Maybe Martin McAndrew was just a property developer with dubious morals, not a monster, and everything they had connected him to was some kind of misunderstanding.

That thought lasted only until they walked in the front door and a hideous creature leaped on Jaide, throwing her against the wall.

CHAPTER FOURTEEN

Scarborough Has Monsters, Too

Jaide reacted instinctively, reaching for her Gift. A gust of wind rushed down the hallway, slamming doors in its wake, and the light above them went out. By then it was all she could do to stop herself from being covered in drool.

"Fi-Fi! Fi-Fi, stop!" Tara cried, tugging at the collar of a very large and slightly shaggy gray-haired dog that weighed at least twice as much as she did. Jaide managed to get out from under its paws and stagger away.

"*This* is Fi-Fi?" gasped Jack. When Tara had said *puppy*, he had imagined something more like a Pekingese.

"Yes, and she's very naughty — aren't you, you bad girl! Oh, yes, you are. Yes, you are!"

Scolded, but also lovingly scratched between the ears for a moment, the dog turned around and ran up the hallway and back again with claws scrabbling madly on the floorboards. She skidded to a halt just millimeters before them, and Jaide realized that the wild light in the dog's eyes was joy, not bloodlust.

"She's . . . big," Jaide observed.

"Irish wolfhound," said Tara proudly. "Her full name is Feliciana Adelaide Waterford Champagne the Second.

She's a champion, but we got her cheap on the condition we don't breed her."

Jack reached out with a tentative hand to pat Fi-Fi's head. It was easily as high as his. The dog leaned affectionately into him, almost pushing him over again.

"Come on through," said Tara, brushing past Fi-Fi in order to lead them down the hallway. "I'll give you a tour."

This was exactly what the twins wanted, and they paid close attention to everything Tara showed them. The house was L-shaped on a big block, with numerous bedrooms and bathrooms, a shiny metallic kitchen opening onto a huge family area, a study, and an entirely separate entertainment area. Jack's eyes lit up at the sight of the giant television, Jaide's at the swimming pool in the backyard.

"How was the train?" Tara asked them as she poured them soft drinks from the cavernous fridge. "I find it a bit lame, but better than waiting for Dad sometimes. Come see my room. Mom's set up a bed on the floor there for you, Jaide. Jack gets a whole room to himself."

Tara's bedroom seemed almost as big as a whole floor of Grandma X's house. She had two different handheld computer games, a laptop, her own hair straightener, an MP3 player, *and* a mobile phone. A dollhouse sat on a pedestal in one corner. Clothes lay scattered in drifts across the floor, corralling four or five soccer balls. There were two bookcases, each filled to the brim with movies, trinkets — such as the moth she had brought home from Portland, still in its jar — and of course books, all of them well thumbed. Jack scanned the spines: Tara owned a lot of novels about werewolves and vampires. He doubted any of the stories were remotely connected to real shape-shifters or the work of the Wardens.

A space had been cleared on the floor and a fold-out bed was ready for Jaide. She put her bag on it, only half-listening to Tara, and peered through the windows of the dollhouse. There was miniature furniture inside, and a miniature family, complete with miniature dog.

Tara showed Jack to the next room along, which was much smaller, containing only two single beds and another bookcase, this one filled with crime novels and spy thrillers.

"They're my mom's," Tara said. "Dad doesn't like reading. Now, what would you like to do first? Go for a swim, check out the mall, or watch a movie?"

The twins exhibited identical looks of indecision. It was too much to choose from. Visiting with Tara was going to be work as well as fun, after all.

In the end, they went to the mall, where they had another soft drink and an ice cream each, which they ate while checking out the shops. There were other kids doing the same, but the groups didn't talk to each other much.

"Out-of-towners," said Tara. "I mean, I'm new here myself, but they're only in Scarborough for the day. They'll be gone before nightfall, and won't come back until next time the weather is nice. You must see them in Portland, too."

Jaide shook her head. "I think Portland is too small for tourists."

"And the locals are too weird," Jack added. "I think they scare visitors away."

"I think the people in Portland are interesting," said Tara. "Everything here is boring. I've seen it all before. Malls and shops . . . they're all the same."

"But that's what your dad does for a living," Jack pointed out.

"And my mom, too. We'd be broke without places like this, and out-of-towners to sell things to. Doesn't mean I have to like it. I'd love to live in Portland, with you."

When they had run out of things to see in the mall, they went back to Tara's house and worked off what Susan Shield called a sugar-and-food-coloring buzz in the pool. Neither Jack nor Jaide had brought bathing suits, but Tara had spare sets for guests. They were brand-new, with their tags still attached.

When the sun started to go down, they went inside and dried in front of the television. Tara's mother had come home from work, and her father had emerged from his study. The smell of roast chicken was already filling the house.

Jack tore his eyes from the television long enough to remember why they were there. Excusing himself to use the bathroom, he went up the long corridor to Mr. McAndrew's study and, clutching the antique pillbox in his hand, just in case, poked his head through the door.

Inside, he saw a desk with a computer, two filing cabinets, and a wall of glass-fronted cupboards. Through the glass he saw self-help books and several award statues. *Someone* liked Mr. McAndrew's houses, then.

Also on the desk were an in-box full of invoices and blueprints, an old chocolate tin with a bristle of pens sticking out the top, and a photo of Tara and her mother against a white-mountained backdrop. There was nothing to indicate an affiliation with The Evil.

But there wouldn't be, Jack told himself. It wasn't like being in a religion, where people wore crosses or headdresses. Being an agent for The Evil didn't come with a uniform.

Footsteps sounded in the corridor behind him, and Jack backed out of the study, heart hammering. To his relief, it was just Fi-Fi, tongue lolling and tail happily wagging. Jack abandoned his search of the study and went to the bathroom before he could be discovered by someone less happy to see him.

The role of investigator was reversed over dinner.

"Tara tells me you're both interested in buildings," said Mr. McAndrew, reviving the lie they'd offered at school the previous day. "I'm very pleased to hear it. We need young people with bright ideas to keep us moving with the times."

"Yes," Jaide replied hesitantly.

"Some buildings," added Jack. "Uh, old ones mostly."

"There's a lot of opportunity in old buildings," said Mr. McAndrew. "You get a great old property, of really solid make, it's easy to strip out the insides, keep the facade, split it up into a ton of apartments. . . ."

He carried on from there for so long that the twins forgot where he'd started. But that was better than when he started asking questions, with Zena adding her questions in as well. Both Tara's parents wanted to know everything about the twins — where they had come from, why they had moved to Portland, what their parents did, and so on. Neither Jack nor Jaide had faced such a concentrated interrogation since discovering their Gifts and the Wardens, and they found it difficult to keep the lies straight.

"Your house *exploded*?" Tara's mom put her fork down and covered her mouth with her hand. "That must have been simply terrifying."

"I guess," said Jack. "Luckily, our dad was there to save us or —"

He stopped as Jaide kicked him under the table.

"But I thought your father was overseas?" said Tara's father with a frown.

"He is now — that is, he was just back before he went again. I mean, he travels a lot."

"Looking for antiques?"

"Yes. Really expensive ones."

"Well, I think you're very brave," said Tara's mom. "Both of you. And I want you to know that you're welcome here anytime. If there's anything we can do to make this difficult time easier for you . . ."

"If your parents are looking for a permanent home, for instance, or a decent gas contractor who understands the building code —" said Tara's dad, earning a kick under the table himself.

"What?" he said to his wife. "Everyone needs somewhere to live, don't they?"

"They've already got somewhere, dear. Don't be pushy."

"It doesn't hurt to ask. And they *said* they're interested in buildings. . . ."

Tara put on a pained expression while her parents bickered good-naturedly. Jack and Jaide concentrated on eating, now that the attention had shifted from them. The food didn't seem to be laced with anything magical, and it was much nicer than Grandma X's had been recently. Jack had seconds even though he knew there was dessert.

Tara's parents drank a bottle of wine between them with dinner and by the end were performing duets of their favorite old rock songs, much to Tara's horror.

"Let's get out of here before they start digging out their old Van Halen records," she said, putting her plate on the floor for Fi-Fi to lick up the scraps. "I bet you never have to put up with anything like this."

"No," said Jaide, thinking that now she could see what Tara's parents saw in each other. Physically, they were completely different, but they laughed at the same jokes and they liked being together. "No parent is perfect. Our dad's jokes are awful, and Mom couldn't bake a cake to save her life."

"Were you scared of your grandmother when you first came to Portland? She looks a bit strict."

"Oh yeah." Jack resisted the urge to tell her how they'd initially thought Grandma X was a witch.

They played games — proper computer games, not old board games their father had owned thirty years ago — until bedtime, which came much later than the twins were used to now. Because it was a Saturday night, Tara's mom declared they could stay up and watch a movie. Tara had an extensive collection, so it took at least fifteen minutes to decide which one. By the time it had started, Jack was already feeling sleepy. Luckily, it was a girly movie he wasn't very interested in, so he dozed on a beanbag, feeling pleasantly full and contented.

He woke from a dream of being smothered to find Fi-Fi sprawled across him, dribbling into his shirt. The credits were rolling over a pop song he didn't like. Jaide was sound asleep on her end of the couch, snoring softly. He tried to sit up, but Fi-Fi was as heavy as a mountain and refused to wake up.

"Help!" he called out.

Tara blinked out of a daze. "Oh, hey. Fi-Fi, wake up!"

The dog snorted and jerked upright, releasing Jack.

"Thanks," he said, rubbing feeling back into his legs, or trying to. "Are you okay? You were staring at the screen like the movie was still playing."

"I was, wasn't I?" Tara smiled and shook her head. "I was just thinking about those moths. It was weird how they attacked us, like they knew what they were doing. Why would they do that?"

"I don't know," said Jack, hoping his face didn't betray the lie. "Animals are weird."

"Dogs certainly are," she said, giving Fi-Fi an affection-ate pat.

"Pins and needles!" cried Jack, kicking his feet in the air. "Pins and needles!"

Tara laughed. "You're weird, too, Jack Shield. And so's your sister."

Jack bit down on the urge to say, *You should talk.* "Gee, thanks."

"I meant it as a compliment." She wasn't smiling now. "I don't keep friends for long, because we're always moving. Will you be my friends for as long as I'm here?"

He nodded. No matter what her father might be up to, she seemed okay, and of course the pool, television, and great food helped.

They woke up Jaide and went to bed. The twins slept right through the night. There were no weird dreams, no unusual incidents, and breakfast the next morning was perfectly delicious, with pancakes, yogurt, and freshly squeezed orange juice. Tara's dad instantly vanished into his office with a cup of coffee. Tara's mom was in a hurry to get to the shop in order to open it by nine. She left the kids snacks, and strict instructions to remind Tara's dad to get them to the train on time.

"You know what he's like," she said to Tara. "If we didn't keep reminding him, he'd probably forget we're here."

"It's true," said Tara, as they waved Zena off in her zippy little sedan. "Dad once called me Fi-Fi by mistake."

"Ouch," said Jaide, fighting a sense of frustration that had been building in her all morning. They had only an hour or two to go before they left, and so far they had nothing. Being forgetful and self-centered wasn't a sign that someone was secretly working for The Evil. If she couldn't find *something*, they would have to go home empty-handed. Despite all the circumstantial evidence —

the van, the weather vane pointing to the building site, the weird discarded skin — there was nothing that directly pinned anything in Scarborough to the troubles in Portland.

It wasn't until they were actually at the train station that they got something to make the trip worthwhile.

Tara had convinced her dad to let Fi-Fi come with them to say good-bye. The dog took up half the backseat, forcing Jack and Jaide to squash together on the other side. Just as they arrived at the station, she jumped behind the seats into the back, her giant feet scrunching posters and tearing up pamphlets, so the back of the van began to look like a confetti delivery had exploded.

Tara's father twisted around in his seat as he stopped the car, his face red and angry.

"Tara! Get that dog out of here!" he yelled. "Those pamphlets cost me a fortune!"

Tara gulped, then leaped out of the car to open the van's door. Fi-Fi jumped out, licked Tara on the face, then stopped, her huge head snapping around toward the station. She sniffed the air for a second and then was suddenly in motion, galloping off between the rows of parked cars.

"Fi-Fi, come back!" Tara took off after her wayward dog. Jack and Jaide clambered out and ran after her in turn, before she could get herself flattened by cars filing into the parking lot, or even by the train, which was just pulling into the station.

It took several minutes of shouting and calling, but eventually, they had Fi-Fi by her collar. It took all three of them to keep her still. She strained and tugged but couldn't get away from them.

"Sorry about that," said Tara. She was scratched and breathing heavily. "It's the cats. They always get her riled up like this."

"Cats?" said Jaide. "What cats?"

"The train cats. Didn't you see them when you arrived?"

Jack looked around. There was a cat sitting on the parking lot fence, two on the shoulder, another on the platform, and several peering out at him from under parked cars.

"They live under the station," Tara went on. "Dozens of them. The railway's always trying to get rid of them, but they keep coming back. Hey, what is it?"

Jaide had reached across Fi-Fi's quivering back to grip Jack's arm.

"Look!" she said.

Jack had seen it: a perfectly white fluffball of a cat with part of its tail missing. The same one that had attacked Kleo.

"*This* is where they come from," Jack said.

"Exactly. They must be riding the trains in and out of Portland." Jaide noticed more cats arriving as the train readied itself for departure. Ari had said there were rumors of a big fight that weekend. There, right in front of them, was the army assembling!

"We have to do something," Jaide said.

"Do what?" said Tara. "They're only cats."

"It's just, Jaide got attacked by stray cats once," said Jack, with a warning glance at his sister. "They make her nervous. But we're fine here, right?"

"Uh, yeah," said Jaide. She made a conscious effort to look normal. "Thanks for having us, Tara. We really enjoyed it."

Tara brightened. "I did, too! Do you think you'll come and stay again?"

"Sure," Jaide said. "Why not?"

"Great! Sorry about my dad being so grouchy just then."

"That's okay. I hope you don't get in too much trouble."

"Don't worry. He doesn't stay angry."

"Good," said Jaide. "Hey, there's even more cats!"

She pointed toward the station. There were more cats there, but Jaide just wanted to make Tara turn away. In that moment, she reached down and unclipped Fi-Fi's collar. The collar fell off, and Fi-Fi launched herself at the assembling cats once more, barking like a mad thing. The train cats scattered, hissing and spitting.

"Fi-Fi!" shouted Tara in dismay. She took two steps to run after the dog, but stopped suddenly as the train's steam whistle screamed out its departure warning.

"You go," Tara told the twins. "If you miss the train, you'll never be allowed back! Go! Fi-Fi, come back!"

"Thanks," Jaide yelled as the train's whistle sounded again. Jack was already running onto the platform. "See you at school tomorrow!"

Tara didn't reply. She was too busy trying to retrieve Fi-Fi, who had chased the fluffy white cat and at least a dozen others underneath a parked minibus. Tara's dad and several members of the public were trying to help, but the dog kept running around and around the minibus, dodging humans and lunging at any cat that dared show its head.

Jaide hid a smile as she waved at Tara through the window of the carriage. Thanks to the cat-hunting Fi-Fi, not one feline had gotten on the train. That crisis, at least, had been averted.

"You again," said the portly conductor, coming up to punch their tickets. "Looking more cheerful than before, too. Does that mean your trip to Scarborough was a success?"

"Not really," said Jack. Without really thinking, he added, "We thought we'd find something there, but we didn't."

"If that's the worst thing that ever happens to you, then you've reason to be cheerful."

The conductor moved on to the next person in the train, leaving Jack to ponder the echo of Custer's advice. If he had *felt* cheerful, maybe he would have agreed. But The Evil excision was still roaming about Portland, and so was the monster — unless they were the same thing, which seemed unlikely, since the legends of the monster went back so far — and they had come no closer to finding anything that would tell them what was really going on.

But much worse than that, his Gift was still lost.

CHAPTER FIFTEEN
DEAD END

Ari was waiting for them by their bikes when the train arrived at Portland Station.

"Where's Kleo?" asked Jaide.

"It's nice to see you, too," Ari replied huffily. "Clearly you didn't miss me at all."

"Seriously, Ari, where is she?"

"Patrolling," he said. "The attack hasn't come yet."

"We know, and we know why it won't. We found out where the cats are coming from and stopped them from coming today."

Ari looked from Jaide to Jack and back again. "What have you done?"

"We *helped*," said Jaide.

"I know we weren't supposed to," said Jack, trying to buck his own spirits as much as Ari's. "But I really think this time we *have* helped."

"This is not going to end well," said Ari grimly. "You'd better tell me on the way, troubletwisters. Your grandmother is waiting for you at home."

They saddled up and rode out, with Ari in Jaide's basket again. It didn't take them long to tell Ari about the train cats and the way the attack had been foiled. By the time they had reached the sawmill, the cat was completely up to speed.

"From Scarborough, you say — by train? Are you sure?"

"Yes," said Jaide. "We saw that fluffy white cat there, the one who attacked Kleo."

"That's Amadeus. He's Kleo's main rival."

"It was definitely him."

"The train won't go back to Scarborough again today," said Ari. "This may work out. But let me tell Kleo, will you? There are ways to present this kind of news —"

"Wait up!" interrupted Jack, coming to a sudden stop in the middle of the road. "That wasn't here yesterday."

Jaide jammed on the brakes, almost throwing Ari from the basket.

There, on the road in front of them, was a series of thick, red-brown spatters.

"Is that . . . blood?" Jaide's gorge rose at the very thought.

"Looks like it," said Jack, following it with his eyes across the shoulder to the building site's main gate. "I think we should have another quick look."

"No, no, no!" wailed Ari. "Not again!"

The cat jumped out of the basket and onto the road, in order to sniff the spatters. He pulled a sour face.

"It's not blood. It's some kind of oil. And what else did you expect? This is a building site. It's full of machines. You humans love your machines, but they never seem to work very well. They're always breaking down — and that's clearly what's happened here. Why do you have to see The Evil everywhere? Can't you accept that sometimes some things in Portland are perfectly ordinary?"

The twins gaped at Ari. He had never spoken to them this way before.

"Well," said Jaide, "if it really is oil . . ."

"Do you accuse me of uttering a falsehood?" Ari challenged, glaring at them with his fur standing on end.

"I don't know, but —"

"I would never lie about something like this. I might bend the truth where missing meals are concerned or suchlike. But never about Warden matters!"

"Maybe we've been jumping to conclusions," Jack said slowly. They had lost control of their Gifts, defied Grandma X, accused innocent people . . . and for what? To chase mythical monsters and fleeting shadows all across Portland and beyond, to no end at all.

Troubletwister, know thyself.

"All right," Jaide said. "Let's just leave it . . . for now. If Grandma really is home, we can talk to her and see what she says."

"She's there," Ari said. "I promise."

He hopped back up into the basket, muttering so softly under his breath that Jaide barely heard him say, "She'd better be!"

Grandma X *was* home, bustling about in the blue room, lifting objects and looking under them, one after the other.

"Welcome back, Jaidith and Jackaran. How was your trip to Scarborough? Did you find what you were looking for? No, I guess you didn't — or else it would have found you, too, and you wouldn't be here now, looking at me that way."

Jack shifted uneasily on his feet. "Looking at you what way?"

Grandma X straightened from her inspection of an apparently normal souvenir ashtray. Her smile was part sympathetic, part amused at their expense.

"Don't feel bad," she said. "When I was your age, I detected The Evil in every dark space and every foul temper. There's no shame in it. After all you've been through, it's no wonder. You just have to learn that there's a fine line between vigilance and paranoia."

"So there isn't an excision?" said Jaide, sitting down on the nearest horizontal surface, a crate stamped ARTISANS OF AFRICA. "Did Custer tell you we think there's one out there?"

"Yes, he did," replied Grandma X. "And . . . you're right. There might well be an excision in Portland. In fact, I'm looking for it as we speak." She glanced at the ashtray in her hand. "Not literally, but that is one of the things on my mind at present."

"Will you tell us what else you've been doing? Because we know *something* is going on."

"Not yet, but it will be resolved soon, I hope, and then I will be able to tell you."

"Why do you have to keep it a secret from us now?"

"Because you are troubletwisters. And with Custer's help, I think you are at last coming to understand what that means."

"That you can't trust us?"

"I can't trust your *Gifts*," Grandma X corrected her. "The difference between the two is significant."

"Will I ever get mine back?" Jack asked in a mournful voice.

Grandma X put down the ashtray and came over to him, resting her hand on his shoulder.

"I'm sure you will, Jackaran. Just give it time. Don't force it. Troubletwisters have been known to explode from trying too hard."

Jack managed half a laugh, thinking she was trying to cheer him up.

"I'm being perfectly serious," she said. "Now, perhaps you two could give me a hand. I'm looking for a sewing needle that I know is here somewhere. It's two inches long and made of silver with a golden eye. It must have rolled away and slipped under something, rather inconveniently."

Jaide got up and joined Jack in looking under random things.

"If there *is* an excision in Portland," said Jaide, "why don't you just find it the normal way you'd look for The Evil? The Oracular Crocodile told us to use the weather vane, and that seemed to work at first, but later it didn't."

"As ever, it's not that simple." Grandma X waved them over and, together, they inched an upright piano they had never seen before out from the wall in order to look behind it. "Were The Evil in its full strength, the weather vane would indeed track it. But an excision is much smaller, and it will be correspondingly weaker. It may also be . . . hiding in something, or even someone. If it is desperate enough, the excision can leave a false trail, by splitting off an even smaller piece and using that to distract us."

"The excision can have an excision?" said Jack in alarm. "How small can a piece of The Evil be and still be The Evil?"

"Very small indeed," said Grandma X. "But don't believe that it's harmless or can accomplish little. Small can sometimes do what big cannot. You must promise me that if you discover its whereabouts, you will immediately report to me, and not try to tackle it by yourselves."

"Yes, Grandma," said Jaide. "We'll try."

"But what if it attacks us and you're not around?" asked Jack, peering under a claw-footed chest of drawers. Without his Gift, he didn't want to meet any amount of The Evil at all.

"Retreat to this house, as quickly as you can. Now," she said, standing with her hands on her hips, "where could this wretched thing *be*?"

"Hang on," Jaide said from deep in a wooden chest. "I think I . . . maybe . . . uh — yes!"

She emerged, dusty and wreathed in cobwebs, clutching a gleaming needle. "I saw it right down at the bottom. Jack, your night-sight really comes in handy."

Jack grunted sourly in response. It wasn't fair. He hadn't even gotten Jaide's Gift to make up for losing his own.

"Well done, Jaidith." Grandma X took the pin from her and tucked it into her sleeve. "Now, I want you to look in the *Compendium* and find the instruction manual for

Cutshaw's Remarkable Resonator, then go up to the widow's walk, where you will find the device itself. I want you to tend it until I come back. Call me if you discover anything untoward. I will be within earshot. Ari, you go with them."

She hurried up the steps to the elephant mural and the door leading back into the house. Ari stirred from the ball he'd curled up in and stretch-yawned so vigorously, it looked like he was going to separate limbs from body.

"We're going where?" he asked.

"Upstairs," Jack said, "once we figure out this Cuthbert's Magical Regurgitator, or whatever it is."

He crossed to the *Compendium* and began flicking through pages.

"I still don't know how she knew Tara's dad was innocent," said Jaide, leaning against the hat stand with her arms folded. "I mean, everything pointed to him — literally, in the case of the weather vane. And who tried to run us over, if it wasn't him?"

"I can't answer the last one," Ari said, "but I know she checked him out when he first came around town. Your grandmother distrusts developers as a matter of principle. They knock down beautiful old things and build ugly new things in their place. And what's worse, they can interfere with the wards."

"That's what *I* said," Jack told the cat.

Ari nodded. "And that's why she makes such a nuisance of herself in council meetings."

This definitely pricked Jaide's interest. "So one of the wards might be near the old sawmill?"

Ari ducked his head down so far it almost disappeared into his fur. "I didn't say that. I didn't say that *at all*."

"Here it is," said Jack. For once, the *Compendium* had opened immediately to the right place.

" 'Asta J. Cutshaw's Remarkable Etheric Resonator,' " he read, " 'for the detection of Evil Corpuscles and Remnant Influences.' I guess that means excisions and stuff like that."

He skimmed the page. "Okay. It emits a puff of colored smoke if it detects something, and the color indicates whatever it is. Blue smoke is for a 'dangerous excision or relict of the first order' and then there's green and yellow for ones that aren't so bad. So all we have to do is watch for it to send out a smoke signal."

They trooped up the widow's walk, where the Etheric Resonator rested on three widespread legs, taking up most of the space. It was a machine of brass tubes, glass bulbs, and snaking copper cables. A snoutlike protrusion at the top rotated once every minute, like a very slow radar crossed with a telescope. Every now and then, something clicked loudly inside it, as though a mousetrap had gone off. The snout protrusion had a small chimney or funnel, but there wasn't any smoke coming out of it.

On the house's highest turret, the weather vane turned easily with the wind.

"So we just sit here and wait?" Jaide asked.

"Yes," said Ari. "She was very clear about that."

The twins sat in silence for about five minutes, watching the Resonator turn and snap. Ari yawned and settled down near Jaide's foot to have a nap.

"What if that *was* blood on the road by the old sawmill?" asked Jack, kicking the toes of his right foot against the walk's wooden rail.

"I told you it was oil," said Ari, raising his head, his ears pricking in annoyance.

"You might have thought it smelled like oil because it was monster blood. Isn't that possible?"

"Ridiculous," huffed Ari. "I could not be mistaken in such a matter. Not unless —"

"Unless what?" asked Jack.

"I suppose if The Evil is involved, there could be some doubt about even common olfactory experiences," replied Ari.

"You mean things might not smell like they usually do," said Jaide.

Ari nodded.

"If the monster is the excision," said Jack, picking up the thought, "then it could be made up of all sorts of weird creatures, and The Evil might have changed its blood as well."

"But why would it be bleeding on the road? Could Grandma X have done that?"

"That makes perfect sense." Jack brightened at the thought. "She's been fighting it. That's what she's been busy with. She's been hunting the monster and trying to kill it!"

"And that's not all. It must have been nosing around the old sawmill because that's where the West Ward is! Right, Ari?"

"I have no idea where the wards are," Ari said. "As for what your grandmother has been up to . . . well, she'll tell you when she's ready, and not before. But let me just say you would be wise to wait and get more information —"

"I wish she'd let us help her," interrupted Jack, hopping with frustration.

"You *are* helping her," said Ari firmly.

"Staring at this old thing isn't doing any good," said Jack in exasperation. He waved his arms in the air, toward the Little Rock. "We could be watching the sawmill instead. We should be over there right now and . . ."

A weird feeling rose up in his stomach as he gestured wildly, and the wind rose with it. Suddenly, his feet were off the wooden deck, and he was flying up into the sky.

"Jaide!" He clutched wildly for the rail, and caught it barely in time. His legs lifted up above his head. The world turned giddily around him.

"I've got you!" Jaide caught his shirt and pulled him back down. He was as light as a feather. "Jack, how did you do that?"

"I don't know," he said, putting both hands around a wooden post and holding on for grim life. "I must . . . I must have *your* Gift now."

Jaide stared at him in surprise and dismay. Was that even possible? She supposed it was, since for a while there she'd had both their Gifts and he'd had none.

"This is why you can't help," said Ari, not without sympathy. "Until you have yourselves under control, you will do much more harm than good."

Jack closed his eyes and sighed. It was exhausting, not knowing what his Gift was going to do next.

"How am I going to get downstairs?" he asked. "I'll blow away if I let go of the railing!"

"Think heavy thoughts," Jaide suggested.

Jack thought heavy thoughts. The heaviest thing he could think of was the huge rusted red ship anchor that was down at the fish market, as a kind of public sculpture. It was a hundred and twenty years old, weighed two and a half tons, and had been retrieved from the wreck of a whaling ship that had been lost in a storm just off Portland. He imagined himself being as heavy as that anchor, secure on its concrete plinth.

Rather surprisingly, it worked. Rather too well, as Jack's legs suddenly gave way and he collapsed onto the roof, feeling his normal weight once more, with a bit extra on top.

"Sorry, Jaide," he said. "I don't want to have your Gift."

"I don't want yours, either," his sister replied. She sat down glumly next to Jack and added quietly, "But I do want mine."

Jack nodded in agreement, and they sat together in silence for a minute. The Etheric Resonator kept revolving across from them, issuing its now annoying snap every thirty seconds or so. No smoke issued from the funnel. For all it told them, Portland was as peaceful and placid as any small town.

"I thought Grandma might have been making poison to kill the monster," Jaide mused, "but that would mean that she was the one responsible for Kleo's troubles. I can't see her doing that."

"And we still don't know who tried to run us over," Jack said.

"At least your mother's coming back tomorrow," said Ari. His ears fell back flat when the twins both looked sharply at him. "What? That's a good thing, isn't it?"

"I guess so," Jaide said. "That means four days of pretending to be normal, though."

"If there's one thing I know about troubletwisters," said Ari, rubbing the side of his head against her arm, "it's that you'll never be normal."

CHAPTER SIXTEEN

JACK AND THE LADYBUGS

The twins didn't spend all of that day watching the Resonator, but it felt like it. When Grandma X returned from wherever she'd been — with the needle bent and corroded, as though it had been dipped in acid — she took out the gold cards again to test their Gifts. The results clearly demonstrated that Jaide now had Jack's Gifts and Jack in turn had Jaide's, but the ability to control the Gifts hadn't transferred with them, so both troubletwisters were back at square one, with Gifts they couldn't command.

After dinner, Jack and Jaide were sent to work on finishing their first entry to the *Compendium*, concerning their own experiences with The Evil. It was something they were simultaneously proud and resentful of. They had to get it right, but it felt far too much like homework. It was also something they were loath to revisit, except for the ending, where everything had worked out for the best.

"What's another word for *horrible*?" asked Jack, stuck on his description of the sewer, as he had been stuck all week.

"*Awful*?" said Jaide without looking up from the screen. She was typing her own version of events straight into their mother's laptop, while Jack wrote his out by hand first. "Hideous? Revolting? Terrible?"

It had been all of those things, but something more as well. Jack realized that overriding all these things was the sheer terror he had felt at the sight of the waterfall of possessed rats he had seen pouring out of a pipe, all wanting to smother him.

"*Terrifying*," he said quietly, and wrote that down.

There was no way, though, that he could capture the dreadful voice he had heard, and the way it still seemed to whisper to him even now, when everything else was quiet.

"Let me read it," said Jaide, peering over his shoulder.

"No!" He clutched it to his chest. "It's not finished."

"You'll never be finished at this rate."

"You can read it after I type it in."

"Of course I will. So can anybody. Well, any Warden, anyway. It'll be in the *Compendium* forever."

That thought made Jack want to crumple up the pages he had already written and throw them away, but Grandma X would only make him start again, and he couldn't bear that thought, either.

Slowly, he went back to work. Perhaps by writing down his experiences, he thought, he might be able to start forgetting them.

At school the next morning, Tara came running up to them from where she had been quietly drawing by herself. She was always the first there, it seemed, dropped off by her father while he went about his work in Portland.

"Have you heard?" she said. "Work's resuming on the sawmill site. Dad got the word yesterday. The council passed a motion overruling community objections, so he can get started straight away."

"I wonder if 'community objections' means our grandma," said Jaide.

"Probably. Dad said she didn't turn up to the last meeting. That's probably what did it." Tara lowered her voice. "And that's not all. Dad and I looked at the site this morning. You'll never guess what we found."

Jack wanted to say *A giant snake skin?* but managed to keep it in. "Tell us."

Tara drew them into a huddle so she could whisper.

"One of the circular saws had been taken out of the toolshed overnight. The blade was covered in blood."

Jaide's eyes narrowed. "Blood?"

"It looked like blood. I only got a glimpse, though. It was all over the ground. Dad took me away and called the police. Did you know Portland actually has a police station?"

"Yes," said Jaide. "It's next to the hospital. Tell us more about the blood. What happened then?"

"Well, it was gross, what I saw of it, but I had to wait in the van until the police arrived, and then Dad took me to school. You know everything I do, now."

"Police?" said Miralda, who had seen the huddle and come up behind Tara. "What about the police?"

Tara told the story again, and the whole class gathered around to listen. Even Kyle paid attention. When Tara had finished, she was grilled for more information, which she couldn't provide, and the class dissolved into wild speculation that Mr. Carver found very difficult to stop, no matter how much he turned his back and counted to ten in some obscure language.

After that, Miralda asked Tara to sit with her during recess, but Tara chose to stay with Jack and Jaide.

"Dad's going to be busy after school," she said as they exited the classroom. "Want to hang out this afternoon?"

"We can't," Jaide said. "Mom's back today and she'll want to spend quality time with us."

"Yeah," Jack echoed, "by making us do homework and baking another cake, probably."

"What about tomorrow?" Jaide suggested.

"Can't," Tara said. "Guitar lessons. Wednesday?"

"Done!"

They shook hands and laughed when they saw Miralda scowling at them.

"Hey, there's a ladybug!" said Jack on their way home. "And another one . . . two . . . there's a bunch of them!"

"So?"

"Isn't that, like, good luck?"

"Only if they land on you and then fly off your thumb or something like that."

Jack held up his hand. Half a dozen ladybugs immediately landed on his outstretched fingers, and he rotated his hand to try to make them crawl onto his thumb. But they barely crawled an inch before they fell off, one by one, straight down to the ground, where they lay still.

Jack knelt down and poked them with his finger, but they didn't move.

"They're dead," he said, wonderingly. "They were fine, flying . . . now they're dead."

"Maybe they were old," said Jaide. "Or maybe your bad breath killed them."

"I don't have bad breath! Do I?"

He huffed into his palm, but could smell only his hand.

"What does it matter? They're only ladybugs. Maybe like butterflies they just drop dead after three days. You look like you just lost your pet budgie."

He shrugged, wishing she couldn't read him so easily. Maybe he had entertained the thought that he might keep the ladybugs in a matchbox or something. Neither he nor his sister had ever had a pet — an unfairness they now understood to be driven by The Evil's ability to take over animals, and their father's wish to keep them safe at all times. Jack would do anything to have a dog, but some ladybugs would have done for a day or two.

He also didn't like that they had died when they landed on his hand.

"Come on," said Jaide, dragging him up. "Mom's probably back already. Let's go see."

Susan was indeed home. She was in the den, reading the latest *Portland Post*, which came out on Monday afternoons. The headline was all about the bloody circular saw — definitely the most exciting thing to happen since the storms.

After she had said hello to them and given them both a kiss, she returned to the article.

"It says here that there was no body or . . . bits . . . anywhere on the site. Still, they're looking for anyone who might have gone missing overnight, or lost a limb mysteriously."

She put the paper down and looked the twins in the eye.

"This doesn't have anything to do with you, does it?"

"What makes you say that, Mom?" asked Jaide innocently.

"Yeah," said Jack. "We weren't even here most of the weekend."

"I know, I know," she said. "Grandma checked with me about you staying with Tara and of course I approve. I'm all for you having normal friends like you did back home, before . . . *before*."

She pinched the bridge of her nose as though warding off a headache. "I just want to know that you're safe."

"We don't have anything to do with this saw thing," declared Jack, with absolute honesty.

"Yeah, you don't have to —" Jaide started to say.

"We haven't had a murder in Portland for fifty years," interrupted Grandma X from the lounge. "No one's planning to start now."

Susan believed them, or chose to pretend that she believed them, and the rest of the night passed uneventfully. In fact, Susan went to bed surprisingly early, blaming a hard shift and too many mashed potatoes with dinner. The twins sat up playing cards until Grandma X turned out the light, and then they, too, went straight to sleep.

It was Jaide, again, who woke in the dead of night at an unusual sound. This time, though, it wasn't cats.

She opened her eyes, startled by the weird clarity of her brother's Gift. She could see as clearly as though the sun was shining through the window, but at the same time she knew it was dark. There were no shadows. There were no spots brighter than others. She could just see . . . everything.

The low, soft, bubbling moan that had woken her came again.

She sat up, clutching her covers to her throat. It was quite different from the massed cat yowling, and it didn't sound human, either. It was full of pain and anger, but there was fear in it, too, that came to the fore when it finally sighed off into silence.

Jaide sat completely still for a good three breaths, waiting for it to come back. When it didn't, she got hurriedly out of bed and, before she could change her mind, shook Jack awake.

"What now?" he asked, blinking blindly around him.

"Shhh. Listen."

"I can't hear anything."

"I know. Wait."

Jaide held her breath. Beside her, Jack picked up on her nervousness and did the same.

"*Uuuuurrrrghhhhhhhhhhblblllellaaaaahhhhhhhhhhh.*"

By the time it had finished, Jack was clutching his sister's arm.

"What *is* that?"

"I don't know," she said, "but I *think* it's coming from the house next door."

They peered out the window, but even Jaide couldn't see anything unusual in the yard over the fence.

The groaning utterance came again, more terrible than before.

"That has to be the monster," said Jack.

"We'd better tell Grandma," said Jaide.

But when they ran upstairs, Grandma X's bed was empty.

"Maybe she's already doing something about it," Jaide said, just as another terrible, bubbling moan came from next door.

"Then why does it keep happening?"

Grandma X wasn't on the widow's walk, either, and neither were the cats. The Resonator turned and clicked as normal, and wasn't smoking.

The twins went back downstairs and looked in their mother's room, at least in part hoping she would wake up and reassure them that the noise was only the plumbing.

But Susan continued to sleep through it all, just as she had slept through the massive catfight.

"I think we have to check it out ourselves," said Jaide. "I mean, this is our chance to find out about the monster."

"I'm not sure I want to find out," said Jack.

Jaide wasn't sure, either. But with Grandma X and the cats away, she felt it was their duty to investigate.

"We have to," she said. "Who else is there?"

"Okay." Jack sighed. "After you. I still can't see in the dark."

Jaide led the way out of the house and across the garden, to where the fence had still not been properly fixed after the bulldozer had crashed through it. It seemed weird to both of them, her being the guide in the darkness. Jack felt Jaide's Gift lashing away inside him as well, reaching out to the air around him. It took an effort to stop it from whipping up whirlwinds or raising a storm. In fact, it took so much of his concentration that he forgot to think about ghosts and haunted houses entirely — until the next awful, liquid groan. Up close, the house next door was very much like a haunted house, with peeling paint and a sagging veranda. The wind echoed through the empty rooms and out through the boarded-up windows, a soft, whistling counterpoint to the horrible groaning.

"It sounds like it's coming from the basement," said Jack. "Do you think this place has one?"

"I guess it does, if it's the same as Grandma's."

Jack pulled at Jaide's pajama collar.

"Uh, what are we going to do if we do find the monster?"

"I don't exactly want to find it," Jaide whispered. "I just want to get a look at it and see if it's part of The Evil."

"And what if it is?" asked Jack. "What do we do then?"

"We use our Gifts," replied Jaide impatiently, without thinking.

"But I can't control your Gift. And what can you do with mine? Except run away faster than me?"

"I wouldn't!" Jaide protested. "But maybe you've got a point."

The awful groaning sounded again, inside the house. The twins jumped and backed off a few paces. As they did so, Jaide noticed something on the steps that led up to the front door.

"What's that?" she whispered, pointing.

"What? I can't see a thing," replied Jack in a panicky voice.

"There's a little mirror on the step. I saw the starlight reflected in it for a second. . . ."

Jack didn't quite see so much as feel Jaide bend down and pick it up.

"It's a mirror," she said. "Like from a powder compact. Why would —"

"Jaide!" hissed Jack. "Hear that?"

"Hear what?"

"The groaning has stopped. But there's a kind of . . . slithering noise. . . ."

Jaide backed up to Jack and they stood silently together, listening.

There was a shuffling noise inside the house, like a big, heavy carpet being dragged across the floor.

The hair on Jack's neck suddenly prickled. A horrible feeling crept over him, one he had felt before.

Someone . . . or *something* . . . was watching them.

"Jaide . . ." He barely breathed the word, afraid of drawing the unnatural attention any closer. "Jaide . . . can you feel that?"

"Yes." It was her turn to clutch him. "Let's get out of here!"

They turned to run, but stopped in panic as the mirror in Jaide's hand suddenly cracked with a sharp retort, and a shimmering white light blossomed in front of them.

++Jackaran, Jaidith — what are you doing here?++

Ahead of them, the spirit-traveling version of Grandma X coalesced out of sparkly motes of light. As always, she looked much younger than she did in real life, but no less annoyed.

Jaide didn't know whether to be relieved or not that it was clearly she who had been watching them, not the excision, or the monster, or whatever had been groaning in the house behind them.

"We heard a noise," Jaide said. "And you weren't around, so —"

++Did you find anything?++

"No," said Jack.

++Well, you're lucky something didn't find you, particularly since you're not wearing those charms I gave you to take to Scarborough.++

They weren't. Jaide's was under her pillow. Jack's was on his bedside table, under *Jeopardy at Jute Junction*.

++Go back to bed this instant, and please let's have no more wandering around at night, no matter what you hear. I'll return soon, and if you aren't asleep by then, there will be trouble.++

They promised they would. With a stern nod, Grandma X's image faded, taking the light with it. When it was gone, Jack was even blinder than ever.

"That was her mirror," Jaide said as she led him back to their own front door.

"What?"

"That was her mirror. She's been watching out for anyone going in next door."

"Or anything coming out, maybe," said Jack.

Jaide thought about that for a few moments.

"No . . . the mirror was facing out. Like an eye watching the outside."

"So Grandma knows what's in there already?" Jack asked as they got back to their room.

"Maybe," said Jaide. "Maybe there's nothing in there. Just a noise to attract someone."

"Like a trap? But for who?"

"I don't know," Jaide snapped, suddenly feeling very tired. "Nothing adds up. It can't be the excision — I mean, Grandma wouldn't let that hang around next door. And why would she let the monster move in? I mean, if there even is a monster . . . Maybe it was just an injured animal that wandered in there to hide, and it died just as we came in. A possum or something. They sound pretty freaky sometimes."

"That wasn't a possum," said Jack. "Not in a million years."

CHAPTER SEVENTEEN

SLOW-MOTION ATTACK

They were woken again a few hours later, just before the dawn, this time by Ari, who batted with a paw first at Jack's face then at Jaide's until both were blinking sleepily at him.

"What . . . what is it?" Jack asked. He'd been dreaming about the sewers and The Evil's horrible voice, and his first, half-waking thought was that he was somehow back there again. "Ugh . . ."

The cry of disgust was for the dead moth that was tangled up in his hair. Brushing it out, he found several more dead on his coverlet.

Jaide paid him no attention, as Ari circled in the middle of their floor, waiting for them to be fully awake.

"What is it, Ari?" she asked sleepily.

"You're needed on the roof," he said. "Someone has to watch the Etheric Resonator, and Kleo and I have to go out."

"No one was watching it before!" Jaide punched the middle of her pillow and laid her head back down again. "Besides, I thought Kleo didn't want *my* help."

"Grandma X was watching from afar," said Ari. "But she's not now, and like I said, Kleo and I need to go out. *Please* come and watch for us."

"Has there been another attack by Amadeus?" Jack asked. He swung himself out of bed and slapped Jaide on the back. "Come on!"

Jaide groaned, but raised her head.

"Not yet," replied Ari. "But one must be coming. Amadeus won't give up, not when he senses he has the advantage."

"I'm only coming if Kleo says sorry for before," grumbled Jaide. She felt very tired and cross, and not at all inclined to help anybody out, let alone Kleo.

"I would be grateful for your help," said Ari diplomatically, neatly avoiding Jaide's demand.

"Come on," repeated Jack. "It's almost daylight anyway. You'll never get back to sleep."

"Yes, I will," complained Jaide. But she dredged herself up and flung on her father's dressing gown, snarling as one arm didn't go through properly.

They tiptoed past their mother's room even though the snoring from inside confirmed that she was still able to sleep through anything, up past Grandma X's perpetually empty bedroom, and onto the widow's walk, where, posed as perfectly as a gargoyle on the wooden rail, was Kleo.

She turned her head as they approached, but did not narrow her eyes or hiss.

Jack took a step toward her, then stopped. Jaide sniffed and pulled her dressing gown tighter around her, deliberately not meeting Kleo's eye.

They stood in silence for almost a minute in the cool night air, not yet warmed by the hint of the dawn to the east.

Finally, it was Kleo who spoke.

"I'm sorry I was harsh with you, and caused you hurt. It was my frustration speaking, not my true feelings."

Ari let out a soft whoosh of relief, and the twins went forward to stroke Kleo's head and scratch under her collar, tributes that she accepted like the queen she was.

"That's okay," said Jaide. "I was just trying to help — and we still want to help."

"You have told us where the invaders are coming from," said Kleo. "That is important."

"I mean *really* help."

"It is best if you do no more," said Kleo. There was iron in her voice.

"What's the story with that fluffball?" asked Jack, trying to change the subject. "Amadeus?"

Kleo bowed her head and stared out across the town.

"He was a friend of mine once. Amadeus and I ruled this coast together, sharing the territory without conflict or suspicion. Then I met your grandmother and became a Warden Companion . . . and Amadeus changed. He became jealous of the time I spent on Warden business, rather than on our cats. He will never stop punishing me for abandoning him. And now it is a battle, a battle to the death."

She eased out from under their stroking hands and jumped down.

"And like any good general, I must go and put heart into my troops. But I must also not shirk my duties here, so I thank you for watching the Resonator."

"I don't think it even works," said Ari. "But orders are orders. . . ."

The strange contraption was still turning its glass eye, patiently and unproductively, over the town below. Grandma X had told Susan it was an antique weather station, and she had accepted that readily enough.

"Well, we'll watch for you," said Jaide, putting her back against the walk's conning tower and tucking her feet into the dressing gown.

"Speaking of watching," said Jack. "Have you seen anything going in or out next door?"

The cats looked at each other for a moment, and Jack thought he saw one of Kleo's eyes droop in the suggestion of a wink.

"We have been watching the Resonator," said Kleo. "Please do the same, or your grandmother will be displeased. Good-bye."

With that, the two cats were off, slipping down the stairs even as Jack called out to them.

"That's not an answer!"

The twins sat there for more than an hour, until Grandma X suddenly emerged from the conning tower door.

"Where have you been, Grandma?" Jack asked sleepily. He had nodded off for at least part of the hour, despite being cold, uncomfortable, and constantly startled awake every time the Resonator clicked.

"Here and there," she said. "In the blue room."

"No, you weren't," said Jaide. "I listened and didn't hear you."

"Well, I was being quiet. And speaking of which, tread lightly when you go downstairs, or else you'll wake your mother."

"She'd snore through a football game," muttered Jack.

"Grandma," said Jaide, keen not to waste any opportunity, "what was making that horrible groaning noise next door? And why were you watching the *outside* of the house with your mirror?"

Grandma X took a deep breath and looked at her grandchildren.

"I was watching the outside to make sure that no one interfered with what was inside the house," she said at last. "Including troubletwisters, I'm afraid."

"But what was —"

Grandma X held up her hand like a traffic cop.

"I'm sorry, it's not a matter for discussion. You know the reasons why. In any case, there is nothing there now. So please go downstairs."

Jaide opened her mouth, another question on her lips, but it froze there when she met Grandma X's stern gaze.

"Please, troubletwisters," said Grandma X. "I'm sure you are tired, just as I am." Jaide's mouth shut. Jack pushed her gently in the back, and the two of them wearily trudged through the door, back into the house.

"You know those cats we saw on Sunday?" Jaide asked Tara when she came to visit after school on Wednesday. "Are they still there?"

The two of them were sitting in the drawing room playing an ancient version of The Game of Life that had a "Poor Farm" option that Jaide had never seen in the one she knew. A childish hand had written "Henry" next to it, then crossed it out. The Pay Days were ridiculously small.

"Yeah, more cats than ever," said Tara, spinning the wheel and getting a six. "Dad says the council's going to bring in pest control to get rid of them soon."

Jaide nodded thoughtfully, and made a mental note to tell Ari and Kleo later. An even bigger army was building, one that not even Fi-Fi could repel, but there was a chance the council might get them first. That was both good and bad news.

"Where's Jack?" Tara asked, firmly putting a blue peg into her car.

"Talking to Grandma, I think. How are things coming at the old sawmill?"

"Great. Dad seems pretty excited everyone's back at work on it."

"No more blood . . . or other weird stuff?"

Tara shook her head. "It's all been very boring. Much more fun being here. Thanks for inviting me."

They had come home from school to find that Susan had made them another cake, this one a lemon cake with chocolate icing. It was a significant improvement, but a bit rubbery, and stuck to their teeth for an unsettlingly long time.

The girls had gone straight for the games, but Jack hadn't been in the mood for playing. All the way home, he had been buzzed by a pair of dragonflies, and even though they had normal eyes, he couldn't shake the thought that they were somehow sent by The Evil. Then, to make matters worse, he'd swatted one and it had dropped dead as a stone, even though he'd barely touched it. Then the other one had done a kamikaze into his chest and it had died as well, making Jack wonder if he was developing a new and deeply unwanted Gift — attracting insects and killing them.

He wanted to talk to Grandma X about it, and finally found her in the blue room, hand-washing a tub full of what looked like cream-colored clothes. This struck Jack as odd, but he was becoming used to her doing stuff like that.

"What if The Evil has found a way to hide the white-eye thing?" he asked her. "That way, it could be anything or anyone and we would never know."

"Are you talking about Martin McAndrew again?"

He explained about the ladybugs and the dragonflies.

"The eyes are the window of the soul," said Grandma X, standing up and wiping her hands on a now very stained apron. "The Evil doesn't have one, so that's why we see what we see. There's no hiding that white radiance, that absence, except behind glasses or a mask. Otherwise, yes, The Evil could be in anything or anyone, and we would lose the fight for certain. Be thankful it'll never happen."

"Yes, but what *if* . . . ?"

"It's not The Evil, Jackaran," said Grandma X. "It is possible that it is some side-effect of your Gift, one that will doubtless settle down when your Gift does."

Jack looked at his shoes and sighed.

"Well, as I can see it's really bothering you . . ." She went to a cupboard, rummaged about for a moment, then returned with a small ceramic jar. She screwed off the top, releasing a powerful but not unpleasant aroma that made the back of Jack's nose sit up and pay close attention.

"Here." With one finger, she removed a tiny dose of ointment and applied it to the inside of Jack's wrists.

"What is it?" he asked, feeling a tingling sensation rush across his skin.

"Insect repellent," she said, closing the lid of the jar and giving it back to him. "I could say it was something more to make you feel better, but that would not be true."

Jack felt faintly cheated. "Have you ever lied to us, Grandma?"

Grandma X gave Jack a hug around the shoulders.

"You know I have to avoid telling you things, Jackaran. But I do not speak untruths. Not without a very good reason."

That was no more reassuring than the repellent. Jack looked at the door and sighed. He wasn't ready to go back out into the real world, where his Gift was unreliable, unknown threats waited to hassle him, and the girls would gang up on him.

"Do you mind if I stay here with you and read the *Compendium*?"

"Of course you may. But when your mother returns from the shops, we'd both better put in an appearance or she'll begin to wonder where we've gotten to."

Jack sat himself at her desk and pulled out the fat, fact-filled folder and put the image of Amadeus firmly at the front of his mind. Maybe he could find something that would help repel the invasion that Kleo thought was coming.

Despite Ari's confident assertion that cats were too sure of themselves ever to be controlled by The Evil, the

Compendium reported otherwise. There were numerous instances in which cats had been taken over, and numerous case studies of how they had been dealt with. The examples ranged from Wardens summoning waterspouts to drench the cats, magically growing catnip to distract them, whipping up sheets of static electricity to rub their hair the wrong way, and even scaring them off with illusions of giant birds or rabid dogs. None of which Jack could do, but he read on anyway, hoping to find a solution for Kleo's problem.

They had homemade hamburgers for dinner, followed by more rubbery cake and strawberry ice cream. Jack, Jaide, and Tara played hide-and-seek on the two lower floors, and Tara was surprisingly good at it. Jack couldn't think of anywhere to hide that she couldn't immediately find him in, and she even found Jaide under her own bed, despite Jaide using Jack's Gift to blend into the shadows.

When Jack was it, Jaide hid behind a curtain in the study, and was concentrating on trying to breathe very shallowly when she saw Tara's father's van sitting on Watchward Lane. She was about to call for Tara when she hesitated. Something about the van didn't look right. It wasn't moving and its lights were off. It was just waiting there.

Puzzled, she pressed her face against the glass in order to see better. The driver's seat was in shadow; she couldn't even tell if there was someone behind the wheel. She had just come to the conclusion that it was parked there while Tara's dad looked over the house next door, when suddenly, it started up and backed down the lane, out of sight, all without turning its lights on.

Five minutes later the van returned, headlights blazing, driving up the lane and straight into the drive to honk for Tara to come out. The game of hide-and-seek was abandoned as Susan called them down, and the twins accompanied Tara outside.

Her dad didn't get out of the car. He just waved with one hand, while holding his phone and typing with the thumb of the other. He didn't even say anything more than a glancing "Hi" to Tara as she got in, though Jaide half expected him to say something about waiting in the lane.

"Do you want to come over Friday night after school?" Tara asked after she wound down the window of the van.

"Mom?" Jack asked Susan.

"If it's okay with your grandmother, it's okay with me. I'll be back at work then."

"Sure!" Jack told Tara.

She beamed. "See you tomorrow!"

The van reversed out, Mr. McAndrew still trying to text or e-mail and drive at the same time. The twins saw Tara scolding him, and were surprised that he smiled and tucked the phone in his pocket and put both hands on the wheel.

As they went back inside, Jaide gave Jack a puzzled look.

"You're weirdly keen to go back to Tara's," she said.

Jack drew her into the den and explained that if the train cat invasion hadn't happened by then, it would be the perfect opportunity to do something about it.

"Do what?" Jaide asked.

"Something," Jack replied weakly. Then, a little more strongly, "We're bound to have come up with a plan by Friday."

That night the twins were woken again, though it took several cat-licks on Jack's face to bring him to consciousness.

"What!" he exploded, wiping his face with his pillow.

"I'm sorry to wake you," said Ari. "But we need your Gift."

"What for?"

"To see something that eludes our sight."

Jack blinked, sighed, and put on his reading light.

"Then you need Jaide. Our Gifts are still the wrong way around."

Together they shook Jaide into something resembling consciousness. She barely grunted when Ari explained the situation, and stumbled all the way up the stairs before she really woke up.

There was a strange haze at the top of the stairs, as well as the smell of incense. It wasn't until the sleepy twins staggered out onto the widow's walk that they realized this was caused by the Resonator, which was not only puffing out a dense stream of bright blue smoke, but two hitherto unseen eyes had lit up in the snout part and were flashing red and orange. The snout itself was swinging back and forth across a short arc rather than scanning the entire horizon, and it was clicking away like a Geiger counter scanning something horribly radioactive.

"Where's Grandma?" Jaide asked immediately as she peered out into the night.

"She is on her way," said Kleo.

The blue smoke intensified and the clicking of the Resonator became almost a continuous drone. Jack brushed the smoke away and coughed.

"Does this mean it's getting closer?"

"Maybe," said Kleo, her ears twitching. Ari, too, was looking out into the night, watching and listening, all senses alert. "What you can see, Jaide?"

"Just Portland," replied the girl, squinting. "Nothing out of the ordinary . . ."

The Resonator puffed out a particularly thick cloud of smoke and swung a few degrees to point due north. Jaide scoured the dark expanse of the bay for any sign of sea monsters or some other evidence of a major attack.

"I still can't see anything," she reported.

Jack looked up at the weather vane, which creaked and slowly swung around in a complete circle.

"The weather vane doesn't agree with the Resonator," said Jack. "It's just going in circles."

"It must be close," said Kleo urgently. "Everyone, be ready!"

"I can't see anything," protested Jaide. "Are you sure?"

She stopped as the Resonator emitted a series of sharp clicks, then abruptly turned to point south, sending its smoke eddying in spirals up to the sky.

Everyone ran to the southern railing of the widow's walk, to look out past the shoulder of the Rock to South Beach.

"There's nothing here, either!"

The Resonator clacked again, and this time swung to point northeast.

"It must be something flying," said Jack. "Flying around us. Like a bat?"

"We would hear bats," said Kleo. "They squeak."

"Like mice," said Ari, licking his lips.

Jaide looked up into the sky. She looked everywhere, not just in the direction the Resonator was pointing. If the device was slow to react to something fast-moving, it might be pointing in the direction something *had been* rather than where it was now.

A dark shape slid across the moon, closely followed by another.

"You're right, Jack," she said. "There are at least two bats out there."

"Flying silently," said Kleo. "That is most unnatural."

"It has to be the excision," said Jack.

"But what does it mean?" Jaide asked, thinking of the van parked outside the house earlier that day. "Is The Evil spying on us?"

"We're not *doing* anything."

"Trying to draw us out, then?" suggested Ari.

"That is precisely what we're *not* going to let it do," said Kleo. "I think it's lost, and trying in vain to find the rest of itself."

"We'll never know without asking it," said Grandma X from behind them, making them jump. "And I for one would never trust a word it said. Now, back to bed, troubletwisters. My Companions and I will handle the excision from here."

They said good night and did as they were told. They were too exhausted to argue.

"What do you think the excision is doing, Jack?" Jaide asked as they drowsed in the dark, thinking about the bats circling endlessly around them. "You didn't say, but it looked like you were thinking something."

"I think it's *trying* to frighten us," said Jack.

"Is that all?"

"Yes," lied Jack. He didn't want to admit that he was well on the way to being terrified. The Evil had got to him once before. What if it happened again?

CHAPTER EIGHTEEN

THE GATHERING OF THE GLASS

The twins nodded off several times during school the next day. As a result, Mr. Carver gave the class a long lecture about the importance of diet and spiritual well-being in maintaining healthy energy levels, but it wasn't either troubletwister's fault they kept being woken up at night, or that they couldn't tell anyone about the excision without revealing the existence of The Evil. If they so much as hinted at the existence of talking cats, they'd be laughed out of town.

The bats had been gone by morning, but they hadn't forgotten that weird midnight performance, the second confirmed sighting of the excision in Portland. During the day, Jack was plagued by a swarm of mosquitoes that flew around him but never landed. They dissipated only when he remembered Grandma X's repellent and put it on, and even then they still hung about, just farther away.

Twice Jaide saw the MMM Holdings van go by, moving slowly and deliberately, then suddenly speeding off when the person behind the wheel saw her looking at it. She presumed it was Martin McAndrew, but there was something not right about it, and she couldn't see clearly through the windows. The interior of the car seemed oddly shadowy, as though full of smoke — *or thousands of bugs*, she thought with a shiver.

Tara left them alone, sensing their foul moods and exploring other options in the classroom, now that she had some. Jaide felt bad about that, and sought out Tara to say good-bye when the going-home tune sounded.

"I'm looking forward to coming over tomorrow," Jaide said, not adding that for the troubletwisters it wasn't entirely a social trip.

"Me, too," said Tara brightly. Their surliness was clearly forgotten. "Shall we catch the train together?"

"Sure, why not?" It wasn't until they were on their bikes and riding home that Jaide stopped to think about how this might interfere with any plans they had about the train cats, if they ever came up with one. They had twenty-four hours to scour the *Compendium* and see what they could find.

When they reached Watchward Lane, there was a police car outside the house next door. Martin McAndrew was talking to the officer, who was taking notes down in a tiny black book.

The twins stopped to hear what was going on. Maybe the missing body had been found!

". . . when I passed this afternoon, I saw the damage and called the station immediately. I've been waiting here ever since."

"I see, sir," the officer said, making no apology for what Mr. McAndrew clearly thought was a significant slight. "And what damage is there, sir?"

The police officer was a surprisingly young woman, with an untidy blond ponytail. The back of her shirt was hanging out under the straps of her equipment vest, which was absolutely loaded with equipment: pistol, Taser, cell phone, walkie-talkie, pepper spray, handcuffs, baton . . . all the stuff that Jack and Jaide couldn't imagine being needed in Portland.

"I've already told the station, Officer . . . um . . . Haigh. And this is the second time I've made such a complaint. Why don't you just come see it for yourself?"

"Very well, sir. I will."

Officer Haigh and Tara's dad went up the driveway and into the house. Jack and Jaide hesitated only for a moment, then sneaked over. The MMM Holdings van was in the driveway. Jaide peered into it as she went by, but there was no sign of bugs.

Voices came from inside the house.

". . . scratches and scrapes, and, see here — they go out the back door and into the garden, where the back fence, too, has come down. And I only just repaired it!"

The twins resisted the urge to interject that the bulldozer had damaged the side fence, not the back, and it still wasn't secure. While the police officer and Tara's dad were busy in the backyard, the twins darted across the hall and into the front rooms, one by one. They were empty, and looked like they had been for decades. There was nothing but dust and lots of cobwebs.

"There's nothing weird here," whispered Jack.

The sound of voices grew louder, so they made a hasty escape.

"Shouldn't we tell Officer Haigh?" Jack asked. "Maybe there's some test they can do to prove that Tara's dad is up to something."

"Who says he is? I don't think he'd call the police if he was guilty of anything that happened in the house."

Jack was nearly too tired to think at all. "Couldn't he be double-bluffing?"

They put their bikes in the laundry room, where their mother insisted they keep them so they wouldn't rust any further. Susan was out somewhere, so they dumped their bags in their bedroom, and then went to find Grandma X. She was in the blue room, looking into a long, framed mirror that normally stood upright in one corner of the crowded space, but was now lying on its side, resting against the backs of two sturdy chairs so she, sitting in a chair opposite, was looking into it. The twins could see only the back of the mirror, where various letters and numbers had been drawn in white chalk.

"The troubletwisters are here," Grandma X said, glancing at Jack and Jaide and then back into the mirror.

"Yes, sorry we're late," said Jack. "There was a pol —"

He was interrupted by a deep, masculine voice.

"I understand. We will be circumspect."

The twins looked around, but saw no one else in the room. Grandma X waved them over.

"These are my grandchildren," she said, pulling them in to stand next to her, one on each side. "Jaidith and Jackaran, say hello to some of my colleagues: Phanindranath Puthenveetil of Bombay, Roberta Gendry in Montreal,

Andreas Barlund from Stockholm, currently stationed in Hobart . . ."

The twins weren't listening to the names. They were staring in amazement into the mirror, from which the faces of no less than a dozen people stared back out at them, as though the mirror were a window into another, very crowded room. Most of the people smiled and waved, but some just nodded seriously, almost impatiently, as though keen to get back to what they had been discussing.

"This is how Wardens talk to each other, rather than using the telephone or the Internet," said Grandma X. "We call it a Gathering of the Glass. One day you will learn how to do this, in times of need."

"We have been discussing the matter of the excision," said a round-faced woman with tightly curled black hair. She was one of those who hadn't smiled. "Such things are rare, and they are rarely a problem. Usually, they fade to nothing within hours, days at the most, or pop like a soap bubble in an instant. That this one has lasted this long marks it as extraordinary."

"It must have a psychic anchor that keeps it alive," said a thin-faced bald man. "A focus of will, something it has found in a human host."

"But that in itself is no cause for concern," said a young woman with eyes that twinkled with warmth. "This one is obviously not particularly strong in other respects, or else it would have shown itself openly, perhaps even attacked."

"Something's coming," said Jack, feeling that the Wardens were downplaying the issue. "I don't know what, but I can feel it."

He didn't add that the insects that kept following him and dying were surely a sign of this impending doom. He felt that they were, but he didn't want to say so.

"You have no reason to be afraid," said the woman with happy eyes. "Your grandmother will protect you, and we're here to help her do just that."

"How?" asked Jaide. "You're all so far away."

"That's what we've been discussing. There are several ways to B&B . . . um, that's 'bind and banish' . . . an excision —"

"They do not need to know the details, Claudette," interrupted Grandma X. "Particularly if you will insist on using your deplorable acronyms. Suffice it to say, troubletwisters, that we have listened to you and are taking action. Now, I want you to attend to the Resonator. I will join you shortly."

Jack lingered, staring in wonderment at the Wardens in the mirror.

"Hey, could we talk to Dad through this mirror?"

"No. You must not."

The voice was the same one they had first heard. It belonged to a man with a broad face and even broader beard that was the same bright yellow as his thick mane of hair. He looked like a lion, and just as dangerous.

"Not until you have your Gifts properly under control," he said sternly.

Grandma X shooed the twins in the direction of the secret door.

"Aleksandr is right. Now, say good-bye and attend to your duties."

"Good-bye, Jack and Jaide," said the woman with the smiling eyes. "It was nice to finally meet you. Hector says such wonderful things about you!"

Jack wanted to go back and ask her what exactly their father had told her about them, but Jaide was tugging at his arm.

"Come *on*," she insisted, and he had no choice but to follow.

Instead of going up to the roof, however, she detoured back to their room and opened her school bag.

"What are you doing?"

"I want to look in that dictionary Rodeo Dave gave us. I want to look up *circumspect*."

Jaide pulled the thick book from her bag and thumbed her way to the Cs. "I have a vague idea what it means, but I want to make sure."

She found it and quickly read through the definition while Jack peered over her shoulder, wondering what was going through his sister's mind.

"That's it," she said, closing the book so suddenly she made Jack jump. The bang echoed through the otherwise silent house. "It means to be careful about what you're saying. To keep something secret."

She looked up at Jack. "They're not telling us everything about the excision."

Jack didn't feel as affronted as she did.

"Is that so surprising? They're not telling us a lot about *anything*, Jaide."

"But —"

"Come on. Let's go do what we're told before she tells us off. I'm too tired to get into trouble."

"All right."

Ari was on the widow's walk, but Kleo was out patrolling. The Resonator was wildly active, shooting to a new direction every few minutes, as though an army of The Evil was swarming all around them. Fortunately, Grandma X had turned the smoke off. Or maybe it had run out of fuel. Now its little eyes just winked, weak in the daylight.

Despite the Resonator's activity, there was nothing visible under the afternoon sun, and the weather vane hardly twitched.

"It's been like this all day." Ari yawned. "You didn't bring any food by any chance, did you?"

"Sorry," said Jack, who could have used a bite himself. "I can go get you something."

"No, you have to stay up here until they finish talking about the ward."

"The what?" said Jaide.

"The *excision*," said Ari, suddenly finding the energy to sit up straight. "That's what I meant to say."

Jaide came right up close to him. "You said *ward*."

"Slip of the whisker," replied Ari. "I meant excision, of course."

"*Which* ward?" asked Jack. "Not ours, I hope."

"If there was anything wrong with that ward, you would feel it," said Ari hastily. "That's what happens when you make a ward. You're connected to it for life, and —"

"Don't try to change the subject," said Jaide, poking him in his furry chest. "If there's something important going on, we want to know about it."

"There's always something going on here," Ari said. "I mean, look at that contraption, will you? But I honestly don't think there is anything for you to worry about. It's not even a problem anymore, mostly. Everything's almost exactly back the way it was before."

"Except for the excision, and Amadeus and the train cats, and the monster that everyone seems to have forgotten about." Jaide flopped back onto the wooden deck. "It's like there's a spell on everyone in this town, making them forget what's important. Something is coming. Jack can feel it, and so can I. Why won't anyone listen to us?"

"You are being listened to, Jaidith." Grandma X ascended wearily from the stairs. "I would never have called a Gathering of the Glass otherwise."

She handed the twins half a sticky bun each, and gave Ari a slice of cured meat, which he swallowed in one giant gulp.

"We've decided to conduct a binding and banishing on the excision this Friday night, while you're in Scarborough." She pulled a small silver flask from her hip pocket, opened the top, and took a swig. Then she offered it to Jack. He sniffed suspiciously at it, and she said, "Pure water. There's nothing better."

"Can't we help?" asked Jaide after she, too, had had a sip.

"I . . . that is, *we* . . . believe that it would be too dangerous for you, and not only because of the threat posed by your uncontrolled Gifts. The excision has been too busy to worry overmuch about you this week. But now, with its plans thwarted, it will seek to hurt us another way. Through you. If it can turn one of you, or kill both of you, it could break the East Ward and reestablish its connection with The Evil."

"What has it been too busy with, Grandma?" asked Jaide innocently.

Grandma X smiled.

"Never you mind," she said.

But Jack thought he understood now. The excision, in the form of the monster, must have attacked one of the wards, but its efforts had been in vain. How the weird potions and poisoned rats fit into the plan, Jack didn't immediately know.

But then he had a flash of inspiration.

What if Kleo is the living ward?

That way, the poisoning of the cats made sense. And Kleo's anxiety about Amadeus and the other cats, too.

The insight was so powerful and obvious that he could have kicked himself for not working it out sooner.

The train cats were working for The Evil. They wanted Kleo out of the way just as much as *it* did. That was how it had turned them. When they had what they wanted, the wards would fall and Portland would be exposed.

No wonder Grandma X was so worried.

She and Jaide were still talking, but not about anything real. The story about the excision wanting to attack them was obviously a cover to hide the Wardens' real concern. That was okay; Jack didn't mind as much as Jaide did that things were being kept from them. They were smart enough to work it out for themselves, eventually. And smart enough, too, to find ways to be part of the solution.

"Are we having dinner soon?" he asked. The half a bun had barely touched the sides of his empty stomach.

"Of course, dear boy." Grandma X ruffled his hair. "Let's go downstairs now. Ari can watch a little while longer, then I'll take my turn at the Resonator. You are getting an early night tonight, and sleeping right through if I have to tie you to the beds to make sure of it."

Neither of them had the energy to argue with that. After a week of disturbed rest, it was all they could do to stay awake through dinner, even with the excitement of the police car next door to report. Their mother expressed alarm at the thought of trouble so close to the house, but assumed it was only minor vandalism of the kind she was used to from the city.

"There's a bad element in every town," Susan said. "Although I'm surprised we haven't seen any graffiti at all in Portland."

"I don't approve of it," said Grandma X primly.

"Of course you don't. Neither do I. But there's not much we can do about it."

The smallest hint of a secret smile touched the corner of Grandma X's mouth, gone so quickly that Jack and Jaide almost missed it. But they saw it, and wondered what particular fate the Warden of Portland reserved for graffiti vandals.

Susan yawned, setting off the twins, which made them all laugh.

"It's weird," she said, stretching. "I sleep so well in Portland, but I hardly sleep at all when I'm on shift. Too much to worry about, I guess. It's so peaceful here. I could get used to it."

She smiled as though in surprise at the thought, and the twins smiled back, thinking, *If only you knew!*

CHAPTER NINETEEN

CATS ON A TRAIN

The twins slept so well, they wondered if Grandma X had slipped them a potion before putting them to bed. They didn't even dream, which made it something of a relief for Jack. He woke feeling nervous but confident, as if ready for a test at school, one he had prepared for well in advance.

They said good-bye to their mother and went to school, Jack lathered in Grandma X's repellent in order to keep the bugs at bay. They barely thought about anything other than finding ways to repel the train cats so Kleo would be safe.

Jack had told Jaide his theory before they had nodded off the previous night, and she agreed that it was watertight. Why else was Kleo hardly to be seen these days? She was in hiding, not patrolling.

"She doesn't seem the hiding type, though." That was Jaide's only doubt.

"But she has to obey Grandma" was Jack's counterargument. "That's what it means to be a Companion. They took an oath, remember?"

"I wonder what it means to be the living ward," she mused. "Does it feel . . . weird?"

"Maybe she can never leave Portland," said Jack. "It'd be like a prison."

That was a gloomy thought, alleviated only by Tara's relentless good cheer. She had prepared a whole schedule of fun things for them to do that night, starting with a swim and finishing with another late-night movie marathon. Her parents were so less strict than Jaide and Jack's that it was like they were from another planet. It made even Jaide feel a lot more positive about Martin McAndrew, despite all the weird things that had accrued around him.

That was the only thing Jack couldn't fit into his new understanding of Kleo and the living ward. If she *was* the living ward, then what did it matter if MMM Holdings was building near a particular site? If she had any kind of fixed abode, it was with Rodeo Dave in the Book Herd.

"Eww," said Miralda as they came in from lunch. "What's that on your back?"

Jack twisted and turned, but couldn't stretch his neck far enough. "I can't see. Get it off, whatever it is!"

"It's just a worm," said Tara, flicking it from him. Perhaps by accident, perhaps by intention, it landed right at Miralda's feet. "It doesn't take much to scare you Portlanders, does it?"

Miralda flushed in anger. "I'm not scared. I just think it's unhygienic."

"Nothing wrong with worms," said Kyle. "They're not even slimy, like most people think."

"And you know all about worms, I suppose," said Miralda with a sneer.

"Well, some. We've got a worm farm at home. I could bring it in for show-and-tell one day."

"Spare me." Miralda turned to the rest of the class for support.

"That'd be cool," said one boy.

"Can you really cut them in half and make two worms?" asked another.

"That's an excellent idea, Kyle," said Mr. Carver, overhearing. "*Lumbricus terrestris*, the humble earthworm, is an essential part of organic gardening. A day discussing the many beneficial creatures living in our backyards would be an excellent addition to your learning. Let's make it Monday, shall we?"

Kyle looked startled by Mr. Carver's enthusiasm for anything he had uttered, and Miralda practically had steam coming out of her ears from the way the tables had been turned on her. Jaide couldn't hide a smile of triumph when Tara shot her a quick wink.

Jack didn't share their satisfaction. Whatever the excision was up to, he was still the main target. He couldn't bear the thought of bugs coming in wave after wave, day after day. What would it be next — centipedes in his clothes? Scorpions in his bed?

That thought kept him subdued and distracted even after the home-time tune sounded and the weekend had finally arrived.

The twins had brought the stuff they needed for Scarborough with them to school, so there was no need to go home. They went past the old sawmill, all three on foot, with Jack and Jaide holding their bikes by the handlebars rather than riding on them. Tara chattered happily about the night ahead, then stopped when she saw the MMM Holdings van among others parked outside the building site.

"That's weird," she said. "Dad's supposed to be in Scarborough today."

"I saw him drive past the school earlier," said Jaide. "Maybe something came up."

"But he promised he'd pick us up at the train station in Scarborough." Tara looked as though she might want to go find him, but at that moment the train whistled, telling them that they had only moments to catch it.

"I guess Mom will be there instead," Tara said as they ran the last hundred yards to the station. "That must be it."

They stumbled onto the train, red-faced and out of breath. They had barely collapsed into a seat when the train lurched under them and they were off.

"Well, well, well," said the portly conductor as he clipped their tickets. "And then there were three."

"Three's company," said Tara, smiling up at him.

"Or a crowd," he said, tapping the side of his round nose.

"He's always like that," Tara whispered when he had gone. "I think it's how he stops from being bored."

"Whenever our dad says 'Well, well, well,'" Jack told Tara, "he always follows it with, 'And that was the story of the three holes in the ground.'"

Tara laughed. "That's terrible. But at least your dad cracks jokes."

"And your dad buys you stuff," said Jaide. "That's something."

"Oh, yes, but still no horse. I ask him every year. Maybe one day, when we settle somewhere permanently."

"Do you think you'll stay in Scarborough long?"

Tara shrugged. "I don't know. But I hope so. I like it here better than the last three places combined."

She glanced at Jack when she said this, but he didn't seem to notice. He was staring out the window, deep in a thought that Jaide couldn't read. She felt a tiny twinge of jealousy, but didn't know whom she was jealous of, exactly. She told herself not to be jealous of anyone, since Jack would always be her brother and Tara didn't have to choose between them. They could all be friends, just as they were now.

They talked nonstop the whole way, so it seemed like only moments had passed before they arrived at Scarborough station. There was no one waiting for the return trip: People came *to* Scarborough for the weekend, not the other way around. Tara looked around when she stepped off the train, but neither of her parents was in evidence. Reaching into her school bag, she pulled out her phone and checked the screen for messages.

"Dad's coming," she said, "but he'll be late. We're to wait until he gets here."

"That's okay," said Jack, slouching off to the nearest bench. His bag was heavy and his feet were sore, even though he'd been sitting down the whole trip. That happened a lot. His mother said they were growing pains, but he never seemed to get any taller. "Do you think he'll let us get donuts again?"

"I'm sure he will," Tara said with a grin. "He always buys me stuff when he's feeling guilty."

They sat in silence for a while, watching cars come and go along the street outside the train station. Jaide kept an eye out for Amadeus and the train cats, but they were nowhere to be seen. Perhaps, she thought, the council's countermeasures were working.

Then she saw a pair of pointy ears poke up from the coal tender behind the locomotive, followed by two amber eyes. Seeing her looking, the cat ducked immediately back out of sight.

Jaide grabbed Jack's arm.

"They're on the train," she whispered into his ear. "They must've gotten on the other side!"

Jack broke off a conversation with Tara about his favorite computer games and turned to look. He couldn't see anything, but he knew better than to mistrust Jaide's eyesight. It had once been his, after all.

"What are we going to do? We never decided what to do, exactly!"

"We have to go warn Kleo!"

"How?"

"You're whispering again," said Tara, folding her arms tightly across her chest. "I know it's a twin thing and all that, but I reall —"

"Can we borrow your phone?" asked Jaide, seeing it still in her hand.

"Well, sure, but —"

"Thanks!" Jaide took the phone and walked to the other side of the platform to call home.

She got the answering machine, which was just a computerized voice telling the caller to leave a message.

"Hello? Grandma, are you there? Pick up, it's urgent!" She waited a second, but no one picked up, so she kept talking. "You have to tell Kleo to get ready. The train cats are coming, right now!"

The machine beeped and cut her off. Jaide hung up and rang the number again.

"It's me again, on Tara's phone. You have to get this message soon. You have to tell Kleo! If the train cats get to Portland and she's not ready —"

Again the machine beeped.

"Gah!" Jaide gave up on the phone, but she wouldn't give up on the situation.

"Is everything all right?" asked Tara, coming up behind her.

"Yes, I mean, no." Jaide gave her back the phone. "There's a problem. We have to go back."

"What?" Tara blinked, startled. "But you've only just gotten here."

"I know. It's Grandma. She's . . . she's not well."

"How do you know?"

"I just called her."

"But how did you know you had to call?"

"Because she's really old and . . . frail. . . ."

"And she always forgets to take her medicine," said Jack, coming to her rescue.

"Yes, that's it. If she doesn't take them, she'll get sick."

"Really?"

Tara wasn't buying it, and Jaide didn't blame her. The excuse sounded weak even to her, but what else could they do? The train cats were coming to Portland, and someone had to stop them.

"I'm sorry, Tara," Jaide said. "I really am sorry. We'll come over next weekend — maybe even tomorrow night, if Grandma is feeling better again. We'll call you, I promise."

The train blew its whistle and let out a great cloud of white steam.

"What if I come with you," Tara said, "and Dad brings us back later, when he's finished whatever he's doing?"

"Here he is now," said Jack, pointing. The familiar van was nosing its way into the parking lot. He frowned. "How did he get here without us seeing him pass the train?"

Tara ignored his question, her face screwed up in frustration.

"But the donuts, all the things we were going to do —"

"I know. We can do it all next time."

"But —"

Tara's dad honked his horn. The train hissed mightily again.

"We have to go!" said Jaide, pulling Jack to the train.

Tara stood on the platform, torn between her father and her friends.

With a squeal of metal, the heavy iron wheels of the train began to turn.

Jack and Jaide jumped aboard and fell into a seat, dragging their bags behind them.

"Change your mind?" asked the conductor from the back of the car. "Or change of heart — what *is* that cat . . . those cats —?"

His eyebrows shot high up on his domed forehead as a tide of cats swarmed from underneath the railway station, ran across the platform, and leaped onto the moving train.

The conductor fell back as the cats swarmed through the windows of the cab and landed on him, knocking him to the floor. Three crashed into Jack and two on Jaide, all of them with their sharp claws out, slicing through clothes and flesh as they slid to the floor. The sound of feline feet scratching the top of the train heralded dozens more leaping from the station roof.

The twins fell back from the cats, who simply ignored them and went to sit on the seats, as if they were legitimate passengers. The conductor slowly got to his feet and bent over, holding his nose.

"Achoo!"

He sneezed very loudly, and then sneezed again, as he fumbled with a spotted handkerchief he had pulled from his uniform pants. "Achoo!"

The train whistled again, and slowly chugged out of the station. The driver obviously hadn't noticed all the cats swarming aboard.

"Allergic," wheezed the conductor. He slumped into a seat and waved his hand in front of his face as if he could somehow dismiss all the cats. But even more of them appeared, jumping down from the roof and entering the carriage at both ends. Again, they were silent, and they moved slowly but purposefully, which made them even creepier.

"This is crazy!" exclaimed Tara, suddenly appearing behind the twins.

Jaide looked around so quickly she hurt her neck. In all the rush and tumble of the cats' arrival, she hadn't seen Tara skip aboard the train just after them. Now their friend was caught up in the train cats' invasion of Portland, and who knew what else?

"Uh, yeah," said Jaide, who was frantically trying to think of what she could do with Jack's Gift to get the cats off the train. More and more of them kept coming in, and even though they just sat down, there was something very threatening about their silence and the way they were all looking at the twins.

Jack didn't try to think about what he could do with Jaide's Gift. Instead, he calmly reached up and pulled the old-fashioned emergency cord.

It came away in his hand, leaving Jack with a three-foot length of rubberized cable that wasn't connected to anything.

"Uh-oh," said Jack. The train kept right on rolling, steaming indefatigably for Portland. "That should have worked."

"They must have cut the cable," said Jaide.

"Or bitten through it," Jack said.

"Who? The cats?!"

The twins stared at Tara, and she stared back at them. Neither Jack nor Jaide knew what to say. If they said *yes*, it would sound mad. If they said *no*, they would have to come up with another explanation. And it would be a lie — a lie that would soon be revealed, if the troubletwisters were to use their Gifts to stop the invasion.

Jaide chose to ignore the question and went to the stricken conductor. His eyes were puffed up like marshmallows and his breath, when he wasn't sneezing, was thick and raspy.

"Are you going to be okay?" she asked him.

He tried to talk but couldn't, and ended up simply nodding.

"Can we talk to the driver? The emergency cord isn't working."

He pointed to his side. There was a leather holster for a phone or a walkie-talkie there, but it was empty. At the same time, Jack saw one of the larger cats drop something out of its mouth, through an open window.

"It's gone," said Jaide urgently. "But we have to talk to the driver!"

The conductor waved at the front of the carriage. There was a connecting door marked NO UNAUTHORIZED ENTRY that had to lead to the coal tender and then the locomotive.

Jack ran to the door and tried the handle.

"It's locked!" he called back.

"What's going on?" asked Tara plaintively.

The cats stirred, and all of them turned their heads together, looking back along the carriage.

"Have you got a key?" asked Jaide.

The conductor didn't answer. His head slumped to one side, and his puffy eyes closed. He was still breathing, but with a horrible rasping noise, and his lips were slowly turning a pale blue.

"Check his pockets!" shouted Jack. He tried the handle again, putting all his weight into it. But the carriage was old and very solidly built, and the handle and lock were bronze and completely resisted his efforts.

Jaide made a face and started searching the conductor's pockets, starting with his waistcoat, and was immediately rewarded by pulling out a big, old key on a chain, which was fastened to a button.

"I've got it!" she cried, fumbling with the button.

At that moment, something white streaked down the aisle, jumped to a seat, and catapulted itself onto her shoulders.

Sharp claws dug into her skin. Even sharper teeth fastened onto her ear and a harsh feline voice whispered:

"Hold it right there, little girl, or I'll bite your ear off."

CHAPTER TWENTY

OFF THE RAILS

Jack saw Amadeus jump onto his sister and reacted instantly, reaching for his Gift, not even thinking about which Gift that might be.

A savage wind rushed up the length of the carriage. It blew up and over the seats, knocking cats in all directions, and struck the white cat square in the back. Amadeus went flying, legs and tail splayed out like a starfish, yowling like a kitten.

But Jaide went flying, too, tumbling along the aisle with a screeching mass of frightened cats.

"Stop it!" shouted Jaide desperately, as she tried to grab hold of a seat leg. "Jack! That's enough!"

Stop, thought Jack to the wind that was now howling backward and forward along the carriage, just stopping short of where he stood in front of the connecting door.

"Stop!" he shouted.

But the wind didn't stop. His Gift, formerly Jaide's, was thoroughly out of control.

The carriage shook as though in an earthquake. And then the lights went out. The sun dimmed, as if a deep, dark cloud had passed in front of it. At first Jack thought that Jaide was using his Gift somehow, but then he realized that he was doing this, too. His Gift had jumped back to him, and now *both* of them were out of control.

"Stop it!" he yelled, completely frightened now. "Stop this now!"

The Gifts didn't obey him. The air was full of cats, and the entire carriage was in danger of being swept away. That would solve the problem of the train cats and the troubletwisters, but it might also rid the world of one innocent conductor as well, not to mention the only friend they had made since coming to Portland — a friend who was now wailing in terror as the wind inexorably pushed her toward a half-open window. She had a grip on an armrest, but as soon as she lost that . . .

Tara would be gone.

Jack gasped as he realized she was moments away from death. Something shifted inside his head. The mad rush of his Gifts faltered. Cats fell out of the air like furry, overripe fruit, and the darkness ebbed away. Jack rushed to Tara and pulled her away from the window, staggering with her back to the connecting door.

Jaide landed on her side with a thud and was momentarily winded. Her face was stinging, and when she raised her hand to touch it, her fingers came away red. Amadeus unwound himself from a tangle of three cats not far from her, but before he could make good on his promise, Jaide forced herself up and pointed a shaky, bloodstained finger at him.

"One more step," she gasped, "and we'll blow you all into the sea!"

The white cat lowered his head and hissed at her.

"I know all about your Gifts," he said. "And I know you can't control them properly."

His eyes were innocently blue, but Jaide picked up a definite glint of The Evil in everything about the cat.

"Don't be so sure about that," she said, backing up against the locked door to stand next to Jack and Tara, who was obviously in shock, her body shaking despite Jack holding her up. "I presume The Evil told you about us. What did it promise you?"

"Satisfaction," replied Amadeus. He advanced a few steps, his followers jumping across to form up behind him. "Dominion. *Revenge*."

"I bet you were a nice cat, once," said Jaide. Her fingers fumbled with the key, trying to fit it into the lock behind her, while at the same time she kept a close eye on Amadeus and all the cats that were swarming up behind him. "Have you thought about using your powers for good instead of evil?"

"Good and evil are human words, human concepts. I just want what's rightfully mine. Kleo stole the Portland catdom from me. I want it back."

The key turned silently in the well-oiled lock.

Jaide glanced sideways at Jack. He lowered one eyelid, confirming that he'd seen what she was doing, and took half a step sideways, bringing Tara with him closer to the door.

"And I just want to help my friend," Jaide said. She turned the handle.

A rush of perfectly ordinary wind swept through the gap, carrying with it a cacophony of sound, the harsh beat of metal wheels on metal rails, combined with the *choof-choof-choof* of the engine up ahead. Ragged clouds of smoke rushed past, swept backward by their speed.

Jack dragged Tara through the door and out onto the narrow metal step that projected out of the passenger carriage. Jaide followed, slamming the door behind her.

The three of them could barely stand on the metal step, but there was no easy way to get to the broad steel step at the rear of the coal tender ahead. The two cars were connected only by an interlocking coupler and a safety chain of thick iron links, and they could all see the railroad ties flickering past underneath.

The train appeared to be going much faster than it had when they'd been inside.

"We have to jump across!" shouted Jack. "They'll come over the roof!"

Jaide nodded, and looked back down at the flickering ties. If they jumped and fell, they'd be cut to pieces. . . .

"Now!" insisted Jack. He turned Tara around and pointed at the ridiculously small platform ahead of them, which jerked around and up and down with the train's movement.

Before Jaide could protest that they should leave Tara behind, she jumped, leaping elegantly across the gap. Jack followed, but the wind whisked around him and carried him up like a feather, so he landed on top of the coal tender. It wasn't full, so he disappeared from Jaide's sight with a frantic yelp.

Jaide didn't hesitate after that. She jumped, too, landing heavily next to Tara and smacking herself into the rear wall of the tender. Rebounding, she almost fell off before grabbing a handhold.

Tara looked at her fearfully.

"What . . . what's going on?" she asked. It was almost a mantra from her now.

"We have to get to the driver," said Jaide. But there was no obvious way forward, except by climbing up into the tender, and there was no easy way to do that. Unless you could fly, like Jack almost had.

"Jack!" Jaide called, looking up. "Jack!"

But it wasn't Jack who looked over the edge. It was the coal-dusted face of Ari, closely followed by several other cats, and finally her brother, who was significantly more smeared with black dust.

"Behind you!" he shouted.

Jaide turned just as three large, heavy cats plummeted into her and knocked her off the narrow step.

"Jaide!" screamed Jack, almost going over the side himself as he lunged down, holding out a hand that would never stretch so far, nor arrive in time.

Jaide twisted and stretched as she fell. Her hands hit something and closed desperately around the lever that controlled the coupler between the passenger carriage and the coal tender. It immediately gave way, but moved only a few inches before juddering to a stop again.

With her toes still on the back step of the coal tender, and her hands gripping the lever on the passenger carriage, Jaide was stretched out between the two carriages.

Only the coupler stood between her and the lethal track below.

Jaide tried to tighten her grip, but there was grease on the lever. The sound of the train wheels was so loud it felt like someone hammering on her brain, and the lurch of the carriages was making her toes slip.

She closed her eyes and fought a rising sense of hopelessness. If she'd had her Gift, it would've been a simple matter to rise up on the wind to safety. Now, all she had were her hands around the slippery handle, and a very strong and reasonable wish not to die.

"Jaide! Hang on!" shouted Jack. She could hear the fear in his voice. "Hold her feet, Tara!"

She opened her eyes and looked back. Ari and several Portland cats had jumped down and dispatched the cats who'd knocked her off — forcing them over the side. Jack was still up in the coal tender, balancing on his stomach as he leaned over the edge, obviously trying to work out how to climb down.

Tara was kneeling down on the step, and a moment later Jaide felt a grip around her ankles.

"I've got you!" shouted Tara nervously.

But she hadn't, not really. Tara would never be able to stop Jaide from falling, and she was stretched too far across for the other girl to help her back up.

The lever suddenly dropped another couple of inches. The coupler squeaked and groaned, and the feeble-looking safety chain danced wildly off to the side.

Jaide looked below her. If the lever went completely

down, she would lose her grip, she knew. She would fall to the tracks and be run over by the train.

I need my Gift, she thought. *I need it like I've never needed anything before.*

Jaide shut her eyes and remembered. She remembered flying off the widow's walk, being caught in the wind, to fly up and up and up, her body lighter than a feather —

Wind blew across her face. A cool, night wind.

Jack was shouting something, but Jaide paid no attention. Every part of her was focusing on the wind, on the memory of her Gift.

The locking lever suddenly lurched down an inch. Jaide's hands slid down with it, grease splurging out between her knuckles.

Slowly, but surely, she began a slide that would end under the wheels of the train.

All this had come about because she had tried to stop the train cats. How could she help Kleo when she couldn't even help herself?

The wind was a roaring all around her, louder now than the train itself. It was her Gift at work — she could feel that now, her Gift in Jack's hands, if it could ever be said to be in *anyone's* hands, really. It was like something outside of her, an arm or leg that occasionally decided not to obey her brain's commands. Or a living thing in its own right, something that existed outside of her, and which, for a joyous, brief while, had shared its power with her.

Not being part of it was like losing her best friend — or even closer than that. Like losing her *brother*. It had been with her for her entire life, and she had never noticed it. And now, somehow, she had lost it —

The lever dropped. Jaide's fingers slid, and grasped nothing but air. She fell, screaming, her eyes clenched tightly shut against the inevitable.

It didn't come.

Her Gift cupped her in fingers of living wind and spun her like a sock in a dryer. Jaide shot up a good forty feet, right up through Tara's grasping hands, then slowly glided down to land in the coal tender, next to Jack.

Below them, the coupler to the passenger carriage dropped to the track in a shower of sparks. Tara clung to the back of the tender with her eyes tightly shut. The tender lurched forward, and the safety chain took up the slack with the screech of metal being tested well beyond its capability.

"If the chain breaks, we'll leave all the train cats behind!" said Jack excitedly, as he hugged his sister, both of them almost falling over as he slipped on the loose coal underfoot.

"I don't think so," said Ari, as he and his Portland followers swarmed up and over the end of the coal tender and turned to yowl defiantly behind them.

Jack followed Ari's glance.

There were lines of train cats pouring out through the windows of the passenger carriage and climbing up the sides to the roof. Amadeus was already on top, yowling at the biggest and meanest-looking cats to move up and attack, though he himself was not coming forward.

The cats would have no difficulty jumping the gap, and though the chain was groaning, it hadn't given way.

"I'll stop them," said Jaide. She was flushed with confidence. Her Gift had saved her; now it would do her bidding again. "I'll make us go faster and snap the safety chain."

She raised her arms above her head and called to the wind, visualizing it coming down, making them go faster, pushing the locomotive and the coal tender so hard it would snap the chain.

The wind answered her, a great gust sweeping in along and under the train, almost lifting it from the rails as it picked up all three carriages — locomotive, coal tender, *and passenger car* — and hurled them forward.

Jaide and Jack fell over with the sudden acceleration, sending up a great billow of coal dust that threatened to choke them.

Coughing and spluttering, they staggered upright and looked over the edge.

The passenger carriage was definitely still with them, the chain not even taut now that the wind was pushing the entire train along.

"Uh, that wasn't what I meant to happen," said Jaide. "I'll stop it now."

She shut her eyes and reached out to the wind. But she felt no response inside, no Gift leaping to her aid.

It was just like before. Her Gift was gone.

But the wind remained, pushing the train on faster and faster.

"Jaide!" Jack shouted.

Jaide opened her eyes. On the step below, Tara was staring back at the cats who were now streaming down onto the forward passenger carriage step, readying themselves to jump across to where she was standing.

"Tara!" yelled Jack. "Hold up your arms!"

Jaide blinked and reached down to Tara.

Together, they pulled Tara up just as Amadeus and the first wave of train cats jumped across to the coal tender's step.

CHAPTER TWENTY-ONE

COLLISION WITH THE EXCISION

I'll hold them off," said Jack, picking up a jagged lump of coal. "Jaide, you and Tara go ahead and get the driver to stop the train! Ari —"

"We will stand with you, troubletwister," Ari said calmly. His cat followers lifted their heads and swelled up their chests. "They shall not pass."

"Tara, you stay, too," said Jaide, after a quick glance at her friend, who looked in no shape to run forward across a loose pile of coal.

"Do you . . . can you . . . talk with that cat?" asked Tara in a whisper. "And, Jaide, did you . . . fly?"

"Yes," said Jack. "Look, we'll explain later. Grab some coal and throw it at any cat that tries to get past."

A whole row of paws with claws extended like grappling hooks suddenly appeared over the lip of the coal tender.

"Here they come!" spat Ari. "Stand fast!"

"Go, Jaide!" Jack shouted as he fired off a chunk of coal and picked up another.

Jaide hadn't waited. She was already clambering up the pile of coal as fast as she could. It was piled high in the middle, so she needed to get over the peak and down the other side. Jaide had never seen coal before. She had heard about it, of course. She knew it was black and some people burned it in power stations, which was bad for the environment. But she'd never held a chunk of it in her hand, and certainly never tried to cross over a small mountain of the stuff.

It *was* black, and it smelled of charcoal, and it made every footstep treacherous. The coal was dancing, jiggling energetically from side to side because the train was moving beneath it. No matter where she put her sneakers, the coal shifted underneath her weight, trying to tip her over.

Finally, she got to the other side, and reached the front of the tender accompanied by a small avalanche of coal. Unlike the gap between the passenger carriage and the tender, the one to the locomotive ahead had a kind of metal bridge of two plates that were joined by a concertina section of rubber.

Jaide gasped with relief that she wouldn't have to jump across, a gasp that turned into a choking cough of surprise.

She could see clearly into the cab of the locomotive, with all its hissing pipes and dials and wheels and levers. But there was no one in it. The driver was missing, the only sign that he had ever been there a cap on the floor.

Jaide took that in and then gasped again, as she saw a small gray shape next to the cap.

"Fall back to the ridge!" Ari commanded as more and more train cats swarmed up and into the coal tender. Though they were not all that keen to attack, the sheer weight of their numbers meant that Jack, Tara, Ari, and the other Portland cats were constantly beset by wave after wave of enemies. "There are too many!"

"What ridge?" asked Jack, kicking at a cat who was trying to bite his foot, while simultaneously throwing lumps of coal with each hand.

"The top of the coal pile!" answered Ari, following that up with a battle-yowl as he slashed the ears of two cats who had temporarily outflanked him. "Go!"

The defenders scrambled up the coal slope to the tarpaulin and re-formed in a line. The train cats didn't immediately follow up, at least not until Amadeus himself jumped down among his troops and pointed up with his paw, one shining claw extended.

"Swarm them!" he yowled.

"Oh, no," said Jack. Not because of what Amadeus had said, but because of what he'd just seen.

Amadeus's eyes were entirely white.

The gray shape was a cat, who lifted a paw in greeting.

"Kleo? What are you doing here? It's not safe!" shouted Jaide. The thumping roar of the locomotive was really loud here, as was the noise from the tracks and the rattling carriages, all of it amplified because the train was going way, way too fast.

"It was safe enough before someone raised this wind beneath us," replied Kleo. "I presume that is your work, troubletwister?"

"Uh, yes," said Jaide, flustered. She looked ahead and saw that not only was the train going at least twice as fast as it usually did, it was terrifyingly close to Portland. There was only about a mile to go before they would crash into the buffers at the end of the Little Rock tunnel. If the train didn't jump off the tracks before then. "We have to stop the train! Where's the driver?"

"He was leaning out the side to look ahead when the wind came up, and it knocked him off," replied Kleo. "I suspect it would be a good idea to . . . ahem . . . stop it."

"I can't," Jaide confessed. "My Gift's gone again. I have to use the train's brake!"

As she spoke she looked wildly at all the wheels and levers in the cab, bewilderment in her eyes. Why wasn't there something simple like the foot brake of a car?

"I believe the brake is that long lever with the red handle," said Kleo calmly. "At least, that's what they used to slow down coming into Scarborough."

"Scarborough?" asked Jaide. She moved forward and gingerly reached for the lever. "You've been on the train to Scarborough and back?"

"How else would I be here now?" asked Kleo. "I needed to reconnoiter the opposition."

"But how can you leave? Aren't you supposed to be in Portland all the time?"

"Why?" asked Kleo.

Jaide took a firm grip on the lever and started to pull it down.

"Aren't you the living ward?" she asked, just as the lever slid down, the brake engaged, and the wheels of the locomotive locked up with a screech worse than anything Jaide had heard from fighting cats or the Monster of

Portland, as at the same time everything that wasn't tied down and everyone who wasn't holding on were thrown violently forward.

The shock of the sudden braking sent everyone in the coal tender flying, both friends and enemies. Jack narrowly avoided going over the side, along with several cats who were not so lucky.

As it was, he fell down the forward slope of the coal pile, landing in a heap with Tara and Ari, along with a couple of Portland cats and four or five train cats. Coal dust went flying, and for a few moments, there was an informal ceasefire as everyone got up and brushed themselves off.

The squeal of the brakes continued, but despite this the train had not slowed down anywhere near enough to actually stop. Sparks were cascading up on both sides of the locomotive, the wheels jammed rigid.

The train was now effectively skating toward the Little Rock tunnel and certain destruction.

"Jack! Look out!" cried Tara.

Jack whirled around just in time to fend off two leaping cats, striking out with wide blows of his arms. Before any others could attack he picked up the long-handled shovel near his feet and brandished it.

But only one enemy cat was in sight. Amadeus stood on top of the coal pile, looking down at him, his white eyes bright.

++Hello, Jackaran Kresimir Shield,++ said The Evil.

Jack lowered his shovel and touched his pocket with his elbow, checking that the pillbox charm was still there. Though he doubted it would do much for him now that The Evil was actually present, it was still a little comforting.

"Go away!" he shouted. "You're not meant to be here."

++But we are here, little troubletwister. Have you changed your mind?++

Jack knew it was talking about him joining The Evil.

"No," he said. "I'll never change my mind."

++Excellent. We are pleased that you still wish to join us.++

"That's not what I meant!"

++We know what you mean better than you do, troubletwister.++

"You don't know anything about me!"

++I know what happened to your father in the place you call the Pacific. I know what he lost. Don't you want to know, too? Don't you want to know all the secrets the Wardens are keeping from you?++

Jack stared into the cat's horrible white eyes and suddenly didn't know what he wanted. He stood frozen as Amadeus slowly began to come down the coal pile, as sure-footed as ever despite the jerking and rattling of the still-speeding train.

"That voice?" said Tara, clutching at Jack's arm. "That voice in my head — stop it, Jack! Please make it go away!"

Her cry cut through Jack's paralysis. He turned to her and spoke urgently.

"Don't listen to it, Tara! Think of something else, something happy. Think of donuts!"

"Donuts," murmured Tara. "Really great donuts, hot, with cinnamon, just cooked . . ."

Thinking of donuts made Jack feel better, too.

++Such small thoughts, so soon to be lost to the world.++

Amadeus blinked and shook his head. His eyes had returned to their normal bright blue. His voice was normal, too, notwithstanding that he was a cat.

"What? Why are you leaving me?" the cat cried.

Jack had no idea why The Evil had left Amadeus, but he tried to take advantage of the cat's temporary befuddlement. Running up the slope, he swung his spade, only to lose his footing as the train suddenly lurched, the sound of the wheels changing from a shriek to a sickeningly loud *thump-thump-thump*. Amadeus jumped out of the way, and Jack rolled back down, losing his weapon.

Tara dragged him out from under a layer of coal, just as Jaide and Kleo ran in from the locomotive.

"Grab hold of something!" Jaide yelled. "We're going to crash!"

CHAPTER TWENTY-TWO

WHAT LIES UNDER LITTLE ROCK

Everything went into slow motion. Jack and Tara dived for the front-left corner of the tender as Jaide, Kleo, and Ari went for the front-right. Amadeus jumped back over the coal pile, shouting to his followers.

Jack wedged his legs against the side of the tender and looked across at Jaide. The train was shaking violently, the tender bumping up and down, the brakes still letting out occasional shrieks.

"How long?" yelled Jack, meaning how long until they hit whatever it was they were clearly going to hit.

Any answer she might have given him was lost as they went into the tunnel. Everything went dark, and the sound around them was both muffled and magnified at the same time. But there was no impact, and for a moment Jack thought there wasn't going to be.

He had little more than a second of feeling relieved. Then the train hit the buffers blocking off the Little Rock tunnel, smashed straight through them, and left the track.

The locomotive collided with the rock wall of the tunnel,

screeching along it like a giant metal finger running down a blackboard before it finally tipped over and came to a stop, a hundred yards inside the tunnel.

The tender did not tip over, but it, too, scraped along the tunnel wall, one entire side getting peeled off like the lid of a sardine tin, Jack pulling his feet back just in time. One of Ari's Portland cats was not so lucky.

The passenger carriage did not follow, the safety chain finally breaking as the front part of the train careered off the rails.

Finally, everything stopped.

In the darkness, steam vented with a melancholy howl. The survivors in the coal tender slowly dragged themselves upright, coughing out coal dust and pushing away the drifts of coal that had almost buried them.

"Jaide? Tara?" whispered Jack. "Ari? Kleo?"

There was a terrible silence for a few seconds, then three voices answered. But Kleo did not.

"Jack," said Jaide, coughing. "Can you see?"

"Yeah," said Jack. He *could* see. There were Tara and Jaide, and Ari trying to lick coal dust off his own eyes. . . .

"Can you make us a light?" Jaide continued. "Be careful."

"Make a light?" whispered Tara. "How?"

Jack didn't respond. Despite everything, despite the situation they were in, his heart was swelling with hope and relief.

His Gift was back!

He thought about a soft, gentle light. Like the light cast by the big lamp in their old living room, the one with the gold patterned paper shade that his father had brought back from a trip to Japan.

A steady, golden light grew above his head and slowly spread, illuminating Jaide's relieved expression and Tara's gobsmacked one.

"How are you doing that?" she asked. "Are you . . . are you guys some sort of superheroes?"

"I wish," said Jack. "Oh . . . Kleo!"

Jaide looked where he was pointing. A familiar, sleek blue-gray tail was poking out from under a pile of coal. It wasn't moving.

"No!"

The cry came from human and cat mouths, and the next second there was a frantic, mixed-up melee as everyone tried to dig Kleo out at the same time. Jaide got to her first, picking her up and cradling her to her chest.

"Kleo! Kleo, don't die!"

Ari sniffed at her, then sat back on his haunches with a sigh of relief.

"She's not dead," he pronounced. "Just stunned."

"That's a relief," said Jack. "I mean, obviously for herself, but also since she's the living ward as well . . ."

"No, she isn't," said Jaide and Ari together.

Jack stared at them.

"Well, who is, then?"

Somewhere outside the wrecked train, a horribly familiar groan sounded over the hiss of escaping steam.

"*Uuuuuurrrrrghhhhhhhhhhhhblblllellaaaaahhhhhhhhh.*"

Everyone rushed to the front of the tender to look out, and there they all stopped.

They were in a cave. The train had opened up a great gash in the side of the Little Rock tunnel, and the coal tender had run into a vast hollow chamber that lay behind it.

Slowly, led by Jack, they climbed down. He expanded his light without even thinking about it as they left the tender behind and looked around. High above, long stalactites sent back flickering reflections. Black shapes wheeled and turned in a panic between them, hundreds or even thousands of bats, rudely woken from their daytime slumber. Fifty yards away, a wide pool of dark water lapped at the white limestone of the cave floor.

"Uuuuuurrrrrghhhhhhhhhhhhblbllllellaaaaahhhhhhhhh."

The sound filled the cave, making everyone's hair stand on end.

Jack looked at Jaide.

"That's whatever was next door," he whispered.

"What is it?" asked Tara. She stayed close to Jack, apparently convinced that he was indeed a superhero, no matter what he said.

"That . . ." said Jaide, pointing to the underground lake.

There was something in the shallows, near the shore of the lake. A huge creature, half fish, half worm, that was pulling itself feebly along with the flipperlike appendages that sprouted near its front. It had two small-looking black eyes and fanlike fronds where its ears should have been, and there were numerous scars and stitches in its pallid, glistening flesh. There was a new, bleeding wound in its side, with a piece of train embedded in it.

Its mouth opened, and the gurgling groan came again.

"That has to be the monster," whispered Tara.

As she spoke, there were footsteps behind them. Everyone whirled around.

A woman walked across, between the wreckage of the locomotive and the tender. She wore coveralls that were so cut and stained, they were little more than rags, but no one noticed that, because her eyes were shining white, without pupil or iris, and her mouth was set in an unnatural smile.

++Thank you, troubletwisters,++ said The Evil. ++Once again, you have opened the way for us. We could never have gotten in here without your train.++

Jaide felt her blood stop in her veins, and not just because of the voice. She knew the face The Evil was wearing.

It wasn't Martin McAndrew. It was Renita Daniels.

++Do not be afraid,++ said The Evil. ++We are here to protect you.+

"You can't be here," shouted Jack. "You're dead!"

++You should know better, Jackaran,++ said The Evil. ++We would never leave you. We have so much love for both of you!++

"You're the excision," said Jaide, finally understanding. "The leftover that stayed behind when the wards were reestablished. Rennie was the focus, her will to stay alive kept you here. . . ."

"What's going on —" whispered Tara.

++You do not know the meaning of love,++ interrupted a stern voice that came from the silvery, spectral form of a young woman in a white robe that had suddenly materialized near the edge of the lake.

"Grandma!"

++Stay back, troubletwisters,++ Grandma X warned them. ++You are in grave danger. ++

++We will keep them safe,++ said The Evil, its mental voice sliding insidiously into the children's minds.

As The Evil spoke, Rennie stepped closer, moving farther into Jack's light. Tara gave a cry of horror, and even Ari shuddered.

It wasn't just the white eyes that distinguished Rennie now. She was truly a creature of The Evil. Her ears were made up of bits of bugs and nightcrawlers. Her entire left hand was composed of dozens of rat paws, melded together to fashion palm, thumb, and fingers, a ghastly jigsaw where the original rat parts could still be seen in outline.

Falling from the lighthouse must have done that, Jack thought. Hiding, probably underground, had done more. All the injuries that must have caused . . . all had been repaired by The Evil, in its own horrible way.

Rennie took two steps forward, and her hair swung strangely. Jaide gulped as she realized it wasn't hair at all but was composed of hundreds of small black spiders.

"You're Rennie?" asked Tara unexpectedly. "You're the builder who disappeared with Dad's second van?"

"There've been *two* MMM vans all this time?" asked Jaide.

"Yeah. Dad lent one to her, and then when she was missing, so was the van. . . ." Her voice dropped back down to a whisper. "What happened to her? What does she want?"

++If she still exists anywhere inside that shape, she wants to replace her lost children,++ said Grandma X.

++That's how The Evil twisted her mind into joining it originally. Thus it ever goes — love is turned to hate, and the world is poisoned once more. But we know you now, excision, for what you are. You are a pathetic remnant, and we will see you gone!++

Other glowing figures appeared around the lake. In amazement, Jack recognized Custer, the mane-headed Aleksandr, and several others from the Gathering of the Glass. They were all in spectral form. Some glowed white, like Grandma X. Others were blue, green, yellow — every color of the rainbow. All were young in appearance, just like Grandma X. Only the woman with twinkling eyes looked the same, because she had been young anyway.

Rennie took in the new arrivals with her white, lifeless eyes.

++You will not. The living ward will die, and we will triumph!++

"What?" asked Jack.

The Evil laughed through Rennie's damaged mouth, echoing it within their minds.

Over in the lake, the monster's groan suddenly changed. It rose up on its flippers and tail, and roared in defiance.

"No," said Jaide. "That?"

The light of the Wardens brightened, forming a ring of silver fire around the monster. It didn't seem to slow it, however. It slid on as quickly as before, dripping rank water and slime as it advanced upon Rennie, who retreated back into the darkness.

The monster stopped, its blunt head turning as it tried to work out where its target had gone.

"Watch out!" shouted Jack as a wave of train cats burst out from the remains of the train. He reached for his Gift, trying to maintain the light while also raising a line of shadow that would cloak him and his friends.

He failed. The light disappeared, but its loss was not noticed, the brightness of the silver ring around the monster and the glowing Wardens more than enough to banish the darkness. The shadow also didn't work, for some reason wrapping the coal tender in impenetrable blackness rather than Jack.

But Amadeus's cats weren't coming for Kleo and the troubletwisters. Instead, they swarmed right past them and threw themselves at the monster.

The white ring flared. The train cats who hit it bounced off and fell senseless to the floor. Amadeus himself twisted in the air and somehow managed to avoid that fate. Hissing, he ran on, disappearing into the cloud of steam around the fallen locomotive.

"The monster is the living ward?" said Jack in disbelief, stepping back out into the light. "All this time?"

++You shouldn't be here,++ said Grandma X, disappearing and reappearing beside them. ++Move back up the tunnel, as quickly as you can.++

"But why didn't you —" asked Jaide.

++Go! You must take Tara to safety and await my arrival. I am on my way.++

++Enough,++ said The Evil, and Rennie's twisted form once again came into the light. ++We grow weary of this dance.++

The composite woman stood stock-still. The white in her eyes faded, and her left hand began to shiver.

"It's leaving her," whispered Jaide.

++Watch and ward!++ called Grandma X.

High above them, hundreds of bats chirped all at the same time. Then they moved together in a great cloud, but not down toward the monster. They flew up and began to hurl themselves at one of the stalactites. Bat bodies smashed into it and fell like a ghastly rain.

A sharp splitting sound followed the *thump, thump, thump* of impact. A stalactite as long, thin, and sharp-tipped as a spear fell, guided and directed by yet more white-eyed bats. It dropped with a whistling noise, and skewered the monster just behind its head, going right through its body before embedding itself deep into the ground.

The monster howled, a howl that was worse than any noise it had made before.

It was a howl of mortal agony, a death-cry.

The images of the Wardens flickered.

++Troubletwisters . . . go to the —!++ Grandma X was cut off as her shining image vanished.

Rennie flinched and straightened up, the white luminosity returning to her eyes as The Evil left the bats and returned to her.

She looked at the twins and smiled.

Her teeth were not human.

"Go to what?" asked Jack. He was trying very hard not to panic.

"The ward," said Jaide. "We have to do something for the ward."

The Evil laughed inside their heads as they ran to the side of the giant creature. It was still breathing, but only just. Pinkish blood pulsed from its terrible wound, forming a puddle around its feet. Its black eyes stared out, unseeing.

"Don't die," said Jaide, clutching its slick, clammy side. "We need you."

"You *can't* die." Jack didn't want to think what it would mean if another ward failed. They had only just managed to repair the last one. "You're the Monster of Portland. We didn't realize what that meant. We didn't know *you* were the living ward!"

"It's stopped breathing," Tara said.

No one said anything.

There was a moment of absolute stillness between the monster's last breath and the failure of the living ward.

But it was only a moment, and when it passed, The Evil came rushing through to join its excision with a deafening cry.

++Yes!++

CHAPTER TWENTY-THREE
THE LIVING WARD

It's in my head," muttered Tara.

Jack looked at her in horror. A white film was slowly washing across her eyes.

"No!" he shrieked. "Donuts! Think of donuts! And . . . shopping!"

++You have interfered for the last time, troubletwisters.++

The mental voice was like a sledgehammer blow to the head. Jaide actually fell down on one knee and dropped Kleo. Jack raised his arm as if he could block the attack.

The living ward, the West Ward, had failed. Now Portland was exposed to the power of The Evil. It would flow in, unstoppable, and destroy the other wards, and then spread across the whole world —

"No!" shouted Jaide. She reached for her Gift and it was there again, rising up in her like an overflowing spring. She spun up a tornado and sent it at Rennie, only to see it wither and fade, breaking into small eddies of air that merely lifted the spider-hair on Rennie's head.

++You are right to doubt your Gifts,++ said The Evil. ++They are weak. You do not know how to use them. We will teach you, when you are with us.++

Rennie raised her arms. A vast cloud of moths and bugs flew to her middle, and were absorbed. She grew taller, and relished in it, twisting and flexing as bats flew to join her, too. Then the train cats came, slinking and writhing, resisting to the last. But they, too, were taken.

Amadeus was the last, stalking proudly, as if it were all his idea. Rennie reached down for him and picked him up. When she stood straight, Amadeus was no more, but there was a ruff of white fur around the giant Rennie's neck.

At Jaide's feet, Kleo stirred. Ari was at her side in an instant, licking her face, but she pushed him away with one paw and stood up.

"Back away and run, troubletwisters," she whispered. "Ari and I will try to hold it off."

Jaide looked behind her. There was only the dark lake, and the body of the monster.

"Too late," she whispered.

++ Warden Companions. You may join us, too.++

Jack felt just the fringes of The Evil's mental might focus on Kleo and Ari, and he staggered back once more. Kleo fell again and kicked her legs, turning herself in a circle, but her eyes stayed clear.

"No!" she gasped. "No! I am stronger . . . I will not fall. . . ."

Ari remained standing, but did not speak. His eyes, too, remained clear.

Rennie growled and grew larger still, as hundreds more bats flew down and were taken in. A carpet of insects enlarged her feet.

++You will all join us! Troubletwisters, too!++ came the mental voice. ++It is time!++

Now the force of The Evil really came to bear. Jaide fell and doubled over, clutching her head. Jack groaned, feeling his every emotion and thought being squished out his ears.

A small hand slipped into his.

"I'm feeling better, Jack," said Tara. "I think the donuts did it. And shopping."

He could barely remember her name, let alone think of anything he liked.

Ice cream? Hot dogs? Chocolate?

They were just words, as dry as ink on an ancient page.

Hector? Susan? Jaide?

They might as well have been names on gravestones in the Portland cemetery for all the emotion they aroused in him.

But there was part of him, his deep inner self, that refused to give in. It was the part that doubted, the part that had listened to The Evil and been tempted before, the part that understood exactly what it would mean to give in because it knew The Evil best of all.

Troubletwister, know thyself. Only then will you know your enemy.

"Never," he said. That single word took all the energy he had, but getting it out mattered more than anything. "Never!"

++Ah!++ The Evil sounded more amused than surprised. ++You are not the weak one after all.++

"Neither of us is weak!"

++You are wrong, troubletwister. One always falls. Thus it has always been, and thus it always will be.++

Jack forced his eyes open. His sister was lying on the ground, gasping like a fish. Her eyes were open, but they didn't see him. Was that a faint swirl of white curling in them already?

He closed his eyes again, forcing The Evil from his mind. It was messing with him — he was sure of it. First it made him doubt himself, then, when that failed, it turned on the person who mattered most to him. If he let it, The Evil would eat at his confidence from the inside until he was hollow all the way through. And then it would take him over.

Jack would never let that happen, to either him or his sister.

He was still carrying the remains of his backpack. Reaching inside, he sought and found the jar of insect repellent Grandma X had given him. He brought it out, unscrewed the top, then drew back his right arm to throw.

"You'll never beat us!" he cried, opening his eyes just enough to aim.

++Then you will die.++

Rennie raised one enormous hand to strike him down.

He threw the jar into the insect maelstrom that was her midriff and watched the moths scatter.

She staggered backward, beating at the chemical fire in her belly. **++Foolish troubletwister! You have but delayed the inevitable!++**

Before she could recover, six brilliantly colored bolts of light stabbed through her, their passage leaving black spots on Jack's eyes. Rennie staggered again, swatting at them.

++Confounded Wardens, pricking us from afar.++

The bolts of light struck again, blasting out hundreds of insect corpses, and burned rats and bats. The giant Rennie reeled backward, roaring and snarling.

"What's going on?" asked Jaide. Her mind was a fog. She remembered The Evil declaring that it would take her and Jack first, followed by the rest of the world.

"The Wardens are fighting back," said Jack.

"Jack started it," said Tara proudly.

"Uh, not really," he said.

"Either way," said Jaide, "let's work out how to finish it."

It looked for a moment that the job was being done for them. Rennie's giant body was slumping against the cave wall, disintegrating into its component parts, which scurried, flapped, or ran away as fast as they could. What remained of Rennie herself was little more than a scrap of humanity, blinking around her in alarm and horror.

Her eyes were clear. Her pain was real.

"*What have I done?*" she cried.

But there wasn't time to think about her, for at that moment the locomotive suddenly lurched into an upright position. With a grinding, scraping sound, it jerked backward a yard, stopped, then jerked backward again. The clashing of pistons and hissing of steam rose to a crescendo.

++We will smash you! We will crush you!++

"It's in the train!" exclaimed Jack.

The Wardens' multicolored lightning played across the locomotive, but without effect.

"It's backing up for a run at us," said Jaide. She looked around wildly, but they were trapped against the pool of water within the cave.

"What are you going to do?" asked Tara anxiously.

"I don't know," said Jack. "But I can't feel it anymore in my head. I think it's using all its power on the train."

Ari and Kleo were getting up, though they moved in a daze. The eyes of the bats they could see flying around in a panic were normal. Only the train was possessed by The Evil.

"We have to fix the ward!" said Jack.

"But it's a different ward. We can't just pick something at random and say, 'Be the ward!' It has to be someone living."

"What about one of us — could we do it?"

"I doubt it. You know how afraid they are to allow a troubletwister anywhere near a ward — imagine what it'd be like if we were one of them!"

"Then who?"

"What are you talking about?" asked Tara. "Is there anything I can do to help?"

They turned to face her. She was as smudged and dirty as the two of them. She didn't know anything about wards and Wardens and excisions and The Evil, but here she was, in the thick of it all.

Volunteering for more.

"No," said Jack.

"What do you mean, 'no'?" said Jaide. "She's the only one who can do it!"

"No, she's not. What about all these bugs and bats and things?"

The locomotive vented steam and edged forward, rubble shifting under its wheels.

"It's changing shape," said Tara. Her voice was almost conversational, as if there had been so many shocks in the last half hour that nothing more could scare her.

The locomotive *was* changing shape. Steel railway tracks were rising up behind it and slithering forward to join the boiler, where they attached themselves and then sprang out like cruel, grasping arms. Its pistons were withdrawing from the driving wheels and slanting downward, to turn into legs. Legs that flexed, eager to dash forward.

The boiler itself was splitting at the front, separating into jaws. . . .

"We have to let her do it!" said Jaide.

"She can't!"

"Don't I get a say in this?" asked Tara angrily.

"No!" they both yelled at her.

The train was backing up like an enraged bull, snorting and furious. More piston-limbs were forming at the rear. Once they were functional, The Evil would be able to charge forward like a living battering ram, a living weapon, intent on just one thing:

Killing the troubletwisters who had defied The Evil once again.

"Let me do it," said a weak voice off to the side. "Let me be the ward."

They turned to see Rennie crawling toward them. She was conscious, and free of The Evil, but horrible to behold. Worms and insects crawled all over her. Her left hand was gone, leaving only a putrid stump. Her face was so ravaged by what The Evil had done to her that she was barely recognizable. Only her eyes were the same — full of a terrible sadness that could not be put into words.

"Oh, no," said Jack.

"You must be kidding," Jaide agreed.

Rennie coughed up a bug and spat it out.

"I . . . I lost . . . lost my children. The Evil took my grief and turned it into a desire to hold you in their place. I thought I was doing the right thing. I thought that bringing The Evil into the world would unite us, bring us together in one happy family."

She twisted uncomfortably on the stony ground. Dark fluid leaked from her eyes. Jack realized that she was weeping.

Behind her, The Evil locomotive grew its last piston leg. It rose up and opened its nightmarish jaws to reveal the firebox still burning within.

"Now it has tossed me aside and left me to die. I want to make amends. It is the only way I can make up for the mistakes I've made."

Jaide looked at the locomotive. They had only seconds before it charged.

"What if we trust you and you betray us?"

"Please let me! I failed to protect my children, so let me protect you, this town, the people . . . give me a reason to live."

"We don't know how," said Jaide uncertainly.

The locomotive vented steam in an unholy scream that sent ripples flying across the lake. With it came the return of The Evil's mental voice.

++What are you doing?++

Rennie stiffened. A fleck of white appeared in her eyes. "Now!" she whispered. "Now!"

The locomotive shuddered forward and struck rubble. It backed up, moving ponderously on its steely legs. Then it rammed forward, exploding the fallen rocks, but not quite all of them. Not enough so it could pass.

It backed up again, snorting and steaming.

Jack and Jaide both took what remained of Rennie's right hand.

"Rennie," said Jaide.

"Renita Daniels," corrected Jack.

"Renita *Cassidy* Daniels," Rennie whispered.

". . . be the living ward of Portland," the twins said in unison.

Rainbow-hued light flared between them. Rennie's back arched and her mouth opened in a silent cry. Jack and Jaide shook as their Gifts were ripped from them in a wild, sudden rush. They had forgotten that the creation of a new ward would temporarily rob them of their powers.

Even as what made them troubletwisters rushed into Rennie, making her into the living ward, The Evil fought back. The whiteness was spreading in her eyes, and the locomotive was smashing against the fallen rocks.

"Come on, Rennie!" Jaide cried.

Jack gripped her hand more tightly than ever. "Don't give in!"

Tara joined in, unflinchingly reaching out to touch her palm to the side of Rennie's ruined face.

"Please," she said. "You're a mom. We're kids. And we need you."

The white vanished from Rennie's eyes in an instant, and the black tears became clear. She smiled, and her eyelids slowly closed.

The living ward was restored. Portland was safe again.

The locomotive, reversing for its final charge, kept going and rammed backward into the tunnel beyond the cave. Its boiler burst, and red-hot coals exploded out of its firebox, falling like a shower of meteorites.

++No! Come back to us, be one with us, forever. . . !++

The mental voice of The Evil faded, and then was gone.

CHAPTER TWENTY-FOUR

SMOKE AND MIRRORS

A few seconds later, the shining forms of the Wardens returned. Four of them bent over Rennie and laid down a cloth of something so white that the twins and Tara couldn't bear to see it and had to look away.

When they looked back, Rennie and the four shining figures were gone.

++Quickly,++ said Grandma X's voice. ++There is little time.++

The twins turned to see her sylphlike, youthful form standing directly behind them.

"Are you a ghost?" asked Tara.

"Where did Rennie go?" asked Jaide at the same time.

++No, I'm not a ghost,++ replied Grandma X. ++Rennie has been taken to a place where we will heal her, at least as much as we can. But right now you all must listen very closely. Emergency services are on their way.++

"Uh-oh," Jack said.

"Mom!" exclaimed Jaide.

++Yes, your mother, among many others. We must get you out of the cave before she arrives.++

Two more shining figures appeared next to her. One

was Custer, in human shape, and the other the big-haired Russian. Aleksandr.

++We must act fast to seal up the cave again,++ said Custer. ++And restore the locomotive pieces to a more usual form. You children need to get out now.++

Jack nodded.

++Tara,++ said Aleksandr. ++One moment. Jack, stand next to her, please.++

Tara turned to look at the Warden. Something flashed in his hand and she went limp for a moment and would have fallen if Jack hadn't propped her up.

++She will remember nothing of what transpired here,++ he said. ++You must not remind her.++

"But she was part of it," said Jaide. "We couldn't have done it without her."

++You may talk of the crash, but not what followed. She saw too much. It would do her no good to remember.++

He waved his hand, and Tara followed the gesture like a puppet, heading toward the hole in the cave wall.

Ari and Kleo appeared, no longer looking quite so worse for wear.

"We must follow," Kleo said. "The Gathering is going to work their magic, and they wish you well away before they start."

"I get it," Jack said. "In case our Gifts make things go wrong."

He set out after Tara and the spirit of Aleksandr, his hands shoved deep into his pockets.

Jaide followed, but paused as she saw a bedraggled, white-furred body in the rubble. Amadeus had no visible wounds, but he was clearly dead. He appeared to have died from shock.

"Poor Amadeus," said Kleo. She licked the top of his head, in a final farewell.

"What happened to the other train cats?" she asked.

"Most ran away," said Ari. "We'll just go and make sure that *all* of them did so."

"Good."

"Would you carry Amadeus for me?" Kleo asked Jaide. "He should be properly buried, not left here like this. He was not always as you saw him."

Ari sniffed, then stifled it suddenly when Kleo looked at him.

"All right," said Jaide, swallowing a flash of mixed sympathy and revulsion. She put her hands under the dead cat and, with one quick movement, picked him up.

++Hurry!++ called out Aleksandr, turning back to the cave. ++Out through the tunnel!++

The twins ran to him, took Tara by one arm each, and led her out into the night air.

"Along here," said Kleo, guiding them across the tangled tracks and past the passenger carriage, which was only half off the railway tracks.

Behind them, with the sound of a great stone door slamming shut, the cave was once again sealed off from the tunnel.

Sirens approached. Two police cars, one fire engine, and an ambulance screeched around the corner into the station parking lot. Jack shielded his eyes from the bright lights.

A car door slammed and Susan almost catapulted out of her seat and was with the children in an instant.

"Jack? Jaide? What on earth are you doing here?"

Before they could even begin to answer, she gathered them into a frantic hug, then pushed them back to peer at their filthy faces, looking for blood, bruises, broken bones, and possibly worse things the twins couldn't imagine.

"We were on the train, Mom," Jack told her. "But it's okay. We're all right."

"Are you sure? Your face is scratched," she said to Jaide.

"It doesn't hurt," she said, and indeed it didn't. After everything that had happened, she had completely forgotten about it.

"And you, Tara? You poor girl. Look at me."

Susan swung Tara around so the light caught her full in her face.

"Uh, what?" she said, as though waking from a deep dream. "Where am I?"

Susan held her face and looked into her eyes.

"No obvious sign of concussion," Susan said. "But I think we'd better take her in for a full checkup. Just sit down here, Tara, for a few minutes."

She turned back to the ambulance and raised her hand above her head.

"Hobo, stretcher!"

"I'll take the twins home," said Grandma X, the real, physical Grandma X, coming forward out of the light. "You have work to do."

There was something in her voice that made the professionally repressed fear in Susan's eyes fade.

Susan looked the twins over again, then nodded.

"In a moment. Do you two know if there was anyone else on the train?"

"We were the only passengers," replied Jaide. "There was a conductor. . . ."

"Okay," said Susan. "Well done."

She kissed the twins and gave them another hug each.

"Call me if you feel any pain developing, headaches or stiffness in the neck . . . Anything out of the ordinary. And clean those scratches up. I will be back as soon as I can."

"We will," promised Jack and Jaide. Tara smiled dreamily and yawned.

"Just when I thought Portland had gone quiet again," muttered Susan.

Another paramedic trundled a stretcher up, and he and Susan bent down over Tara again, Susan shining her penlight into Tara's eyes. Other emergency workers were picking through the wreckage, looking for anyone else who might have been injured.

"They already found the driver," said Grandma X as she led them to the idling Hillman Minx. "He broke a leg but he's fine."

"What about the conductor?"

"He was unconscious through the whole thing. Custer made him comfortable, and the paramedics will find him in a minute or two."

"He'll forget, too, won't he?" asked Jack.

"People always forget what they don't want to remember."

"Especially if they're helped," added Jaide.

Jack thought of the old living ward, and the stories of monsters that had leaked out despite how secretive it had been.

"But where there's fire, there's smoke, right?"

Grandma X put a finger to her lips.

They got into the car, Jack and Jaide together in the back.

"Poor Rennie," said Jaide. "Just think of everything she went through."

"And now she's the living ward," said Jack. "I mean, how's that going to work out for her?"

"Very well, I imagine," said Grandma X. "It will give her a vital purpose to live, something that she had lost and never thought to find again. She will not be a builder again, though, I fear. Phanindranath is a wonderful healer, and a fine . . . ah . . . mundane surgeon, but even a Warden cannot replace a missing hand."

Jack was about to ask a question about what a Warden healer *could* do when they were suddenly beeped from behind, by a car that also flashed its lights to high beam.

"Ah, that will be Mr. McAndrew," said Grandma X. "We are so close to home I think he can meet us there."

When they arrived at Watchward Lane, Martin McAndrew's van pulled up behind them. He jumped out and ran to the car, desperately peering through the windows to see his daughter, who wasn't there.

Grandma X wound down the window. She spoke at the same time as he did, their words overlapping.

"Tara?! Where's Tara? I'll never forgive myself —"

"Tara is perfectly fine, Mr. McAndrew," said Grandma X.

"But where is she?"

"She is perfectly fine," repeated Grandma X sternly. "However, she has been taken to the hospital to be absolutely sure."

"Perfectly fine," echoed Mr. McAndrew. "At the hospital. Uh, thank you. Thank you."

He turned to run back to his van, stopped, spun around, and leaned in through the window in a clumsy attempt to give Grandma X a hug.

"Thank you," he said, with a kind of dazed expression. "If *you* say she's perfectly fine . . . she must be. . . ."

"Indeed," said Grandma X, gently pushing his hugging arm back with one long finger. "Off you go."

"Yes," muttered Mr. McAndrew as he backed away. "To the hospital. Perfectly fine. *Perfectly fine.*"

"I wonder if this will make him think more about his family," said Grandma X as she climbed out of the car. "Come along, troubletwisters."

Grandma X took Amadeus's body from Jaide and led them back inside. The twins' heads were whirling with their new understanding of recent events.

"So the vandals next door were actually the living ward coming and going," said Jaide, "except for that day we were locked out, because you had it here while the excision was next door, watching us?"

"And that needle you were looking for was to stitch up

the living ward's wounds," said Jack. "And what I saw you washing that day was bandages, not clothes?"

"And the snake skin we saw was left by the monster as it healed from the first attack?"

"All correct," said Grandma X. "I kept the ward in the cellar next door, and was careful to replace the cobwebs when I was done. There wasn't time to repair the damage, though, before Martin discovered it."

"I guess that's why Mom has been so sleepy lately, too," said Jaide, adding one more secret secret to the list. "You've been knocking her out to stop her from hearing anything in the night — such as the monster when it was hurt."

"True."

"But why do you and all the other Wardens look so young when you appear as spirits?" Jack asked, thinking more generally.

"We appear exactly as we did when we became Wardens," said Grandma X, "for that is the day we attained our true selves."

"So we'll be like that, too, one day?"

"Yes, Jaidith."

"But why?"

"I'm afraid that's one of the mysteries, Jackaran."

"Almost everything is a mystery," Jack complained.

"True," said Grandma X. "I am pleased that you realize it. Now go and wash."

They trudged upstairs and took turns in the shower. When they came out, Grandma X painted bright yellow ointment on Jaide's scratches, which made them sting anew.

Neither of them was hungry, but, remembering Custer's advice about taking sustenance after using their Gifts, they forced down some leftovers for dinner.

By the time that was done they were both practically nodding off at the table.

"Your mother could be hours yet," said Grandma X. "Do you want to go to bed or lie down in the living room and wait for her there?"

"Down here," said Jaide.

"All right. You go on in and I'll get some pillows and blankets."

The twins stretched out in their own, very different fashions; Jaide lay on the room's only couch, and Jack curled up on the floor with his back against the base of the couch, studying the pattern on the carpet. Like so many other decorations in the house, it featured a four-pointed motif, not unlike a compass.

"What ward was the living ward?" he asked Grandma X when she returned. "South or West?"

"West, Jackaran."

"And what *was* it? The monster, I mean. Where did it come from?"

"It was a pet."

"A what?"

"The previous Warden of Portland kept an axolotl. It was much smaller then, of course. Becoming a living ward initiates change, though it is not always physical. It is similar, though more pronounced, to the way inanimate things take on special characteristics when they're around Wardens.

This is also true of some living things. Companions, for example. I think you've noticed this, too, in recent days. Although perhaps in ways you'd rather not."

Jack puzzled over this for a second, then remembered. "The insects? I thought that was The Evil . . . the excision —"

"They are drawn to your Gift as moths are to a candle, with similar results. It's not your fault. It may extend beyond insects, too. You might find animals acting oddly around you in the coming weeks as your Gift settles — but they won't die. Only the tiniest minds are completely overcome by the power we possess."

Jack thought of Fi-Fi the dog and was glad. Imagine if he'd patted her and she'd dropped dead!

"Now shush," she said. "Your sister is already asleep."

Jack sat up to look. Jaide's eyes were indeed tightly shut. Grandma X laid a blanket over her and put a pillow by her feet, in case she woke up and looked for one. Then she gave Jack the same, and he arranged himself back down again, resting his head more comfortably against down and cotton.

Grandma X crouched down next to him and brushed a lock of brown hair from his forehead.

"You look just like your father did when he was a boy," she said. "So serious. What are you thinking about, Jackaran?"

He hadn't known he *was* thinking of anything, but it was there in his mind when he looked.

"What did The Evil mean when it said 'One always falls'?" he asked.

"It said that, did it?"

"Yes, and I suppose it's one of the mysteries, too. . . ."

"No, it's not a mystery, but it is something I hope you won't need to learn about for a good while yet." She smiled. "No more questions, now. You've earned a rest, don't you think?"

Jack nodded, even though she had blatantly dodged his question. He *was* tired, and they *had* saved Portland for the second time in a month.

"Yes," he mumbled. "I reckon we have."